ASPER

This novel is a work of fiction. Names, characters, places, and incidents are either the products of the author's imagination or used fictitiously. Any resemblance to actual events, locales, or persons, living or dead, is entirely coincidental.

Copyright © 2017 by Rhonda Smiley

All Rights Reserved. No part of this publication can be reproduced or transmitted in any form, electronic or mechanical, without permission from the author or publisher.

ISBN: 978-0-9984492-0-3

Cover Design by Damonza

TWO WORLDS. ONE HOPE.

ASPER

RHONDA SMILEY

CHAPTER ONE

MILLA EASED HER BLADE into its sheath, strapped it to her hip, and tiptoed toward the door, squeaky sandals safely in hand. She had at least two hours before her father would surface from his morning incantations and she wasn't about to waste them indoors. A trace of guilt nudged her, but she recovered and turned the knob. With a deliberate heart-stopping blast, her *Quodex* fanned its pages like a maniac, and she spun, both bracing herself and glaring at that snitch of a book. But her father—gifted with the concentration of a desert vole—was still pacing the study area, levitating candlesticks, vases, and canisters around him. Milla sank at the sight of him stooped in a question mark, beaten by the harshness of life. No, the harshness of being born a conjurer. She'd do anything to hex him happy, but even her *Quodex* didn't offer that spell.

Speaking of, she pinched that no-good, loud-mouthed compendium of nonsense tighter than her brow. "Rat me out again and I'll dog-ear your chapters, beast."

Her *Quodex* had the nerve to exaggerate a shudder, so she whacked it off the table. She had no choice. The book flew across the room, intentionally knocking every jug—potions and brews, elixirs and tonics—off the rickety shelves before slamming into the dirt floor melodramatically.

Oh, broth—

"Milla Saofia Joviana Langstromer!" Her father was in her face instantly, giving her no time to come up with an excuse. Worse, his wafting bric-a-brac crowded her.

"I was framed," she said, swatting at the chorus of candlesticks, vases, and canisters.

"When will you learn to get along with your tome?"

"When it gets along with me."

He folded his arms, waiting, and when she feigned ignorance, he said, "Come now. You're sixteen and seven moons. Surely you can mend the pottery?"

"Surely." *Not.* "But Father... Really? Do we need another jug of archaic potion?"

"Potions are not archaic."

She raised a skeptical eyebrow. "When was the last time you used one?"

"You fail to see the point."

"That's what *I'm* saying."

He shook his head in a way that made her feel worse than any spell of remorse, and reconstituted the pottery with the swipe of his hand while keeping his objects afloat. "I worry about you, Milla. You squander too much time outside and devote none to studying."

"I studied all morning."

"And what did you accomplish?"

"You didn't say I had to accomplish anything."

"Oh, Milla," he groaned, adding to the lines that had appropriated his youth years ago.

"It's not my fault I have the attention span of a bush possum."

"You don't apply yourself."

"Blasted, I'm tired of hearing that."

"Mind your language, or I'll lock away your Earth books."

She grumbled apologetically. "It's the stuffy air in here. It affects my manners."

Her father sighed and his floating objects dipped—a sign of defeat. Or victory, as she preferred to think of it.

"You may take a respite," he said. "But you'll study when you return."

"Yes, Father," she said, lacing her sandals.

"You'll learn a new spell which you must enchant without the aid of your *Quodex*."

"With pleasure."

"And you'll return posthaste should you sense an inkling of danger."

"I insist." She propped up one of his candlesticks before it hit the dusty ground.

He retrieved her *Quodex* and handed her "the compilation of every verse every conjurer should know." If she had a spell for each time she heard that, she'd be more powerful than the queen.

"Until you've studied them all, you must never travel without your lessons."

"My thoughts exactly." She tucked the velvet-covered text inside the waistband of her pants, inadvertently revealing the tear in her seam.

"Did you unravel your stitching?"

I'm innocent, she wanted to plead, but how could she tell him it unraveled itself now that he was using such thin burlap or that his sewing these days was on par with her sorcery? "I'll mend them tonight."

As she turned to run out, he took her hand, stopping her, and held it sentimentally. The shimmer of his marking between his thumb and forefinger drew her eye: the three moons—one crescent, one half, and one full circle—signifying him a sorcerer. He wore his lineage proudly. Another difference between them. She kissed his cheek and positioned his lips in a smile with her fingers.

"Worry not. That's an order," she said and rushed out before he could change his mind.

She beelined to the stone wall that served as a prep area next to the fire pit, retrieved a wooden figurine hidden inside one of the cauldrons, and dashed into the forest. When she was far enough away that her father couldn't possibly call her back in, she stole a moment to appreciate their home. Coddled in a cluster of towering pines with low-hanging, thick-needled branches, the shack of mud and grass melded organically with its surrounds. If she didn't know better, she'd suspect he had conjured an invisibility spell on it, but even he hadn't mastered that skill.

Milla sat cross-legged near the edge of the pond, shaded by her favorite tree; the one with boughs that meandered here and there, nearly touching the ground, and flourished with citrus flower blossoms. She sucked in the fragrance of the blooms, the grass, the lilies on the water, and wondered why no potions ever required the nice-smelling stuff, only roots and stalks and bulbs.

She unsheathed her knife. Straight-edged on one side, serrated on the other, the white-metal blade—as long as her hand from wrist to fingertip—came to an extended point. Aside from the twine and burlap around the handle for gripping, which could use replacing, it was as pristine as when her father had handed it down to her.

Milla wiped the blade clean on the hem of her pants, careful not to slice the cheap material, and got to work on the details of the figurine. She barely shaved a layer off the cheekbone when a rush of shadowy movement jolted her to her feet. On instinct, she fled behind the tree for cover (instead of returning posthaste, as promised), and a hand clutched her calf, fast and hard, from out of nowhere. She shrieked, kicking to free herself while lamenting how her father would take the final disappointment of her demise because she didn't listen to him… until she realized who was squeezing her leg. His color and texture matched the environment, making him mostly imperceptible, but she could see him now that he bobbed and fidgeted right in front of her. She stomped her foot.

"Tobly, you scared me!"

Waist high to her, the craggy-skinned boy smiled from ear to ear, which was always a spectacle since his ears lay near the back of his head.

Derg. That was the idea, he communicated telepathically.

"You're lucky I didn't use my sorcery."

He chuckled.

"I could if I wanted."

Go ahead. Start with your burlap.

Milla grumbled and stretched her top down to cover her tattered pants. "Don't tempt me. Besides, I have other talents."

Tobly held his hand to his forehead and searched the land for them.

"Oh, har har," she said, not the least bit amused, and showed him the carving. "Look."

You have some kindling. Congratulations.

"It's not kindling, it's a gift I created for my father. With my own hands, no sorcery necessary, thank you."

He took it and inspected it this way and that, right-side up and upside down, and scrunched his nose as if catching a whiff of the Hinterland Marsh. She snatched it back.

"You don't have to like it. It's merely an object he can levitate during his incantations." She sighed. "I can't bear the thought of his loneliness. He spends all his time indoors; studying, preparing, and fearing. He's wasting his life."

With the sensitivity of a log, the little imp burst into laughter and snorts, spraying her with his spittle.

"Honestly." She wiped her face.

I just noticed. He gestured to the carving, recognizing that the features resembled his.

"So now you see the mastery of my work?"

But I'm more pleasing to the eye.

"Provided we overlook your personality."

At least I have one.

Milla gasped in alarm, pointing behind him. "Tobly, duck!"

He spun on the aggressive, kicking up sod, and she stuffed the carving in her pocket, laughing as she clambered up her favorite tree.

Cheater.

He scrambled up, hopping over her like a jungle squirrel, and won the race to the top, no surprise. He always did and he always had to make a deal of it, too, pretending to be asleep or acting shocked to see her. Some silly commentary, and today was no different as she pulled herself onto the branch, taking a perch next to him.

What a relief. I thought you got lost.

"I did, but then I caught the stench of your feet and followed that."

Tobly raised his foot to his nose, like an animal would, no hands, and sniffed it. *Smells fine to—ooh, grub.*

He picked a fleshy larva from between his toes and popped it in his mouth.

"So uncivilized."

Tobly stuck his tongue out, the larva still on it. *My blunder. Did you want some?*

She laughed and shoved him. "Ew. Swallow it."

He ate the insect and forced a wet burp afterward.

Milla leaned back, looking out to admire the view, and instead spotted the eccentric bald man, in his usual baggy cloak, beyond the shrubs of Lost Creek. She elbowed Tobly in the gut. "There he is, that man with his silly white bird."

He's harmless.

"How do you know?"

Derg. I can hear him.

"Why does he wander so? And always by the Creek."

You don't own the Creek. 'Sides, he has no family anymore. What would you like him to do?

"It's odd, that's all. And have you ever seen a white crow before?"

No. Looks delicious.

Goodness, Squeeds had a one-track mind.

When the dense flora devoured every trace of the bald man and his white bird, Milla settled back against Tobly's shoulder and watched villagers on the outskirts go about their lives, oblivious to the plight of sorcerers, the scourge of the army. She guessed most of them had probably never seen a soldier in person. Or a Squeed for that matter. Blissful ignorance, how wonderful. No cares, just living to live. Oh, her father would be disheartened—dedicating his life to educating her and here she sat begrudging her knowledge. Her lineage.

Like a scratch in the fabric of time, repeating over and over again.

"No eavesdropping, Tobly."

Was that private? Many sorries, Mill, he offered, insincerely.

"I'll remember to keep my thoughts quiet in your company."

You? You can hold your thoughts about as well as you hold your tongue, meaning—

"I know what you mean. So what? I speak my mind. It's a virtue."

Then I guess you told your father about me? Being proud of your candor and all.

"Soon, Tobly."

He frowned. *'Soon' is your favorite word.*

"It's my least favorite word. I feel everything terrible lies within the realm of 'soon.' Besides, he doesn't know I visit the Creek."

Tobly almost fell from the tree, flabbergasted.

"As if you tell your mother about your escapades."

Every minutia.

"Hogswaddle."

If you visited, you'd see.

"Right. Me, in a Squeed habitat. I hardly think Father would approve."

Apparently, he needn't know since you keep many secrets.

"Why I ever befriended a pushy, little—" She stopped midbarb when a silver-coated bear cub hobbled out of the brush below with an arrow lodged in its haunch.

Tobly jumped to a predatory crouch, salivating and ready to pounce, but Milla plucked him back by the scruff.

Hey!

"You promised, no hunting when we're together."

What hunt? It's waiting to be eaten.

Milla hurried down the tree, ignoring him.

I hope you value the sacrifices I make for you, Mill.

I do, she assured him silently. She landed as softly as she could and the cub growled—more whimper than ferociousness. She squatted to its height and held out her palm to gain its trust, and after it sniffed her open hand (without baring its teeth), she examined the wound. The head of the arrow was buried in the meaty part of its haunch, impossible to remove without ripping the inside out with it.

Tobly leaned over her, unnoticed by the animal. *If you have to keep this perfectly suitable meal from me, at least do it fast, and with the help of your Quodex.*

"Not everything requires a verse." Milla retrieved her knife and wiped it on her sleeve to clean it, cutting some of the burlap in her haste. She separated the cub's flesh, ready to operate, and discovered the arrow had penetrated deeper than she'd thought, halfway into the bone. The young bear yelped and Milla let go.

"Please, Tobly, you're distracting me."

Yes. I'm the problem.

"I can hear you slobber."

He wiped his mouth, but his stomach gurgled. She glared at him.

My stomach speaks for itself.

"Oh, very well." She sheathed her blade and leafed through her *Quodex*, finding the verse she needed in Chapter Three. Three. A child could do such an early spell from memory.

Stop exaggerating and do it already. I've yet to win an argument with my appetite.

Milla let out a growl and Tobly took the hint, stepping back two paces. She hovered her hand over the arrow. "*Boga abugan fram eower ofslean. Lif ge-laestan se foldweg.*"

A pale shimmer emitted from the nock, moved past the fletching, down the shaft, and into the haunch of the cub. Following in the path of the shimmer, the nock, then fletching, then shaft disintegrated into particles and drifted off in the stock-still air.

Milla stood inert, in disbelief. Tobly gawped openmouthed, which only accentuated his disgruntled stomach. The cub bounded to its feet and stumbled backward, as shocked as they. It licked the gash in its leg and burrowed through the thick brush, disappearing from view. Milla bounced with joy.

"Ha!" She held the carving high. "Two feats in one day." Her smile flatlined, killed by a sharp hollowness in the air.

Run!

"Tobly?"

The Squeed was gone. The soil rumbled softly at first. Then louder. Closer. The clang of armor punched her eardrums. She dropped the figurine and ran. Through the brush, the forest, the trees, the streams, through nature's maze, she sprinted as fast as hunted prey, pounding with terror.

Milla raced out of the leafy canopy, shocked breathless by the sea of sinuous black armor surrounding her home. A wave of heat rushed through her, triggering those horrifying images in her mind's eye: cages, beasts, swords, soldiers. Her legs weakened and she fell to one knee.

"No, not now, not now." She pushed her way out of the haunting visions and ran toward the barricade of sickening metal. Soldiers encased from head to toe in their impenetrable membrane of armor had aligned their horses, equally-shielded, in tight formation, but Milla shoved her way through, breaking free on the other side, inside the circle of evil. She raced toward her shack, calling for her father, but a hulking figure whose vileness seeped from his armor, exited before she got there. The sight of him stopped her as effectively as an immobilization spell. The captain of the army—the only soldier with a crest of the queen's castle on his chestplate—grinned, his dull matte metal moving like skin.

Lightheaded with fear, everything warped in front of her, but Milla had to get inside her home; she had to see her father. She stumbled out of her daze, toward the doorway, and the captain grabbed her by the throat, hoisting her up against the wall with her feet off the ground.

"Where's my father?" She swung her arms and legs, but they rebounded off his armor.

"Where is the scroll?" His voice echoed from the helmet and Milla spat through his open eyeshield.

"Pig," he said, smashing her head into the wall.

The crack rang louder than the pain, spiking her ears with a shrill buzzing. She ransacked her foggy mind for a spell. Anything. "*Faran o' onweald fracod...*"

"Do you attempt sorcery on me?" He laughed. "The queen will be charmed."

"*Geanlaecan eall seo god... seo god...*" The captain squeezed her larynx to the back of her neck, cutting off her vocal cords, but she couldn't recall the rest of the spell anyway.

"Last chance," he said, squeezing harder.

A thousand pins pricked her face, lighting it on fire, and her eyes were sure to pop from their sockets, but if she was to achieve only one thing in life to make her father proud, it would be protecting the scroll. A blistering whorl of electricity struck the captain, sparking his metal, and Milla fell from his grasp.

"Run, Milla!" Her father levitated behind the throng of soldiers, shooting another sizzling whorl, but the captain dove for cover this time. A soldier leaped off his horse and tackled her father midair, slamming him to the ground. "Run!" he yelled again and the soldier stomped on his chest, silencing him.

Milla panicked with indecision, then ran into the forest behind her.

She broke through curtains of ferns and leaped over thorny bushes that shredded her pants up to her thighs, scratching her legs bloody. Galloping hooves closed in on her and she about-faced, darting into an area populated with thick scrubs, and lost her bearings. The *clatter* and *clang* and *gallop*. Deafening. She scrabbled out of the scrub and her shoulder pinched in agony, nearly jerked out of its socket, as the captain yanked her off her feet. He dragged her by the wrist—her legs slamming into rocks and her head banging against his horse's metaled flank—all the way back to her shack.

Her father, facedown in the dirt and kept there by the boot of a soldier, had surrendered the fight. Milla struggled to free herself, but the captain threw her into a barbed shrub and heaved her father to his feet.

"Where's the scroll, Filimore?" the captain said.

Her father didn't answer and the captain backhanded him with a blow to the face that sent him into the dirt. Milla scrambled over, but the captain whipped his sword to her father's throat, stopping her short.

"My patience wears thin," the captain said, his blade drawing blood from the crease in her father's neck. Milla couldn't steady her legs, and her eyes burned with the rise of tears, but her father remained stoic. Another trait she didn't inherit.

"You may present me to Lucrecia for interrogation," her father said.

"Present you to the queen?" The captain smirked and turned to his soldiers. "He wishes to be presented to the queen."

The soldiers laughed.

"You have two options, Filimore, neither of which is an audience with the queen. If I ask again, I'll be talking to a corpse."

When her father didn't respond, the captain swung his sword to strike, and in a haze of nausea, Milla grabbed his arm.

"I'll give you the scroll," she said, not recognizing her own spineless voice. "I'll give it to you, just don't kill him." She released her grip on the captain's arm and looked into her father's woeful eyes. "Forgive me, Father. I meant to be strong. I did."

"Forgive *me* for not protecting you."

The captain propelled Milla toward the shack. "A count of ten and then his head will join you in there."

Milla raced inside. The cots were slung across the room, mattresses sliced open and straw spilling out. The table was flipped on its side and the chairs torn apart, like firewood. Splintered shelves littered the floor, broken pottery everywhere, and the canisters, candlesticks, and vases in the study area were chopped, smashed, or flattened. Milla traced her hand along the crooked seam on the wall where the cots used to be, releasing a concealed door. She bolted into the secret passageway, running the interminable distance to their hiding place, snatched up the wooden box, and sprinted back. She ran out of the shack breathless but in time, holding out the box for the captain as she went to her father's side.

The captain motioned to a young soldier, no older than Milla, and said, "Open it."

The young soldier obliged. Inside the box, rolled up and bundled with lace woven of gold strands, the iridescent piece of parchment swelled, then settled. "It's here."

"You have it, now go. Go!" Milla screamed.

The captain thrust his blade at her so fast she hadn't time to react, but the shiny steel passed her neck by the width of a hair and pierced her father's chest, so powerfully, so viciously, it emerged clean, blood free, out the back. Milla froze—everything inside her stopped. Time stopped. The distorted mutter of shock and confusion filtered through the soldiers and pounded her ears incomprehensibly. Time shot back and her father gasped and wheezed for air. The captain withdrew his sword, now bloodied, and placed it to her heart.

"Beg me, you pathetic witch. Beg me to die."

She wanted nothing more than to end her anguish, but the young soldier intercepted the captain's blade with his own.

"Our orders," he said. The captain's sword was gone in a flash, faster than wizard speed, and he was mounting his horse, his soldiers following. Except the young one, who stayed a moment longer and said, "Find a new place to hide," before riding off.

Milla turned to her father, wiping the sweat from his brow. The threads of his cloak went from brown to red as if dyed from lingonberries, but it was his blood. So much blood. She pressed on his wound to stop the flow, drowning her hands in the stickiness.

"Forgive me, Father. I had premonitions I didn't share with you. Visions too horrible to speak, but I'll never keep secrets again. We'll heed their warnings and—"

"Milla," her father said weakly. "Take this. Go." He held a folded piece of parchment in his shaky hand.

Milla fought her tears. "Yes, we'll go."

A stream of blood seeped from the corner of his lips and Milla's tears broke free. She wiped her face and took out her *Quodex*. "I'll heal you."

He struggled to speak and nothing came out but labored wheezes.

"Save your strength, Father. Please. Let me find a spell." She rushed through the pages of her *Quodex*, the verses blurred by tears. "Help me," she said in a whisper, but the book wilted in grief, giving her nothing.

Her father coughed up a mouthful of blood and Milla cried out in horror.

"Go," he pleaded, his last breath strangling hers. His head fell limp and his eyes dimmed, the light, the life, gone. The three moons on his hand faded from existence. Gone. Milla's world, gone. She lost all feeling and felt everything. Ice cold and burning up. Dead as stone, and so alive, every fiber of her being ached. She gasped a breath and grabbed her father's cloak, pulling him to her.

"Father, don't leave me, please. I need you. I'll be a better study, I'll do as you say. I'll do anything. Please!" She shook him frantically, but he didn't respond. "Father, please!"

His lifeless body hung heavy, like he was nothing more than a sack of grain. She fell onto his chest and sobbed. She sobbed until her eyes dried of tears, and then she wept with her soul, until that, too, emptied. When she was a shell of a frame, when she had nothing left to give, she lay there, his blood caked on her palm. She wasn't paralyzed with pain exactly, but she couldn't move a muscle, not even to blink. The sun broiled down, a comforting blanket, and she waited for death to take her as well. She had no will to live, nothing to live for.

But then a fire ignited in the pit of her abdomen, so foreign a feeling she thought she had just inherited her father's spirit. Her veins boiled, her heart raced, an electricity shot through her, sparking her back to life. She wasn't ready to die. Not yet. She pocketed the parchment he held, kissed his cold cheek, and got to her feet. She had one thing to do first. Kill the queen.

CHAPTER TWO

THE FULL MOON tinted the cerulean sky with its silvery glow. Next to it, the faint shadow of a half-moon, smaller, childlike in comparison, strained to break through. Zanub steadied his eyes on the horizon and pushed his steed faster, uninhibited by the winding path through the Hinterland Marsh. The dreary swamp popped and hissed, releasing the rot of luckless travelers, but the stink rolled off his armor. He had smelled it enough times to not notice it anymore. Or perhaps his victory scented everything with sweetness. He had stopped the captain from slaughtering Milla, and so close to the third moon. Plus, he had the scroll. Without consulting his map, he headed for the Shift, knowing precisely where it waggled despite its unseeable presence.

He kicked his horse into a jump over a bubbling mire and, passing through the Shift, emerged in the Desert of Riftinad, landing on the soft powdery grains without missing a gait. The sun, bronzed with spirals of flames circumnavigating it, hung large and low and obscured the moons.

Zanub glanced back. Ripples of heat. And then the captain broke through the ether, catching up. *Cursed!* He was faster than Zanub expected. The captain had detoured off-route, chasing a young sorcerer, a child really, to kill—his savagery was pathological—and Zanub had stayed on track, hoping to beat him to the castle.

He lowered his eyeshield, activating the holographic map on the periphery of his left eye. Moving the map with his thoughts, he rotated it and zeroed in until he oriented himself in its coordinates. Once he had his bearings, he located the next Shift and adjusted his course. He jammed his heels into his horse's belly, galloping faster over the rolling sandbanks, and when he breached the invisible passage, emerging into Ravaenwood Forest, the captain was by his side, his face screwed in its ugly, tedious snarl.

The captain yanked Zanub's reins, causing his horse to buckle and Zanub to leap off to save himself from being crushed.

"Know your place, second," the captain said, snatching the scroll from him.

Zanub righted his horse, inspecting its legs for injury and its metal for cracks, as the captain kicked his charge into a gallop toward the first set of gates leading into Castle Hill. Behind the tall iron bars, an armored sentry unlatched the entrance into the hold and the captain rode in. Zanub mounted his horse as the rest of the army sprung from thin air, a maelstrom of metal. He followed at the rear, jostling for space inside the hold, and the sentry closed the exterior gate behind him.

Zanub checked his eyeshield for gaps, making sure it sealed in his scent, and caught the smirk of the captain at the head of the army. He disregarded him. Every soldier was equal when entering Castle Hill, whether or not his chestplate bore the coveted crest. The castle was guarded by the only known pack of scentmongers in existence and those carnivorous beasts didn't know a captain from a soldier. They had no friends, no foes, and certainly no loyalty, not even to the queen. Their needs were simple. Find flesh, eat flesh. Dead or alive, fresh or rancid. And they looked the part; a monstrosity only magic could create, but neither witch nor warlock took credit. The black-and-silver-pelted creatures had oversized angular skulls for their skinny, lanky bodies. Their yellow fangs hung past their sinewy jaws, tapering to a razor edge, and their claws were as sharp and pointy as their teeth. When they were on four limbs, they came no higher than a horse's elbow, but when they stood on their haunches, they were as tall as a mounted soldier. Not quite canine nor primate, they skulked and climbed and loped with the ease and ferocity of both. So the captain could smirk all he wanted; his conceit would be his downfall, not his savior.

The sentry opened the interior gate and 'mongers shot into the hold, weaving and sniffing, snorting and growling, as soldiers filed in. The gate closed behind Zanub, the last one to enter even though he was second-in-command. He wound his way up the narrow path with the rest of the army. Halfway up, the scentmongers lost interest in the odorless mass and rambled back down. As the army neared the castle, chains lowered the drawbridge across a viscous moat to allow passage, and smiles washed over the metal faces; the clacking upon the wooden planks was always a welcomed sound.

Once inside the castle, the mounted soldiers descended into various stairwells off the vestibule, returning to their quarters, but Zanub guided his horse up. When he reached the antechamber below the Ebony Tower at the top of the castle, he found the captain's horse obediently waiting. Zanub dismounted and ran up the narrow rungs to the rooftop tower. The queen's fiery menace shot out of its flume in the center of the floor and coiled around him, from foot to head, preventing his approach. He couldn't see through the flames but heard the captain laugh.

"You mustn't bully, Inferno. It's most unbecoming," the queen said.

The fire receded, freeing Zanub to take his place next to the captain, but he hesitated when he saw Queldar by the queen's side. The poor warlock had no idea. And the captain, unaffected, like the barbarian he was.

"Shall I order tea while we wait for you, Zanub?"

"No, Majestic Ruler." He moved to the rear right flank of his captain, head down to avoid Queldar's stare.

The captain held out the scroll and the queen plucked it from his hand, unrolling it with a flick of her wrist. The words and symbols faded until the parchment was naked. Unshimmering. Zanub glanced to the captain, but he appeared as shocked as everyone else.

The queen spun to her warlock. "What is this?"

Queldar shrugged, his ill-fitting cloak shivering for him. "A hex I imagine, my queen."

"You imagine? Do you?" She snaked down to his height. "And is this the first you hear of this?"

"I'm deeply offended you ask."

She turned to the captain. "Bring me the wizard."

Zanub tensed, then blurted, "He was slain by the captain." It had to be said.

In a blur, faster than wizard speed if possible, Queldar slammed the captain against the wall, strangling his neck with both hands.

"You fiend!" the wet-faced Queldar spat out.

The captain drew his sword and plunged it into the rabid warlock's side, but the blade broke apart like thinly spun glass against the burlap tatters. The queen's doing, not Queldar's. With tears and snot running down his face, the broken warlock pounded the captain's metal, evoking a quiver from Zanub's lips. But the warlock deserved to know.

"Let it be, Queldar," the queen said.

"Let it be? Let it be?" He must've known it was futile, for he dropped the captain and addressed the queen. "He killed my brother. Against your oath. What kind of leader are you that you cannot control your own soldier?"

The queen launched Queldar across the expansive tower, toward the exit. "Your grief is all that spares you, warlock. Had you found the scroll as promised, Filimore would be alive. Now leave before I regret my sympathy."

Queldar slogged out at the pace of a brokenhearted sloth. He didn't remember his armor, but for some reason the queen shot it onto him, suiting him up as he exited.

She materialized before the captain in full ugliness; hollow eyes and thick veins pulsating beneath translucent skin. Her fire arched over her head, spitting embers at him. "Why is he dead when I gave orders to the contrary, Vylkrost?"

"It was the only way to acquire the scroll, Majestic Ruler. The daughter refused to cooperate."

Liar.

She raised him off the ground with a single nail under his chin. "She best be unharmed, soldier. I can be swift now or quite deliberate later should I hear otherwise."

"She's unharmed. My second will attest."

"He speaks the truth," Zanub said with as little reluctance as he could muster.

The queen dispersed and coalesced in the center of the tower, beauty returned. Her gown of spun silver chimed and the three moons on the curve of her back swayed as she paced. "Poor child. She must be devastated," she said with that voice that made her sound kindhearted. "Bring her to me." She disappeared in an ethereal mist.

"You walk the path of an ill-fated soldier," the captain said to Zanub and marched out.

Sweat-soaked hair matted against her clammy neck and face, Milla vaulted over low-lying brush and fallen twigs and forged through shallow streams. She knew where to find the queen. Everyone did. That witch lived in the black stone monstrosity at the top of Asper's tallest mountain under Asper's darkest clouds. Milla spotted the Shift she needed in the distance—that waggle in the air that only sorcerers could see. If her calculations were right, she'd emerge outside the gates of Castle Hill, somewhere in Ravaenwood Forest.

She sprinted, fueled with rage, and was knocked high into the air, blindsided before she breached the Shift. She hit the ground, breathless, and jumped to her feet, knife drawn, sufficiently angry to pierce the impenetrable metal of a soldier, but it was Tobly who stood there, not some soldier.

"Tobly, I've no time for games."

Nor do I.

"They killed my father. They killed him."

I saw. More than I can bear, which is why you need your Quodex. He held out the book.

"My knife will do fine."

Don't be foolish. Your blade will turn to sand at the snap of the queen's fingers.

"Then I'll use my bare hands."

Your drama doesn't sway me, Mill. You can't face her without your craft.

"Stop filling me with doubt, Tobly."

Stop denying your lineage.

"You're one to speak, you minuscule hypocrite."

I'm taller than most for my species and you know it!

She hadn't meant to hurt his feelings; she just needed to win this argument for her own confidence. "Your brothers would feast on my flesh in a heartbeat, but not you, you chose friendship. Because our choices make us who we are, not our lineage, so stop telling me who I am. I don't need magic."

She has the scroll, in case you forgot.

"Of course I haven't forgotten, but it will do her no good when she's dead, will it?"

You lack the talent to kill a desert vole, Milla, never mind the queen.

The ground rumbled, robbing her of a retort, argument lost.

There, are you pleased? The army comes for you. Go with your blade and your bare hands and see where you land.

She wanted to throttle the Squeed for talking sense. She grabbed her *Quodex* and ran, away from the castle, away from the soldiers, away from everything she knew. She had fits of tears, erupting unexpectedly, and drying up as fast. By the time darkness arrived, she had lost both her sandals and traveled an unknown Shift, emerging in an unknown forest. Above the golden umbrella of foliage, the white crow circled, and Milla snatched her knife from its sheath, scanning the brush for the bald man. "What do you want? Show yourself."

The leaves behind her rustled and she whipped around, ready to pounce, but no one was there. Coward. The bird was gone, too. She gathered twigs, vines, and branches, and constructed a lean-to, and still, the night air chilled her beneath the cover of shelter. If she was smart, she'd study her *Quodex*—how else could she rip the entrails from the vile queen and shove them down her throat?—but the parchment from her father tugged at her. Unable to resist any longer, despite what it might say, she unfolded the crinkled page.

My dearest daughter,

As you read this, I'm no longer with you. However, I remain present in spirit. I write this because I must confess a terrible secret. As a child, you were full of vigor and curiosity, I could scarcely keep up. Given the times, I took you to Lost Creek, the safest haven in all of Asper. You played with the leaves, the dirt, and even the insects. I was so moved by your jubilation, I didn't notice the warnings, but you did, and you turned to me, a look on your face I will never forget. The queen's captain crashed through and seized you before my hands reached yours. You cried out, never taking your eyes from me as he dragged you away. Forever, I thought.

Years of unbearable agony ended when you returned like the most precious gift in the universe, like the day you were born. But you were sad. Broken. I anguished over your captivity and what it had done to you. Forgive me, for I cast a spell to bury your horrid memories. Alas, a spell is only a spell. The memories will return. Deny them the power to destroy you now. I beg you to mend your ways with your Quodex and journey the portal for I cannot bear the thought of more torture put upon you by the evil in this land. It's time to embrace your freedom. Be free, my child.

Your loving father.

A million scenarios converged and imploded, drowning Milla's consciousness into a muddle of sea foam, and when she broke out of her shock, she found herself screaming with the anguish of futility. With a hatred for the cruelty of life. She wrenched a batch of vines from the ground and beat the turf, an unstoppable rage unleashed, and when she fell on her face from exhaustion, she yelled into the pile of mossy leaves until her throat bled. *Be free? Free?* His death alone would imprison her heart always, and now, to know his endless suffering? How could she ever be free?

Her *Quodex* fanned and fluttered, but she was too numb to do anything but kick it away. It skittered next to her ear and shuffled and shuffled and shuffled, forcing her to roll over and sit up if she wanted any peace. The book settled on the second-to-last page, revealing single-line verses; throwaway spells from the ancients no longer used by sorcerers today. In fact, these spells weren't in the newer editions if any existed anymore; word was that the queen incinerated the *Quodices* once she absorbed the notes in the margins. Inhumane witch. Milla's father had handed down this one to her, which was handed down by his father, and so on, all the way back to the rift. She'd probably be grumpy too if she were as old as time, she thought, feeling sorry for her book. She wiped her tears and perused the verse for the portal, undecided. Her father, and clearly her *Quodex*, wanted her to take it, but she wasn't ready. There was still the matter of killing the queen.

Vibrations rang off her bones and she slammed the book shut, placing one hand on the ground, the other up to the air. She couldn't hear the rattle of metal, but based on the strength of the pulsations, the army was near, probably in an adjacent plane. Probably about to breach her space. She ran, looking for cover, and forged her way through a thick tangle of grass taller than she. Her feet, already blistered from having lost her sandals, bled as the meadow sliced her soles with the sharpness of a razor, and she dropped to her hands and knees and crawled. The ground pulsed with greater force, pitching her off balance and onto her stomach. She pushed herself to her knees, but the field split down the middle as the army emerged behind her and charged forth. Milla scrambled to her feet and sprinted, decision made.

"*Se readfah beam onwreon se ecg seo heabban se for freo.*"

The verse held no clues as to where the portal would be, except if her Old Asperian was to be trusted, it had something to do with a redwood tree. She recited the verse again and broke into wide-open ground. A redwood tree shimmered into view, from out of nowhere, on the edge of a cliff not a hundred paces away. She pushed herself harder, faster, lungs begging for rest. She had to get there before—

The army soared from the meadow, over her head, and blocked her path. One by one, ten by ten, twenty by twenty, they arrived, kicking up dirt and grass and stealing her escape. She about-faced and fled in the opposite direction, but they divided forces and circled her. She spun, nowhere to go, as they closed in, imprisoning her.

The captain emerged from the horde, atop his steed, and she met his eyes, only this time she had flashes of when she was a child at the pond. Here she stood, frozen once more as he came to seize her. Helpless. But she wasn't that child. She had vengeance on her side now, driving her. She snapped to and scrambled beneath his horse's legs, running toward the tree. The leaves on the branches faded, the trunk faded—the tree was disappearing. Milla recited the verse under her breath. The clatter of hooves was upon her and she glanced over her shoulder to see the captain reach down for her. She ducked—his glove skimming her hair—and bounded toward the cliff's edge without slowing down, taking a swan dive off the precipice. She plummeted, screaming, arms and legs flailing, until a burst of light ignited and swallowed her whole.

Zanub kicked his horse into a gallop, rearing to a halt carelessly close to the edge of the cliff. He peered over but saw no sign of Milla on the rocky terrain below. A stupefied murmur ran through the soldiers as several scanned the chasm.

The captain approached Zanub and asked, "Where is she?"

"I'm not an oracle, Captain." The captain stiff-armed him off his horse and Zanub's armor crunched on impact with the ground, but he was thankful the captain didn't push him the other way.

"Try again."

"Clearly, she used an uncharted Shift," Zanub said as he brushed himself off and surveyed his armor for damage. "I'll report this to Majestic Ruler."

"You'll report nothing. I'll find that wench."

"My loyalty is with our queen."

"You truly are the saddest fool in Asper if you believe she holds any sentiment for you, Zanub."

"I have no desires for the queen."

"I speak not of the queen."

Zanub reacted faster than his wit—the teenage boy in him—and reached for his sword, but the tip of the captain's blade pressed against his neck, scraping the metal membrane, in the time it took Zanub to wrap his fingers around the hilt of his own.

"Do it," the captain said.

A rustling in the tall grass interrupted their confrontation and they both turned. A soldier was knocked from his horse and wrestled into the underbrush.

"Squeeds! The Squeeds are present!" a soldier yelled.

What luck; bad, in most instances, but here and now, a gift. Zanub stood a chance against Squeeds. The captain glared at him, then mounted his steed. Another soldier was ambushed and the Squeeds encased him like ants to a beetle carcass, dragging him away. Zanub leaped atop his horse amid a surge of movement all around and galloped after the fleeing army. The soldiers ahead disappeared into thin air and Zanub breached the Shift seconds later.

Milla clutched her *Quodex* to her chest as she cartwheeled wildly in a vortex. Radiant colors erupted in an explosion of light, showering down vibrant particles, and streamed past in a nauseating blur. Her skin pulled painfully against her bones and she hugged herself, waiting to break apart. The whirlpool stopped suddenly and the fabric of time stretched around her, held still and steady, then boomeranged back in a vertiginous assault. She slammed into the hardness of life.

Sprawled on a plank floor she had hit so solidly that grooves were etched into her aching body, Milla stayed down. It was nighttime and she was inside somewhere, someone's home perhaps, but where?

A distant rumble shook the floorboards. She fumbled for her knife, but her sheath was gone, ripped from her hip. She groped around the darkness, discombobulated, until she caught the gleam of her blade on the floor. She grabbed it, barely able to hold on with her sweaty palms, and crawled toward the noise to find a window behind the objects crowding the room.

The world outside was as dark as her mysterious surroundings but she could make out a wide gray path extending farther than she could see. The low roar grew louder, closer, and when she braced for an attack by the army, two bright lights appeared instead, blinding her. She stumbled back and fell into a stack of breakables, setting off a cacophony of shattering glass.

The room lit up from overhead, and Milla was exposed.

CHAPTER THREE

AN OLD MAN, older than Milla knew possible, pounded down the stairs on skinny legs, muttering unintelligibly. His yellow hair matched his yellow teeth and deep lines crisscrossed his face in a wild pattern, but his gentle eyes defused his otherwise scary facade. At the top of the stairs, where he had left the door open wide enough to reveal shelves laden with dishes, pots and pans hanging from a rack, and a bowl of tree fruit on a counter, an old woman emerged, tying her plush cloak. His beloved, no doubt. They were unfamiliarly adorable, and Milla slid her knife inside the back cover of her *Quodex*.

"For heaven sakes, Walter, slow down," the woman said. Walter rushed directly to Milla without slowing.

"Oh my lord, oh my dear, oh my goodness," he said as he picked shards of glass from her hair. The room, twice the size of Milla's shack, was overstuffed with all sorts of items: vases and pottery (much nicer than the ones she had back home), opulent tapestries and rugs, colorful textiles that looked nothing like burlap, ornately carved tables and desks, upholstered chairs and couches, and armoires and cabinetry. Some pieces were accented with such intricate iron details, she couldn't tell if they were forged by hand or by wizard.

"Betty, hurry up and help me, will ya?"

"I'm trying." Betty squeezed past him and hoisted Milla to her feet. "Upsa-daisy."

"Am I on Earth?" Milla asked.

"Heavens, how hard did you fall?" Betty inspected her forehead.

"Terribly. I've fallen harder from the top of the tree in Lost Creek, but the grass is much softer than the floor."

"I imagine it is."

Walter shook the handle on the front door several times before he seemed satisfied, then stuffed his hands in his pockets and glared at her. "How'd you get in here, anyway?"

She noticed his hair was pushed up on one side and flat on the other. "Were you asleep?"

"Well, what else would we be doing at four in the morning?"

"Don't mind him," Betty said. "His bark is worse than his bite."

Milla stepped back. "He bites?"

Betty laughed. "She's funny."

"Never mind that," Walter said and crossed his arms sternly. "I'm more interested in where you came from."

"I arrived through that portal." She pointed to the claw-foot dressing mirror across the room, where her aura lingered on the beveled glass. The old couple gasped and spun simultaneously to look at it, and exhaled their relief.

"Do you mean the back door?" Betty asked.

"No, the mirror."

"She's all mixed up," Betty said to Walter.

"Perhaps a little. The air is thick." Milla leaned on a table to steady herself, tipping it, but Walter and Betty grabbed hold of it.

"Please, child," Walter said. "This is a George the Third mahogany pedestal tilt-top table."

"It's lovely. Did you make it?"

Betty laughed again, but Walter narrowed his eyes and took Milla by the hand, guiding her to the bottom step of the staircase to sit.

"Now, what's your name, dear?"

"Milla."

He removed an item from his pocket, which lit up when he pressed a button. "What's your number, Milla?"

"Sixteen."

"What? No, not your age. Your phone number."

"My 'phone number?' I don't know. What is it?"

"Why're you asking me?" Walter said, agitated.

Betty slapped him in the arm. "You're confusing her, Walter. Stop it."

"Well, someone needs to come pick her up," he said, and turned to Milla. "Don't you have a phone?"

"Is that a phone?" she asked, pointing to the gadget.

"Oh, for Pete's sake."

"I don't have one of those. Phones."

"How can we get in touch with your parents then?" he asked.

The words sliced swifter than a soldier's blade, freeing her guarded tears, and she buried her head in her hands, ashamed. A lot of good she'd have done facing the queen when the mere mention of her father sent her bawling.

"Walter, what'd you go and do that for?"

"What'd I do?" The old man dabbed Milla's eyes with a wadded-up tissue but couldn't absorb her grief.

"They're dead," she said, wiping her nose. "I have no one."

Betty rocked her gently. "Sweetie, I'm sorry. There, there."

"Look at her feet," Walter said. "They're cut up from the broken china. Geez. Her head and now her feet. We better get her to a doctor. I sure hope the insurance covers this. What a mess. I don't know how this happened." He pressed a bunch of buttons on his phone as he hurried up the stairs.

"You stay put, dear. I'll fetch you some socks and shoes," Betty said and followed after Walter.

Milla sucked up the last of her tears and looked down at her feet. They weren't bleeding—clotted and dried, the crimson had no shimmer whatsoever—and they hurt only the tiniest bit now. She went over to the broken shards, careful not to touch anything along the way since Walter got perturbed anytime she did, and assessed the pieces of glass and pottery on the floor. Like back home, she had no idea how to mend them, but learning menial spells would be a poor use of her time. She had more important verses to study. She unlatched the locked door and exited.

Arms folded for warmth in the early morning haze, Milla ventured to the edge of the wooden deck, stopping at the top of the steps. So this was Earth. Trees and paths and structures similar yet different to the ones in Asper. The leaves were comically dainty, providing little cover, but richly colored, mostly in greens and burgundies. The paths, leading this way and that, were smooth and flat and free of dirt and rocks; a horse's delight for sure. And the structures in varying styles and sizes, unlike shacks or castles, seemed lifeless. Perhaps when the sun rose, the character would too.

She'd imagined it differently having read books, though in fairness, they were hundreds of years old and even Asper had changed over the centuries. She huffed. Ironic she should finally make it to Earth, not to live freely but to master a spell of all things. The Omniscient must really hate her.

The boards under her feet vibrated, alerting her to a distant drone that was getting louder and closer, until two beams of light emerged on the wide path, prompting her to hit the deck for cover. The lights were attached to the front of a metal beast that passed by, growling the entire time. She cocked her head. *What on Earth...?*

Before she could make withers or tails of it, a pair of worn shoes stopped in front of her face, hindering her view, and she looked up to see a boy, about her age, in those shoes. His eyes were deep brown with flecks of yellow, as if adorned with gold, and his hair, dark and glistening like his eyes, was shorter than most boys' hair on Asper and tousled in an oddly attractive manner. "What're you doing?"

Milla jumped to her feet. "I was… there was… did you not see the beast?"

"Beast?" He brushed past her to look down the street and her heart pounded. Flustered, she lost her footing on the edge of the steps and found nothing to grab onto, but he caught her by the wrist before she fell.

"Probably just a coyote," he said. "They won't bother you. My grandma wants me to take you to the hospital." He handed her a helmet. "Bike's out back."

"Bike?"

"Yeah, motorcycle." He opened the screen door in time for Walter to exit and snatch the helmets from both of them.

"You'll take the car."

"Grandpa. That car's an embarrassment."

Walter gave him the stare that Milla had often gotten from her father, and it worked on the boy as well for he marched back in.

Betty emerged, carrying an armload of fabrics and outlandish footwear. "What'd you do to upset Parker?" she asked Walter.

"Why's it always my fault?"

"That's a good question. Why is that?"

Walter grumbled.

Betty motioned to the cushioned swing that hung by the banister. "Here, sweetie, have a seat. You shouldn't be barefoot with those cuts." When Milla sat, Betty wiped her feet with a damp, warm cloth and began wrapping them with layers of another material.

"Are you crafting a pair of shoes?"

"Out of gauze? That would be something, wouldn't it? No, this is to keep your feet clean. God only knows what's in those boots."

Walter sighed. "No one told you to bring her my lucky fishing boots."

"My shoes certainly wouldn't fit her." Betty slid the boots over Milla's feet and leaned in. "The old coot has five pairs. Not one of them helps him catch anything but a cold." Finally, she helped Milla into a thick red sweater with gold buttons down the front. "Better?"

Milla nodded and got to her feet, chagrined by her clumsiness in the heavy boots. The now familiar rumble, accompanied with a clank and rattle, got her attention. This time it was a green metal beast, and she impelled Betty and Walter toward the door. "Go, quickly."

"Oh, come now, it's not that ugly," Walter said.

"That's the Gremlin," Betty said. "Aptly named but harmless. You've probably never seen one because it came and went before your time. We should all be so blessed."

The metal beast rolled to a stop with Parker inside.

"Is that normal?" Milla asked, motioning to Parker.

"You don't expect him to drive from the backseat, do ya?" Walter said.

"I've never seen such a transport."

"Are you Amish, sweetie?" Betty asked.

"Asperian."

"Do they use horses, like the Amish?"

Milla lit up. "Yes. Though I've never ridden. But I'm keen to try if you have one."

"No, no horses."

"Oh." Milla slouched.

"But a car's nothing to be scared of, dear. Even when they look like that."

"A car? I've read about cars. Automobiles." She looked at the hunk of metal. "I pictured them more glamorously in my head."

"Haven't we all?" Betty said with a glance to Walter.

Milla wobbled down the steps courtesy of her new boots and, brushing her hand along the warm nose of the car, peered under the belly. All metal. She stood up and stared in amazement.

"I know. Total wreck," Parker said through the open window. "But grandpa's stubborn. This or walking's the only way to get there and I saw how you handled those boots. Either way, you'll be embarrassed."

Walter hurried down and opened the door for her. "Go on, now. Get in."

Milla crawled in, maneuvering awkwardly into the proper seated position given the tight confines and her crazy boots. Walter pushed down a button on the door, slammed it shut, and tugged on it firmly. Apparently, he liked locked doors.

"Buckle up," Parker said.

Milla started buttoning her sweater and Parker laughed.

"Your seatbelt."

He leaned over and grabbed a strap from the side of her seat, his hair tickling her face and his neck practically touching her lips. She could taste the sweet saltiness of his skin.

"Wow, I can hear your heart pounding. Are you okay?"

She managed a nod. Once he fastened her seatbelt, he repositioned himself and guided the car away from Betty and Walter. Milla clutched her seat with both hands. If he thought her heart raced before, he should hear it now. Goodness, he probably could.

As they traveled, she observed many metal beasts—cars—waiting obediently for their owners. Like the horses of the army, she supposed.

"My parents died, too," Parker said. "Car accident after they dropped me off for summer vacation eight years ago. Been here ever since."

"How do you go on?"

"It's kind of always sad, but you get used to it in a weird way after a while and then it's just a part of you."

"I can't imagine I'll ever get used to it."

Parker nodded. "Got any other family?"

"I have no one, except a friend, but he infuriates me."

"Sounds like a boyfriend."

"He's a boy friend."

"So is that why you broke into the shop? Needed money for a place to stay?"

"I only broke the pottery. I'll study to fix it if you want."

"I don't think you can fix antique china."

"Not yet but with practice."

He laughed. "Don't worry about it."

Despite dark clouds, daylight pushed through as Parker directed the Gremlin onto a path with a sign that read Greene Street. Though spelled differently, Milla presumed it was named for its gardens because the homes on Greene Street had perfectly shorn blades of grass.

"Does no one live in a shack?"

"Lots of people do, just not in this neighborhood." He steered the beast onto Elm Crescent, and the sky cracked with thunder, splashing down globs of rain. Milla leaned back against the spongy fabric, unbothered by the splatter on her face through her opened window. From her periphery, she noticed Parker sneaking glimpses of her, and her stomach squeezed with a wonderful ache. Discreetly, she wiped the dirt off her face and combed through her matted hair with her fingers, finding bits of twigs and leaves. Mortifying.

When the Gremlin turned onto Rose Garden Parkway, Milla bolted upright. The street ended at a gray stone castle that boasted two huge metaled lions—green, motionless—standing guard on either side of the steps leading up. Velvety turf and vibrant blue, pink, and yellow flowers did nothing to warm the structure. Parker eased the car into the U-shaped pathway, rolling to a stop before a sign that read Rose Garden Hospital, and the car shook, then settled into silence.

"Here we are." He got out and jogged toward the castle, covering his head from the rain.

Milla jiggled her seatbelt until it unfastened but couldn't open the locked door. She climbed through the window, her hands hitting the wet ground, half in, half out, when Parker hurried back.

"What're you doing? The door works." He lifted her up anyway, and pulled her the rest of the way out. She about-faced but Parker grabbed her arm before she could get away.

"Whoa. You trying to get me in trouble with my grandparents?"

"I'm not going in that fortress."

"It's a hospital."

"It's evil. Look at it."

"Buildings can't be evil. They're not alive."

"Since when?"

"*Since wh—*" he started but stopped and changed the subject. "Are you afraid of doctors? 'Cause all they're gonna do is clean your feet and make sure they're not infected. C'mon, I'm soaking wet."

He took her hand and somehow thieved her senses because she was willingly running toward the entrance with him. On her way up the steps, she stroked one of the metal lions to show her benevolence, in case she needed an ally.

The double doors, as tall as the structure and made of mahogany, looked more like a drawbridge and Milla fought those invasive visions from Asper: soldiers, ogres, and rats. Parker opened the heavy door and the images burst into oblivion.

An odor, stringent yet sweet, hijacked Milla's palate, souring her glands. For a vestibule so grand, the air was as stagnant as a hidden passageway in an earthen tunnel. Off to the side, a burgundy couch of polished hide and two plush chairs in a burgundy floral fabric were unoccupied. In the center of the room, a round table made of wood, but shiny, displayed an arrangement of white and pink flowers in a glass vase. Overhead, an enormous chandelier with motionless candles lit the room and reflected off the polished marble floors.

Parker leaned in close enough for Milla to feel his breath and whispered, "I know, it's more like a hotel than hospital. They refurbed an old church and built onto it. But past the lobby, it's all medical. Had my tonsils out here." When she thought for sure their lips would touch, he said, "Let's go check in with the nurse."

He strode across the cavernous room toward a woman tucked behind a long oval desk made of the same shiny wood as the table. Milla followed.

"Hi, Parker, I just got off the phone with your grandmother." She turned to Milla. "You must be Milla. I'm Connie. We've been expecting you. Doctor Thorn's on duty today," she said as if it meant something.

"He's the one who yanked my tonsils," Parker said to Milla.

"I don't wish to have anything yanked."

Parker and Connie laughed and Milla was sufficiently discomfited by now that everyone seemed to laugh when she wasn't saying anything funny.

"Noted," Connie said. She emerged from behind the desk and pushed a chair with wheels toward Milla. "Go on."

"Am I to sit?"

"It's protocol."

"I'll wait for you here," Parker said. "See you when you're done."

Connie pushed Milla in her wheeled chair down several corridors, the next the same as the last, until they arrived in a large room with several beds, unoccupied, partitioned by curtains. With a band wrapped around her arm, Milla waited a long time considering they were the ones who wanted to see her. Finally, a short and pudgy man resembling an ogre—the nice kind—approached and introduced himself as Dr. Thorn. He deemed her cuts superficial and nothing to lose sleep over, not that she had planned to. He poked and prodded and asked if anything hurt and seemed less interested in her answers and more preoccupied with peering into her eyes, ears, mouth, and even her nose with a light. He rolled back on his wheeled stool.

"So you have no ID, is that right?"

She shrugged. She might if she knew what it was.

"No driver's license, passport, anything that says who you are?"

"I have this." She showed him the amber gem around her neck, half of a whole. "It fits perfectly with the piece my mother wore. She was killed when I was three."

"I'm sorry. And your father passed away as well, Betty told us. Was it recent?"

"Very." Milla bit her quivering lips. "The army."

"It takes a brave man. You must be proud of him."

She nodded.

"So, where're you from?"

"Asper."

"Is that near here?"

"In a way. It's in another dimension."

"Did you say dimension?"

"Yes."

He rolled closer. "Follow my finger with your eyes, don't move your head, please." She did. "Do you know who the president is, Milla?"

"Is it Parker?"

"No. It's not Parker. Do you know what day it is?"

"I lost track, but I believe it's close to the seventh phase in the full and first quarter moons."

"And can you tell me how you got here from your dimension?"

"A verse from my *Quodex*."

"Codex?"

"*Quodex*. My book of sorcery."

"I see. And you ended up in Walter's Antiques? That's where you fell, right?"

"I was thrown, from the portal."

"So there's a portal?"

"Yes. The mirror with candles on both sides."

"Oh, the cheval. I'm familiar with it. I've tried to buy it many times."

"No. No, you can't! No one can."

"Calm down, Milla."

"You don't understand! The mirror mustn't be moved, otherwise the paths won't cross. I won't be able to go home, but I have to. I have to kill the queen."

The doctor froze so abruptly, Milla thought she immobilized him with a spell, then remembered she didn't know how.

Parker awoke with a start when Hailey plopped down beside him on the couch and said, "Hey, stranger."

She had her long, blond hair in a ponytail, and was wearing the mandatory white hospital coat for volunteers, except hers was adorned with the gold and silver pin Parker had given her for her birthday last year. Two hearts intertwined. He shifted, uncomfortable by her closeness.

"Don't be like that," she said with a pout. "You didn't come all the way over here to still be mad at me, did you?"

"I'm not mad, Hailey."

"Good." She smiled and Parker almost *wasn't* mad anymore. "So'd you get your tux?"

"I'm not going to the prom, I told you."

"I thought you said you weren't mad?"

"I'm not, but we're still broken up."

The happiness drained from her face. "I promise I won't pressure you to get back together if that's what you're worried about. I won't even treat it like a date," she said. "We'll go as friends."

He shook his head. "Sorry."

"C'mon, Parker. Don't make me go alone."

"I'm not making you do anything. You can go with whoever you want."

"I choose you," she said with a huge smile.

Parker rubbed his tired eyes. He didn't have it in him to go head to head with Hailey this morning. "Why can't you just let it be?"

"Because we belong together. And you know it."

"You're wrong."

"Then why're you here?"

Dr. Thorn and Connie emerged from the corridor with Milla, and Parker jumped to his feet. "Good to go?" He didn't have to turn around to feel the heat of Hailey's glare.

"Milla's going to stay with us a few nights," Dr. Thorn said.

"Why? Does she have a concussion?"

Dr. Thorn took Parker aside, speaking quietly. "She's disoriented. She doesn't know what day it is, doesn't know who the president is."

"That's because she's Amish or Quaker or something."

"She thinks she's a sorceress, Parker. She wants to kill the queen."

"Of England?"

"Does it matter?"

Parker deflated. "I'll let my grandma know." He headed toward the door.

"Parker." Milla ran to him, falling into his arms thanks to the unwieldy boots. "I don't want to stay here."

"It's not for long, you'll be okay."

"Let's get you to your room, hon," Connie said, putting an arm on Milla's shoulder.

Parker pivoted to leave but heard Hailey say, "I'll go with. Make sure she has everything she needs." He gave her a cautioning look and she replied with a wink. He stormed out the heavy doors.

Milla sat in the chair with wheels while the fast-moving Connie pushed it down the corridor and Hailey strode alongside.

"Are you a doctor?" Milla asked Hailey.

"I'm not even out of high school. How old do you think I am?"

"Sixteen, perhaps?"

"So, obviously, not a doctor."

"Obviously," Milla said, not because it was but because she didn't favor Hailey's tone. They traveled three corridors, never reaching the end of any of them before taking the next. Along the way, they passed several people, none as hostile as Hailey.

"Here we are," Connie said. "Room one-twelve."

"The Royal Suite," Hailey said with a smirk.

A bed, a side table, a tray on wheels, and a bright orange chair were squeezed into the chamber. By the entrance, a bathroom with a flimsy door provided little in the way of privacy. Milla craved the warmth of her shack and the comfort of objects wafting about while her father rattled off incantations.

"You can get out of the chair now," Connie said, then turned to Hailey. "Please bring her some toiletries and a lunch menu."

"Sure thing." Hailey marched out.

"Are you hungry?" Connie asked.

"No." Milla's stomach was too knotted with nerves to make room for food. Even the way Parker had left made her feel as though she'd done something wrong.

"Well, fill out your lunch request and mark any restrictions. Kosher, vegan, allergies. Your gown's there. If you need anything, I'm a buzz away." Connie took the chair with her as she left and Milla hoped nothing she said was important.

Hailey returned with the menu and a clear bag of items and tossed them on the tray with wheels. "Just so you know," she said, leaning in to the point that Milla thought the girl might kiss her, "Parker is mine."

Milla's *Quodex* squirmed in a miff in the back of her waistband, but she quieted the book with her hand and waited until Hailey's footsteps faded into silence down the corridor.

"What a witch." Milla removed her *Quodex* and her book heaved in agreement. She placed it between the pillows for some much-deserved rest and picked up the gown at the foot of the bed. Softer than burlap, cozy, but too immodest with its minimal clasping. She tossed it back on the bed, crossed the room, and looked out the solitary window.

An area where stationary beasts rested in strict formation was her royal view from this Royal Suite. She tried to open the window, but it was sealed shut; the culprit for the stale air. She leaned against the wall, eyes closed, and listened to the song of rain on the glass. She stayed that way the rest of the day, letting lunch and dinner come and go, untouched, vowing to crack open her *Quodex* any second now.

Sneaking footsteps jolted Milla faster than a sorcerer's bolt and she spun from the window, heavy with anxiety.

"Sorry," Parker said in a quiet voice, standing in the doorway. "Didn't mean to scare you."

"What are you doing here? We must be in the peak of night."

"Thought you'd be asleep. I was just gonna drop this off for you." He held out a thin compendium of pages for her.

"What is it?"

"Comic book. If you like it, I have more."

She shook it. "I would hardly call this a book."

"Well, it's not literature." He smiled. "It's better."

She glanced through the first few pages, taken aback. "This is more picture than word."

"Yeah. You've never seen a comic book before?"

"No."

"I wouldn't call him your typical superhero, but I thought you'd find it relatable in a way. His parents... well, you'll see. Unless you're not into it." He took hold of the book, but she didn't let go.

"Oh, I'm... into it."

He released his grasp on the book and tilted his head in a mischievous way. "Since you're up, wanna sneak out for a bit?"

Does a desert vole covet beetle dung?

Milla carried her squeaky boots and they tiptoed through the corridors until they neared the vestibule. Parker peeked around the corner and she peered over his shoulder. A woman who wasn't Connie snored behind the desk. Parker put his finger to his lips and they escaped, undetected.

Milla slipped into her boots and Parker grabbed her hand and pulled her with him as he ran down the street, around the corner, two more blocks, and through a grassy area until Milla tripped and fell, taking him down with her. She erupted in laughter. Parker, too. The grass was still wet from the recent rain, but they both rolled onto their backs and caught their breaths. Milla stared at the starry sky with its single bright moon and neither said anything for the longest time. Parker leaned on his elbow, looking at her, and every drop of blood from her body funneled into her face, she was so self-conscious. Should she do the same? Should she close her mouth? Why was it open to begin with? Blasted, she must look like a speckled bass gulping for algae. She was saved from herself when Parker noticed her necklace.

"What's that?"

She took the opportunity to copy his casual elbow-lean, and held up the amulet to show him. "A gift from my father. He gave one half to me and the other to my mother."

"That's sweet. Did you ever get the other half back? When your mom died?"

"No."

"Oh. Too bad." He lay back down and she followed.

"Have you anything from your parents?"

"Just my good looks."

Milla laughed. "Pity they weren't more generous."

"Hey." He tapped her with his shoulder and she tingled from head to toe, and then some.

"Where'd you come from?" he asked.

"Asper."

"Yeah, geography's not really my thing. Is that here? Canada? Mars?"

"It's in another dimension."

Parker sat up, his smile gone. "So Doctor Thorn was right, you think you're from another dimension?"

Milla sat up now. "I am."

"There's no such thing."

"There most certainly is."

"Take me there."

"I can't return. Not yet. The army will capture me."

"That's convenient."

"It's most inconvenient."

Parker got to his feet. "Let's go. You need to get back to the hospital."

"Why are you angry?"

"Because."

"'Because' is not a reason. My father has said so many times."

"How come we haven't heard of your dimension?"

"We don't want to be found. We once lived in harmony, but our world was threatened by yours. You wanted our *Book of Knowing*."

"*Book of Knowing*? Like a real book? That knows things?"

"Knows everything."

"Can I see it?"

"It's guarded by a dragon. No one knows where."

"Wow. A dragon. Again, convenient."

"Again, I assure you, it is not."

Parker shook his head. "So, you come from this other dimension where everyone does magic and there's one book, clever title by the way, that knows everything there is to know?"

"Only sorcerers can do magic."

He laughed, but in a way that didn't seem amused. "Only sorcerers do magic." He plopped down on the grass and stared out. "I suppose your book knows the meaning of life. And why good people die tragically."

Milla sat next to him. "I've never read it. I only know the stories passed down and none have spoken on the meaning of life. Or why even the noblest people die tragically."

He plucked blades of grass, as if he needed something to do to avoid looking at her. "So tell me what happened."

"Your world believed our *Book* would dispel the myths of Asper, but in truth, it revealed the secrets of sorcery, and we feared you would use that knowledge to destroy our world. Many sorcerers tried to hex the *Book* so it couldn't be stolen, but it's impervious to sorcery, even a protection spell. One day, the *Book* disappeared. History tells us that's when the Omniscient placed it with the dragon, where it has remained since."

"And you guys pop back and forth, from here to Asper?"

"No. Our ruler forbade it to ensure we'd remain separate and trusted the portals would be buried in time. They were abandoned for thousands of years until nary a sorcerer knew where they were anymore."

"'*Nary* a sorcerer,' huh? You *must* be from another dimension."

"I believe you tease me now."

"But you knew where it was."

"My *Quodex* is passed down from the beginning of my family. I have spells no others have."

"I don't want to tell you how to do your world, but here, dragons and evil queens are kinda cliché."

"Have you no evil rulers?"

"Hm. Good point."

"No creatures to fear?"

"Sure. Sharks, for one."

"We have sharks. They're friendly."

"They are?"

"Compared to dragons."

"Okay, now you're teasing me."

Of course she was.

"But seriously, sharks aren't friendly here, okay?" He took her hand and pulled her to her feet. "Show me some sorcery."

"I can't without my *Quodex*. I wasn't a good study."

"Well, we have that in common. So you're not born knowing magic, you have to learn it?"

"We inherit the verses, knowledge, and spells of our mothers and in rare instances our fathers, but we have to study to hone our skills. Even with the aid of my *Quodex*, I'm not well learned past Chapter Three."

"Between us, I wouldn't know a Chapter Three from a Chapter Twenty spell."

"In that case, I'll perform an impressive Chapter Twenty spell for you when I have my book."

"You're really a sorceress?"

"I am."

"And you want to kill the queen?"

"She killed my father."

"A drunk driver killed my parents, but I didn't go and kill him."

"Why not?"

"Because it's wrong."

"My father was slain because he was a sorcerer. As were the others before him. I lived my life in hiding, far from the castle, but she found us. She'll always find us and when she does, she'll usurp our knowledge, toss our flesh to the 'mongers, and search for the next, until she has eliminated the entire lineage for our power. And now she has a scroll to unite Asper with Earth. Believe me, she'll be the ruination of us all. She must be stopped."

"Do me a favor. If Thorn brings it up again, just say you were confused after hitting your head. No one here will understand the whole sorcery thing. Okay?"

Milla nodded.

They strolled back toward the hospital and along the way bumped each other playfully, alternating between shoulders and hips, and laughed any time one of them lost their balance. When they arrived, Parker held the door ajar for Milla to slip through and, boots in hand, she tiptoed past the same woman sleeping behind the desk and ran quietly back to her room.

"Wow. She's crazy. Like full-on nutcake."

Parker spun, his bliss extinguished by Hailey, leaning against one of the lions.

"Were you following me?"

She clutched her hands to her chest and feigned distress. "Our world was threatened. We hid the book with a ferocious dragon. Save me, my knight in shining armor."

Parker took the steps three at a time, passing her without a word. Hailey caught up and kept pace as they walked down the block. "Oh, come on, Parker. You don't believe her."

"Why were you stalking me, Hailey? That's what's crazy."

She slapped his shoulder. "I'm not stalking you. I went to the park to think, that's what I do. It's not my fault you were there with Miss Delusional. And by the way, why were you there with her?"

"It's none of your business." Parker rounded the corner and stopped before his bike, where he had left it so the nurses wouldn't hear him pull up. He was about to climb on, but Hailey darted in front of him and blocked his path.

"If you're trying to get back at me, it worked okay? It hurt to see you with her, so we're even now."

"I'm not trying to get even. I'm trying to move on."

"Don't." Her pleading eyes crushed his determination. Maybe he did still love her. "I'm sorry, Parker. I hate myself more than you ever could, but I want to make it up to you."

"You can't."

Tears pooled in an instant and trickled down her cheeks.

"Don't cry."

"I can't help it. Every time you look at me with indifference, I want to rip my heart out. Parker, I swear, I'll do anything. Anything. Please, give me another chance."

"You have to stop this, okay? The sooner you accept it, the sooner we can go on with our lives."

Hailey wiped her eyes and nose. "It's because of her, isn't it? You can't wait to sleep around."

Parker glared at her; she had some nerve. He got on his bike and started it, revving the engine to force her out of the way.

She stepped aside but grabbed his arm before he could put on his helmet. "If you see her again, I'll tell your grandmother everything. I mean it."

"Thanks for reminding me why we're broken up." He tore off, fishtailing around the corner.

CHAPTER FOUR

UNFILTERED SUNLIGHT WOKE MILLA and she jumped out of bed, sending her *Quodex* flying off her chest. She splashed her face with water, soothing her dry eyes, and brushed her ebony hair, which stuck out in every direction as if each strand had a mind of its own. She dug the grass and mud out from under her nails, sat on the edge of her cot, eyes glued to the door, and received a whack right in the nook of her ankle.

"Ow, beast." Milla grimaced and scooped up her *Quodex* from the floor, brushing off the velvet cover. "No need to overreact. It was an accident."

Her *Quodex* huffed (because it never believed her) and settled its pages on their current verse—the one she was studying last night.

"Yes, I remember now."

It closed itself with a snort, daring her to perform it.

"I didn't say I completed the study, only that I was... oh, stop chiding me."

The know-it-all was right; Milla hadn't memorized a single line, but she could recite every detail of Parker, front to back, head to toe. She had fallen asleep thinking of him and awoke wanting more. She blushed, her face hotter than a witch's cauldron, and tapped her foot with the perfect amount of fervor to jostle her *Quodex* off her lap and onto the bed. "Apologies."

Her *Quodex* sighed in defeat, and in good timing, too, because Betty entered carrying several paper sacks. "Knock, knock," she said.

"Knock, knock," Milla said back.

Betty chuckled. "I brought you some clothes. I know you don't have much use for them in here, but you won't be here forever." She laid out several shirts with short sleeves, long sleeves, and no sleeves at all, dresses of different lengths and fabrics, and three pairs of pants, one of them scarcely long enough to cover Milla's thighs.

"These are for me?"

"I hope they fit."

Milla hugged her tightly. "You're truly extraordinary, Betty."

"Now, go on. It's just clothes."

Milla dug through them. "How did you make so many pieces so quickly?"

"Heavens, I didn't make them. I bought them. Shopping's a hobby of mine. How do you think we got Walter's Antiques?"

Milla held a lightweight dress to her form. "Parker will be impressed."

"Oh, Parker? I reckon he will, but you don't want to go and impress anyone too much." Betty handed Milla a pair of shoes. "Try these on."

Milla squeezed and stuffed but couldn't cram her foot into the shoe.

"I don't think that's a fight you'll win, dear." Betty collected the shoes. "I'll return them, see if I can't find some that fit. What size are you?"

Milla held her hands apart, eyeballing a guess. "I appear to be about this size."

"So you do." Betty put her foot next to Milla's and said, "Eight and a half ought to do it." She kissed her on the cheek and left.

Milla lingered in the sentiment, then threw off her burlap tatters and slipped into the dress. The supple fabric clung delicately to her frame and revealed a femininity she had never noticed before. It also revealed the three moons on her right shoulder blade.

She flattened her hair in place, stepped into Walter's preposterous boots, and sat on the edge of the bed, opening her *Quodex* to one of the many annihilation spells. The book fought against it, shuffling to earlier spells, but Milla pinned the page she wanted with her elbow. "Stop arguing and let me do what I need to do."

Her *Quodex* had the gall to flip its opposite side, trying to shut itself, but Milla dug in with both elbows now. "Get it through your parchment, beast. I'm the boss of you, not the other way around."

The verse bled into a puddle on the page, flicking a droplet of ink onto Milla's nose. "Very mature." She jerked her arms away, catching the righteous book by surprise, and it slammed shut with a startled groan. Giddy with triumph, she jammed it under the mattress and sat on it before it could retaliate. She rubbed her nose clean. The book jolted, throwing her off the bed and onto the floor as Hailey was rolling a cart of biscuits and beverages by.

"Clumsy, much?"

"Quite." Milla got to her feet, trusting her unruly *Quodex* knew to stay hidden.

"What's with the dress?"

"It was a gift from Betty. Isn't it beautiful?"

"Yeah, well, if you think it's gonna win over Parker, you can put your rags back on. He's not gonna see you again."

"Why do you say that?"

"Because he's in love with me."

Milla sank to the bed, reaching for the comfort of her *Quodex* that wasn't there. Hailey left her cart in the corridor and entered.

"Look, you seem nice enough and I'm not saying this to be mean, but I've been with Parker since junior high, and no matter how many times we break up, we always get back together because we can't live without each other. So save yourself some heartache and find someone else to crush on." She offered a sympathetic smile, the kind that Tobly gave whenever Milla failed at something, and pushed the cart away.

Milla ripped the ridiculous dress off her quaking body. Served her right for getting sidetracked from her goal. The sooner she returned home, the better. She pulled on a sturdy pair of pants and threw a soft short-sleeved shirt over her head. She hurried toward the exit when her *Quodex,* now on top of the bed, wafted its pages loudly. She waved a hand over her shoulder. "Calm down. I'm going in search of cassava root for the elixir."

Milla strode through the corridors, peering into every chamber she passed. Not one bulb, stalk, or root of value. She continued until she reached the recreation room on the opposite side of the hospital and peeked inside. The floor was checkered with black and white squares, and shiny like all the surfaces here. On a plush sofa, several people chatted, none of them Parker. An unoccupied table had a picture puzzle with pieces missing in several places. Shelves brimmed, not with potions and elixirs, but with books and books and more books. They were ratty and torn and probably dated back to the ones she had gotten from her ancestors.

She wandered in, flabbergasted to find a Crystal Beholder, huge, clear, and pristine, mounted on the wall. Not wanting her essence to be drawn in—she'd never entered that realm before and couldn't risk it now—she eased back, but then realized there was no one near the rock, no shell awaiting the return of its aura. Could it be? Beholding without an astral plane journey? And flawless and crisp, image and sound. Even the most practiced conjurers in Asper had murky, short-lived treks.

She scanned the room, searching for the traveler; perhaps an ally from Asper fleeing the queen or a sorcerer who had never left at the time of the rift. From the couch, a woman changed the vision from one world to another, not with a wave or incantation but with a handheld device, and Milla nearly buckled. How easily she and her father could've avoided the army with such a magnificent Beholder. Did Parker not know about this?

She scuttled to the back of the room and watched others battle malfeasance in their lives. At first, she worried for two men who found misfortune at every corner, but she grew to enjoy their antics. They were unflappable; a testament of their courage. When they were captured, they cleverly escaped with a hand-clapping spell about patty-cakes and a baker's man. If her *Quodex* had spells as fun as these, she would've studied long ago. She gasped. Her *Quodex*!

Milla ran through the hallways. Oh, she wouldn't hear the end of it from that book. Honestly, she must be cursed with a spell of distraction. She raced into her room with apologies on her mind and found Hailey riffling through her *Quodex*. "Don't touch that!"

Hailey spun around, startled. Milla leaped over the bed to grab her book and only realized after her arm stung with pain that Hailey was also holding her knife. The straight-edge of the blade dripped with blood, Milla's blood. Hailey dropped the weapon and the *Quodex,* and fled, yelling for Dr. Thorn.

Bright, shimmering crimson droplets hit the sheets and merged into one dull blotch of red. Milla plucked the immodest gown off the railing and wrapped it around her forearm to spare the rest of the bedding. Dr. Thorn hurried in with an orderly by his side and Hailey at the door.

"Milla, leave the knife where it is," he said unnecessarily since she wasn't anywhere near it. He motioned to the orderly, who snatched it up and marched out.

"That's mine," Milla said, but the orderly left without acknowledging her. Dr. Thorn peeled the gown off her sticky wound and seemed relieved.

"You won't need stitches, but we should get you cleaned and wrapped." Milla nodded.

"Is this something you've done before, Milla? Do you cut yourself often?"

"I didn't cut myself."

"Yes you did. I saw you," Hailey said.

"No. Why would you say—"

"I thought I was next, Doctor Thorn," Hailey said through tears. "Why does she have a knife? This is a hospital." She wiped her wet eyes.

"Take the rest of the day, Hailey. We'll make sure this doesn't happen again," Dr. Thorn said. Hailey hurried off.

"Please," Milla said to Dr. Thorn. "May I have my knife?"

"To do what, Milla? Hurt someone else?"

"No. I didn't do this, my oath. It was an accident. You must believe me. I wouldn't hurt myself or anyone."

"Not even the queen?"

Blasted.

CHAPTER FIVE

PARKER RODE HIS MOTORCYCLE along the winding road. Under a moonless night, the two-lane highway was pitch black except for his headlight. His knee grazed the cement as he hugged the hairpin curve and he opened up on the straightaway, gunning for one twenty. Flashing lights moved in on him from behind, followed by the siren blips.

"Oh man." He downshifted and slowed until he pulled off to the shoulder. The sheriff's car came to a halt behind him, lights still flashing. The burly blond-haired, pink-skinned man exited the car and sauntered over.

"Parker," he said with a nod.

"Hi, Hank."

"You're not the only one usin' these roads, y'know."

"Sorry."

"Your grandma know you're out here?"

"No, sir."

"I don't gotta tell you what a tragedy it'd be for them to lose their grandson in a traffic incident, do I?"

Parker dropped his head. "No, sir."

"Son, there are other ways to work out your troubles." Hank took out his ticket pad and wrote him up. "Can't give you any more warnings."

Hank handed him the ticket and Parker waited for him to drive away before heading out. He stayed under the speed limit.

A block from home, Parker cut his engine and rolled his motorcycle the rest of the way. Hailey was sitting on the porch steps. He sighed.

"It's kinda late, don't you think?" he said. She looked up, her eyes red from crying. "What's wrong?"

"She had a knife, Parker. I thought she was going to kill me." She sobbed and threw her arms around him. Parker pulled away.

"Who did?"

"That crazy girl. She cut herself and when I came in and saw her, she tried to attack me. I ran out and got Doctor Thorn. You can ask him, ask anyone there."

"I will."

Hailey sniffled and wiped her eyes and nose. "How'd this happen, Parker? You can barely stand me anymore."

"Can we do this tomorrow? I don't wanna wake up my grandparents."

"Since when do you care about that? We used to hang out all night sometimes. I miss it. Don't you?"

"It doesn't matter if I miss it. That's not the point."

"I'm really sorry, Parker. It kills me that I was so stupid, but I was sad and angry. I didn't handle it right, but we can't throw away what we had because I made a mistake." She took his hand. "We almost had a baby together."

"Stop it. Stop using that to manipulate me." He marched past her, but she pulled him back.

"You're being selfish, acting like it only hurt you, you know? I cry about it all the time. Still."

"So do I. But like everything else, it can't be undone." Parker pulled his arm free and hurried around the back of the shop, leaving Hailey on the porch. He didn't take the stairs to the apartment though; he leaned against the wall and bit down on his trembling lip. A moment later, the screen door in front creaked open.

"You best be getting home now, Hailey," his grandmother said. Parker shook his head, no idea what she had heard, if anything. Hailey left without a word.

He waited for the door to close, but instead his grandmother gasped, still on the porch. "Walter! I thought you were upstairs."

"What're you looking at?"

"Nothing." She exhaled with the heaviness usually reserved for

Parker's Cs and Ds. "It's a different world, Walter. Same rules don't apply. Everything's moving faster and life's not waiting for us to catch up. Can't say I'm of any use at all."

"Parker's a good boy, Betty," his grandfather said as the screen door squeaked to a close.

Parker stayed against the wall, eyes squeezed shut, letting the night air numb his emotions. No good. He grabbed his bike, wheeled it half a block before starting it, and rode at a respectable speed through the neighborhood, not calling attention to himself. A street over from the hospital, he cut the engine and walked the rest of the way.

He opened the door quietly, hoping to slip in undetected, but Connie was working and she never slept on duty, even double-shifts. A lesson he had learned the many times he tried to sneak past when Hailey had broken her leg last year.

"Hey, Connie," he said as casually as he could. "Hailey left her bag in her locker. Do you mind? Told her I'd get it for her."

Connie nodded. "Sure. Is she doing okay? Must've been scary."

So it was true. "Yeah. She's good."

"I'm glad."

Parker hurried off before Connie could engage further. Once he rounded the corner, he ran down the corridor and, looking over his shoulder, darted into the hallway leading to Milla's room.

Milla was staring out the window like she was the first time he had come to see her. He slipped in and stayed by the wall to the side of the door.

"Hey," he said quietly. She turned and his pulse spiked. Hailey wasn't lying about that either; he definitely had a thing for this girl.

"Parker. I thought you wouldn't come."

"Long story." With a nod to the bandage on her arm, he asked, "Did you cut yourself?"

"No, it was an accident. Long story," she said with a smile.

"But you have a knife? Why?"

"Why? For carving, food gathering, and most importantly, protection. Is it unusual to have a weapon here?"

Parker sighed. How'd she always turn it around to make sense? "No, not unusual. Just, you know, not in hospitals. So what happened?"

"Hailey had my *Quodex*. I panicked and leaped for it. I didn't know she had my knife."

"Hailey did this?"

"She didn't mean to. She ran for help as soon as she saw what happened, but I think she feared she'd be punished. She told the doctor I hurt myself."

Parker tightened his lips. Hailey's motives were never easy to read.

"Is she your beloved?" Milla asked.

"Beloved? No. I'm not even sure we're friends. Let's not talk about Hailey."

"Can we go outside again?"

"Can't. Connie's on duty. No one gets past her."

"Like the bridge ogres."

Parker laughed. "Yeah, probably." He motioned to the book on Milla's bedside table. "Is that your book of tricks?"

"Yes."

"Well…"

"Well?"

"You said you'd show me some magic when you had it."

"Of course." She grabbed the book, but when she tried to open the cover, it flipped in her hands, still closed.

"Is it locked?"

"No, simply willful. It fancies itself superior." She sat on the edge of the bed and wrestled it open.

"The book's alive?"

"Mildly sentient." The book snapped shut on her fingers and she yelped.

"How'd it do that?"

"Please, don't encourage it." She pried it open and held the cover down with her elbow. "Material or ethereal?"

"What's the difference?"

"Material requires an object to control or alter."

"Like turning a pumpkin into a chariot?"

"Precisely. Though I'm unfamiliar with that particular verse. Ethereal utilizes the elements of the universe."

"Which one's easier?"

"Neither."

"Surprise me. But don't turn me into a frog."

Milla almost smiled but stopped abruptly, stiffening upright, and Parker didn't have to follow her gaze to know.

"Did you get lost?" Connie said with a stern look.

"Hailey's bag wasn't in her locker. I thought maybe she left it somewhere else."

"In Milla's room?"

"No, I was looking around and saw that she was up, so I popped in."

"Visiting hours end at eight, Parker."

"Sorry." He snuck a wink to Milla. "See you tomorrow."

"You won't forget?"

"They can't release you without someone to pick you up. I'll be here." Milla smiled, which made him smile. He left the room and Connie escorted him to the exit.

"I know it's not my business, Parker, but I've known you since you moved here and, well, we all feel a little protective over you, you know?" He knew. He was the kid whose parents died in a horrible car wreck. "There's something not right about that girl. I know she's pretty and she seems harmless, but something's going on inside her that isn't normal."

"That's because she's a sorceress."

"I hope you're joking."

"I'm pretty sure it was your house my grandma dragged me to so we could wave some magic sage around before you moved in."

Connie flared her nostrils, lips pursed. "Spirits are of this world, Parker, they're real."

He left.

Milla hurried to the window, hoping to see Parker, but he never passed by the stationary beasts. She pirouetted toward the bed and found herself in a dark chamber inside the castle. She choked on a gasp and was back in the Royal Suite, coughing up a fit until her eyes watered. Her *Quodex* beckoned with a tender flutter, but she slapped the cover shut.

"Save your false sympathy. Had you any concern for me, you wouldn't have humiliated me."

The book spun away in a huff and Milla followed with her own, but a boom of thunder startled her onto the bed in a shivering huddle. The hot breath of the queen hit her face before the queen herself appeared, lifting Milla's chin up with her long black fingernail. Then vanished. Milla grabbed the pillows, squeezing them to her chest, as she rocked. "Are you doing this, beast? Stop it."

The *Quodex* didn't respond; instead, her father's spell did. Ethereal glints bled from her pores and dripped off her body. She clutched her throat, smothered by the stickiness of the waning spell.

"No, no, please." She tried to shove fleeing sparks back inside her skin. "I don't want to know, I don't want to know." Her mind whirled with dizziness. She fumbled for her *Quodex,* but the wall pushed up against her back and the bars of the window closed in on her, caging her in.

"Please… stop."

With no esteem for her pleas whatsoever, Earth ceased its rotation and its essence shot past in a blurred trail as Milla was catapulted through time.

CHAPTER SIX

FIVE YEARS OLD, give or take three moons, Milla turned in a slow circle to inhale the beauty of Lost Creek. The pond dazzled, bejeweled by sunlight, and a magnificent tree dotted the air with fragrance. "Mother used to play here?"

"Her favorite place in all the worlds," her father said.

Milla folded her arms and blew the uneven bangs from her left eye, looking from her father to Queldar and back again. What to do, what to do? In a quick burst, she tapped Queldar's arm and ran. "Chase."

He scampered after her and she took cover behind her father, grabbing his cloak and spinning him. Queldar dodged left and right, in pursuit.

"You cannot outrun me, child. I'm swift as a sorcerer can be. Agile and—" He slipped and his arms windmilled for balance as his feet shuffled. Milla shrieked with laughter and her father joined in.

But the air stifled, devoid of movement, of life. The water in the pond may as well have been glass for it was that still. A suffocating chill cut Milla's laughter and she turned to her father, no time to speak; the captain, sheathed in black armor atop his armored horse, burst through the air before her.

"Milla!" Her father ran toward her.

Queldar shot coils of electricity from his fingertips, but the captain plucked her up in his metal-clad arms, unscathed.

"Father!" She reached out as she sank through the cold then warm aura of the Shift. Her father was gone in an unfathomable blink. Lost Creek vanished, replaced with a forest of charcoal trees and gray skies.

"No!" she screamed. "I want my father, I want my father!"

The captain threw her into a cage that was shielded in its own box of metal armor. Droplets of daylight came through a slotted opening above. She pushed on the door, but it stayed in place, perhaps by magic because she couldn't find a lock. She buried her head in her hands and sobbed.

"Quiet," the captain said, kicking the box hard enough to propel her through the air. She landed on her face. Grasping the bars, she stayed down as his horse galloped forth, and still, she was hurled about until her body colored with pain. After sinking in and out of countless Shifts, predatory snarls closed in on her and she was sure she'd been captured as bait. Rabid beasts leaped onto her cage from all sides, sending her cracking against metal. Pungent spit spilled through the slot above, drenching her with its acidic sting, but she didn't care. Nothing hurt anymore anyway. The slot closed, submerging her into total darkness, and the beasts lost interest. She wasn't bait, after all.

The captain ascended a steep incline, and Milla slid back, wedged into the cold bars. When the protective box was finally lifted, a pair of soulless black eyes stared into hers. She scrambled back with nowhere to go.

The eyes welled with tears, happy tears, and the smiling woman flicked her long fingers, melting the bars on the cage. "Milla. My sweet, precious daughter."

Milla jumped to her feet. "You're not my mother."

The woman tilted her head, brows pinched, amused. "They not only kept you from me, they kept the truth from you. I'm Lucrecia, queen of Asper. And you, my little princess, are heir to my throne."

Milla realized where she was now. Inside the queen's chamber in the queen's castle. The castle no sorcerer dared speak of, lest they be found and silenced. Exquisite threadlike gold and silver papered the wall. The smooth marble floor, which Lucrecia's feet barely touched, shone like the pond at Lost Creek. Her bedding was satiny and plush, her crystal brush sparkled as much as her jewels, and her perfumes sweetened the air. The torches, however, boasted the same personality as the queen, warm with underlying evil.

"You're mistaken." Milla marched toward the door, but an invisible force blocked her path. She pounded on it. "Let me pass."

The queen formed in front of her from glittering particles. "Poor thing, you're in shock. But don't fret. I promise you'll have every happiness in your new home." She addressed her soldier. "Show my child to her quarters, Vylkrost."

The door swung open magically and the force stopping Milla vanished. Vylkrost took her by the wrist and exited the queen's chamber. He led her down a labyrinthine stairwell and, at one point, swung her over a long drop to the belly of the dungeon, either intentionally or recklessly, Milla couldn't tell. She held her breath, preparing for him to let go, but he abruptly turned into a corridor, taking her with him.

He marched down the long hallway until he reached the lone chamber on the floor and kicked open the door. Soon as he released her, Milla scurried between his legs and ran. She found the stairwell and descended hastily, slipping and tumbling several levels before catching her footing. Vylkrost gained on her and she ran faster, but the stairwell had no end. She ducked into the next corridor to hide and lost her bearings in the total blackness. A metal hand clutched her neck and she screamed.

Torches sprung to life, revealing an army of soldiers—some on horseback, some on foot, all in their dull metal skin—lining a corridor of opened chamber doors. Vylkrost emerged from the stairwell, scowling, and Milla quavered. He hauled her back to her chamber and slung her into the wall on the other side of the room. She bolted for the door, but it was locked. Screaming and begging, she yanked on the handle until her throat choked her with dryness.

A breeze whispered her name, and she hurried to the window, buoyed, only to encounter a hideous wroder in wait. She stumbled back, falling to the floor, and the giant bird thrust its head into her room. Its human-like eyes, peering out from beneath a brow of fleshy folds, zeroed in on her, but its stout featherless body couldn't squeeze through. Milla scuttled into the corner and hunkered into a ball until the bird flew off with squeals of discontent. The wind whispered her name again, but she rebuffed the trickery. She looked around her new quarters. Her prison.

The chamber wasn't fashioned of gold or crystal, but it was more opulent than anything she had ever known. Plush fabrics and oversized cushions warmed the spacious room, and sheer curtains softened the black stone walls. In the center, a bed four times the size of her straw cot back home had a three-tiered step for access. A vanity adorned with perfumes and silver-handled brushes beckoned to her melodiously, but she covered her ears. An intricately crafted iron chandelier of burning candles hung from the ceiling high above, and watched her, as did the heavy iron torches bordering the door. Milla yearned for the coziness of her shack; the warm embrace of mud and grass walls. The safety of her father.

She stayed in the corner, braving a night of frightful noises in the darkest dark. Every creak, crackle, and footstep reeked of malevolence. When morning arrived and her chamber door was opened, she fled. Vylkrost grabbed her by the scruff of her neck and held her face to face with her self-appointed mother.

"Disobedience will not be tolerated, my sweet." Lucrecia skulked off.

For three long days, Milla refused the sumptuous meals that appeared routinely on the round table where a child's tea set and porcelain doll in fancy clothes were set up. By the fourth night, hunger won out and she devoured the feast and licked the plate. She looked at the doll, filled with guilt, and climbed into bed for the first time since her capture and melted into the plush covers. The softness brought tears.

A plump rat, on its haunches, smiled contentedly and squeezed under the door and out of the room.

"Witch," Milla said in a raspy whisper before slumber eased her pain.

Days became weeks and weeks became months and Milla stopped hoping for freedom as every attempt led to a punishment more severe than the last. She could endure the chores, the scolding, the gruel, the isolation for days at a time, but being thrown in a prison cell to witness a crazed beast devour what appeared to be a little boy-like creature was too much. So she followed the rules. She sat on her bed when Lucrecia recounted stories while brushing her hair, she took her place next to the queen at the table for meals, and she spoke when spoken to and sat silently when not. And she studied her sorcery.

With several books on her lap, Milla slouched in the black marble throne in the middle of the aptly named Grand Hall. The entire room was constructed from marble, not just the throne, and shone brilliantly despite its deep ebony hue. Large and smooth with no visible delineation between floor, wall, or ceiling, it was an infinite pool of blackness. Inferno's presence added depth from time to time as it wafted by its flume behind the throne. Lucrecia paced the floor, or maybe slightly above it, and her metallic gown chimed in song.

"Come now, child. Surely you're not baffled by a Chapter Two verse?"

Surely you're not dim-witted enough to keep asking?

"How do you propose to rule if you cannot conjure?"

"I don't want to rule," Milla said. Lucrecia was eye to eye with her in an instant, Inferno by her side.

"You're my successor. This is your fate in life."

"Because you stole me."

"I created you."

"You're not my mother."

"I am, indeed. Now you'll study until the sun rises."

"I'm tired."

"Then you'll do well to study hard and perhaps tomorrow you can rest." Lucrecia summoned another hefty tome from one of the far-off pedestals and deposited it onto Milla's lap along with the others. She opened the pages to an impossible verse with the waggle of her finger and marched out of the Grand Hall, leaving Milla in the care of Inferno. When the witch's chimes dissipated, Milla closed the book.

"I'll do as I please." She curled into a ball on the throne and closed her eyes. Inferno bullied overhead, singeing her hair, and Milla swatted the fire away. Inferno snarled but receded. Milla fell asleep thinking of the number one hundred and fifty-three. One hundred and fifty-three sunrises seen from her castle chamber.

After a year in captivity, the castle was home. Milla dashed down the stairs, knocking aside a soldier in her haste. On the next landing, Zanub fell in behind her and kept pace. A year younger than her and already head and shoulders taller, he was the only other child in the castle, and the only male not covered in metal.

"Where do you go?" he asked.

"Where do you think?"

She hurried into the stables, lighting up at the rows and rows of beautiful horses, some armored, some not, obediently staying inside their doorless stalls. Malefactor, Lucrecia's steed, nickered with pleasure when Milla arrived.

"See? I told you. She likes me," Milla whispered to Zanub.

"Because you have carrots, no doubt."

She ignored him, even though she did have carrots, and appealed to Lucrecia, who hovered by her armored horse. "May I ride today?"

"May I ride today… what?" Lucrecia said.

"May I ride today, Mother?"

Lucrecia stroked Milla's cheek. "No, you may not." She handed her the reins and left.

Milla punched her fists to her sides and stomped her foot. "How could I give in?"

"Words mean nothing without sincerity," Zanub said, leaning against one of the stalls.

"Are you not going to help?"

"With your chores?" He laughed. "When you take my place in swordsmanship lessons, perhaps."

"Princesses use sorcery not swords," she said in a mocking tone.

"You fight the strangest fights."

Milla shoved bales of hay in front of, behind, and beneath Malefactor, allowing her to reach the horse from poll to tail, barrel to withers, and began stripping off its metal skin. Magicked by Lucrecia, the armor parted easily, and Zanub was by her side to take each piece.

She started at the head, eager to admire Malefactor's chestnut eyes and lively black mane, which danced unreservedly once freed. She patted the splash of white on the horse's forehead before removing the rest of its armor to reveal its glossy ebony coat.

"Perfect, as always," Zanub said. "Now come to the dungeon. We can chase Inferno. And I have water sacks."

Teaching that pest a soggy lesson was tempting but… "Not on my day in the stables, Zanub. But you go."

Zanub—loyal beyond fault—handed her the grooming kit, and sat atop one of the stalls.

Milla slipped a carrot to Malefactor, then put her hand on its side and jumped off the haystack, never losing contact as she moved around the horse. She squeezed above its pastern and Malefactor obediently bent its leg, but there was no mud or debris in the foot, of course. She checked for signs of thrush or injury, perhaps cracks in the wall of the hoof, but found it to be as pristine as the rest of the horse. After assessing all four feet, Milla alternated between the brush and curry comb on the horse's coat. Free of dirt, she took the time to look for lesions or wounds, pleased to find flawless skin beneath the shiny coat. She moved on to the tail and mane and, with no tangles to speak of, combed the horse's hair as if they were friends at a slumber party. Using a damp sponge, she cleaned around the eyes, ears, muzzle, and dock, unnecessarily, and finished by giving the coat a final polish with a soft cloth.

"You work hard for no reason," Zanub said.

She jumped off the bale of hay and regarded the horse. "It's not work."

Malefactor nudged her with its muzzle and Milla hugged its forearm tightly. "One day I'll ride her. Perhaps out of this castle."

Zanub leaped off the stall and tore out faster than a 'monger on the hunt. He hated when she spoke of such things, but he needed to accept that she would leave one day—him, the castle, all of it.

A lightning storm intermittently lit the queen's darkened chamber. Milla sat before a floating mirror as Lucrecia braided her hair with strands of gold. When finished, the queen admired their reflections.

"The image speaks to my heart," she said. "You blossom with each passing day and in my likeness more and more."

It was true. They looked alike, mother and daughter, with their ivory skin, rosy lips, and dark glossy tresses. Only the green in Milla's irises differed from the queen's ebony eyes. Milla lowered her head; she couldn't bear the resemblance anymore.

With a dismissive wave, Lucrecia sent the mirror back to the wall, above her dresser. She rotated Milla toward her and they sat cross-legged, opposite one another, on the queen's overstuffed bed.

"What shall we talk about tonight?"

"I'm too sleepy to talk."

"You? Why, I don't believe it possible," the queen teased, but Milla didn't bite. "Perhaps some cream with biscuits? Shall I wake the kitchen ogres?"

Milla shook her head. "I'm not hungry."

"Such sadness soils your beauty."

"Then I shall be uglier than a warthog."

The queen brushed Milla's bangs aside, off her forehead. "It vexes me to know I cannot bring you cheer."

"You can," Milla said.

"You're rather one note. But you belong with me."

"May I go to my room?"

"Sit with me a little longer."

Milla looked at the woman, fragile, lonely, not a trace of wickedness about her. "Very well."

Lucrecia lit with joy. "Have I shared the stories of growing up with a sister?"

"You have a sister?"

Lucrecia smiled. "We were mischievous as children."

"You mean to say you tricked her into misbehaving."

"Hardly. She was a handful. I was serious and studious, but she was full of merriment."

"Opposites."

"Quite. Unlike me, she loved to use her sorcery for fun. Though not everyone enjoyed her games. Especially poor Argus. I admit I was the one who dared her to quiet the chattering fool, but it was she who came up with the idea of transforming him to a frog."

"Not true."

"I do not lie. A childish prank, unquestionably, but it was the best she could conjure, being a modest study."

"What happened?"

"To this day, I fear poor Argus hops around Asper in search of a lily."

Milla laughed.

"Your joy warms me, my daughter."

A sharp blade pierced Milla's heart and she thought she'd been ambushed before she realized it was her own guilt that stabbed her.

Lucrecia stroked her cheek. "I promise to be the mother you deserve."

"No." Milla shoved her, sending her off the bed in a clumsy fall. "You're not my mother. I hate you for stealing me. I hate you!"

Lucrecia loomed over her in a blinding instant, shadowed by Inferno, her eyes pained with tears. "Leave my chamber at once, you ungrateful daughter."

Milla ran, and the mahogany door swung open on her approach and slammed shut behind her as she fled into the corridor. She fell against the ebony walls and collapsed to the floor, affected by her own betrayal. They came faster and easier. Soon she'd accept the queen as her mother, settle into the castle, and forget to count the days. Four hundred and two. She pleaded for four hundred and three to be the last. But the queen's tears splashing on the marble from the other side of the door and the sob so plaintive, so heartbroken—despite herself Milla cried for the woman.

On Milla's seventh birthday, the castle was lighted to her pleasing, lifting the blackness off the stone walls. Music filled the air, and studies were waived on this day for her and her best friend, Zanub. She received toys and barrettes and perfumes and dolls from everyone in the castle, Vylkrost included, by force certainly. Milla couldn't celebrate, though. This marked the second year of her capture, the second year without her father. Even Zanub hadn't the talent to lift her spirits.

As she prepared for bed, Lucrecia entered her chamber. "I have a gift for you."

"You've given me plenty." Milla climbed into bed.

"This is a tale, my daughter. A tale I believe you're now old enough to hear."

"I'm not your daughter."

"Do you not tire of saying that?"

"It's true."

"I'll tell you the truth if you're prepared to hear it."

"Are you prepared to speak it?"

Lucrecia sat on the edge of the bed and stroked Milla's hair. "You have such fortitude. Pity you use it only to fight me."

"I could say the same of you." Milla rolled away from the queen.

"The land of Asper once knew a beautiful sorceress with eyes as blue as the sky and pure as the stream. Her name was Jovia."

"I know the story of my mother," Milla said. "My father has told me many times. You needn't waste your breath."

"There's more you don't know. You see, this extraordinary sorceress longed for a child, but destiny thought otherwise."

Milla shot upright. "You lie, for here I am."

"Only because she turned to the most skilled sorceress in the land. Her sister."

"No… You're not her sister. I would know if she had a sister."

"Touched by her plight, I offered my own chance of motherhood to her and she accepted."

"Liar!"

"Filimore knows the truth."

Milla shook her head, speechless.

"Oh, my sister and I created a pact of secrecy so the world wouldn't know, but Jovia told her beloved."

"He would have told me," Milla whispered, her throat as dry as the desert.

"Why?"

She looked at the queen but had no answer.

"To bring you heartache?" the queen continued. "To fill you with doubt? To lose you?" Milla blocked her ears but could still hear her. "I searched and I studied until I unearthed a spell that shifted my fate unto my sister. *My* fate. That's how she was favored with child."

"You can feed me to the 'mongers for I will never believe such lies."

"Listen, my child. It's true." Milla swung at her and Lucrecia held onto her arms, embracing her. "The army was poaching every conjurer in the land. I studied longer and harder to rule the barbarous soldiers, but still, they were too strong-willed. Our population thinned, and we came to rejoice in the birth of our future. You were our hope, Milla. Our future."

Milla cried. Lucrecia rocked her in her arms.

"The army set out to slay you and your family. I tried to intervene but hadn't yet the power to control them. I went to your home to battle alongside you and found it abandoned. I feared the worst but searched the lands for you nonetheless. By the time I located you, the word had spread that Jovia was slain by the army. You were motherless. *Motherless.* And still, your father denied me my rights. I couldn't relinquish my feelings of love for you. You're my hope, Milla. My future. How could I not have you here with me?"

Milla ripped free and fled, Inferno on her heels until Lucrecia halted the blaze. She ran up to the Ebony Tower without rest and screamed for her father. When her throat gave out, she crumpled to her knees and fell into a ball, with no more drive.

A feathery wing draped over her shivering frame and she whirled around to see the silver eyes of a white crow. Behind the bird, partly masked by the dark clouds, the eccentric, bald man—Queldar, her father's brother—reached out for her. She jumped to her feet, reaching back, but Queldar was engulfed by Inferno and swept away.

CHAPTER SEVEN

"MILLA." His voice broke through the black mist and everything froze as time stood still. She was encased in crystal—a figurine—along with the strange bird.

"Milla," he said again and the crystal burst into a shower of fragments, releasing its hold. Life rushed back and Milla swayed in the current. She was on the roof of the hospital, more precisely on the ledge, and Parker stood a few paces behind her with his hand extended. He was motionless, as if frozen in time himself, except for his trembling arm. How long had he been there? How long had she?

"Milla, please take my hand."

A crowd was gathered below, looking up at her. She stepped away from the ledge and as soon as she did, Parker pulled her to him. Comforted by his closeness, she inhaled his scent, breathed him in, and was ripped from his arms by Dr. Thorn, who panted from exertion.

"What're you doing up here, Milla?" the doctor asked.

"I'm not sure. Thinking, I think."

"About jumping?"

"No. Why would I jump?"

"I don't know, Milla. You tell me. First the knife, now this? What's going on?"

Milla shrugged. "I must've wandered here, lost in my thoughts." After her conversation with Parker, she didn't know what she could tell Dr. Thorn but suspected her father's waning spell fell into the taboo category.

"You're not allowed up here," he said as he ushered her into the stairwell.

She glanced over her shoulder to look at Parker, but Dr. Thorn was blocking her view and his ogrish expression—of the nasty ilk—stopped her from trying again. When they arrived in the vestibule, he guided her by the elbow to the shiny oval desk and said, "Wait here." He motioned Parker over to the far end for privacy, but Milla could still hear them.

"I'm taking her back to my grandma's," Parker said.

"Do you want to be responsible if she succeeds next time?"

"You heard her. She was just thinking, that's all."

"You're a bright kid, Parker. Go home."

"You can't hold her against her will."

"I can and I will."

Parker glared at Dr. Thorn, who took it for a moment before he about-faced with the curt precision of a soldier and marched toward her. Parker ran over, blocking his path.

"Parker," Hailey said. She was by the corridor on the opposite side of the desk. "What're you doing?"

"Stay out of it, Hailey."

"Parker, go home," Dr. Thorn said again.

"Not without her."

Connie emerged from the corridor now. "Should I call security?"

"Parker?" Dr. Thorn said.

Parker turned to Milla. "You need to show them you're a sorceress."

"Oh my god," Hailey said with utter shock. As if Milla needed someone else to doubt her.

"But you said to not speak of it," Milla reminded Parker, quietly.

"I know, but they think you're crazy. They want to commit you. Keep you here against your will."

Hailey tried to pull him away from Milla. "For godsakes, Parker, stop it before they lock you up, too." He yanked his hand from her.

"Milla," he said, "you have to do something that proves you're real."

"Any spell?"

"Yes, anything."

She felt the heat of everyone's stares and couldn't think of a spell. Not one, not even to freckle Hailey's smirk with warts. "I need my *Quodex*."

"That's enough," Dr. Thorn said. "Connie, take her back to her room."

"Milla?" Parker said, impatient and annoyed, like her father when awaiting a spell from her. "Do something you know by heart. The first thing you ever learned. You must know the easiest spell there is."

"Conjuring is not simple, Parker."

"But you know how to do it, right?"

"Yes." She leaned toward him speaking quietly. "I'm just not very good at it yet."

Hailey snickered and Milla wished Tobly was here to kick her in the shin.

Parker sank in defeat. "Never mind."

No. She couldn't bear the thought of disappointing him. "I'll try. The Nimoom Spell." She went over the verse in her mind, then swept her arms out to the side, palms up. "*Heolstor cuman hider, ligetraesc niht; Awrecan aet se lyft, forpbryccan thy miht.*"

Nothing happened except Hailey tittered, which would've been perfect if that had been her goal.

Milla raised her arms higher. "*Heolstor cuman hider, ligetraesc niht; Awrecan aet se lyft, forpbryccan thy miht.*"

This time Hailey laughed and Milla was ready to kick her herself but somehow found restraint.

"*Heolstor cuman hider, ligetraesc niht; Awrecan aet se lyft, forpbryccan thy miht. Heolstor cuman hider, ligetraesc niht; Awrecan aet se lyft, forpbryccan thy miht. Heolstor cuman hider—*"

"Milla," Parker said, as he put her arms down by her sides. "Forget it."

"But—"

"Forget it." He hurried out and Hailey ran after.

Milla watched until the mahogany door closed completely, then turned down the corridor toward the Royal Suite and uttered not a word to Connie who accompanied her with platitudes of comfort, none of which were comforting.

Parker threw his leg over his bike and started the engine when Hailey hopped on back.

"Get off."

"No."

"I'm not in the mood, Hailey."

"Oh, come on, Parker. So you fell for a pretty face. It's not the first time," she said with a flirtatious smile. "Listen, I'm sorry, really. I know you liked her but she's crazy. It happens, even to pretty girls. Just let it go."

"Hang on." He tore out of the parking lot with Hailey's arms wrapped around his waist. Her body pressed into his, leaning with him as he took the corners, and even when he didn't. He sped up and down the blacktop until he calmed, then turned onto the fire road and accelerated, kicking up dirt.

Painted in big bold black letters, the name of the town spanned half the circumference of the newly renovated water tower—a spherical white steel tank—and Parker stopped at the bottom, killing the engine to his bike.

"Been a long time," Hailey said.

"You up for it?"

"Hell ya."

They climbed the ladder five stories up and sat on the metal walkway in front of the "O" with their legs dangling over the edge. Below, not as big or bold as its letters, Clear Rock was an unassuming town of houses, shops, and restaurants bordered by farmland.

"Might as well be in the middle of nowhere," Parker said.

"I kinda like the middle of nowhere."

He laughed. "You would."

She put her hand on his, but he took it away.

"Don't," he said and she didn't fight him for once. "Did you accidentally cut Milla with her knife?"

"Really? Did she try to blame me? She needs help, Parker. Like serious help."

He wanted to argue but had no case.

Hailey nudged him with her shoulder. "Hey."

"Hey," he replied, like old times.

They sat in silence for several minutes until Hailey asked, "Parker, will you ever forgive me?"

Forgive was a funny concept. He still didn't forgive the drunk driver. He didn't answer.

"It was junior prom, I got drunk. I didn't know what I was doing."

"Yeah, drunk. While you were pregnant."

"It was stupid, I know. But I was upset and you have to take some responsibility. You weren't exactly thrilled by the news, you know."

"We weren't even out of high school. Of course I wasn't thrilled. How could you be?"

"I loved you, that's how. I wanted to spend the rest of my life with you. I still do."

"Funny way of showing it."

"I'm sorry. If I could take it back, I would. I don't want to make excuses, but you gotta know I felt like you abandoned me when I needed you most. I was alone and scared and I made a mistake, Parker, but I'm only human. What can I do to make it right? I'll do anything, you know I will."

"That's not why we're broken up, so just stop."

Hailey looked away. She was probably tired of hearing him say he didn't love her anymore, that their relationship had been based on passion, the destructive kind, and that they never should've been together to begin with, and frankly, he was tired of saying it. They sat in silence for several minutes.

"Were you pregnant, Hailey?"

She jolted as if he had slapped her in the face. "Are you serious? You think I'd lie about something like that?"

"I think you'd do a lot of things to get what you want."

"Wow. I didn't know you could be so cruel."

"I just want to know the truth. Please. Just tell me the truth. Did you lose it? Did you have an abortion? Were you pregnant? I have a right to know."

"Of course I was pregnant." She flooded with tears now. "I wanted that baby more than anything, more than I wanted you." She buried her face and sobbed.

Parker couldn't seem to get anything right today. Maybe he should be locked up. Believing someone was a sorceress from another dimension and attacking the girl he thought he'd be with forever. He put his arm around Hailey. "I'm sorry."

Milla ripped the covers from the bed, hurtling pillows across the room, and kicked the mattress to the floor. She'd pitch the bed frame through the air if it wouldn't make a racket, but she was done dealing with people today—Parker and Hailey, the insipid doctor, that lurking bald man who happened to be her father's brother of all things, and Zanub. *Zanub*! How could he?

She retrieved her *Quodex* from the side table drawer, thankful it knew when to hide, and hugged it tightly as she sat against the wall. It heaved and melted in her arms.

"I need my memories back. Every single one of them." The book snuggled into her but offered no verse. "I see." Wishful thinking. "I suppose I should accept they'll return whenever they feel like it. No doubt, at the most inopportune time judging from everything else going on in my life of late. Well, I'll find the answers myself."

She got to her feet and marched to the door. "We're going home." She pulled the handle, slamming herself into the door and flattening her *Quodex* in the process. The book moaned and Milla rubbed her sore head. "Seriously?" She joggled the handle. Seriously.

She opened the book to Chapter Seven, knowing the spell she wanted, but the pages flipped to the beginning. "Not now."

She went to Chapter Seven again and again the pages flipped back. "So help me, if you don't cooperate, I'll tear the verse right off your spine."

The book opened to Chapter Seven, *Gehaeftednes*; Verse Six, Eryuth Spell. "Thank you."

She faced the door. "*Duru lettan min foldweg na ma, becuman hider and seo eow abidan.*" She grabbed the handle and… *Blasted*.

The book fanned its pages, sending Milla's hair over her face.

"No mood, beast." She brushed her hair aside but the pages flapped more vigorously, whirling her strands into a tornado above her head. "What is it?"

The *Quodex* settled, as did Milla's hair, and opened to: *Geliefan*.

"Yes. *Geliefan*—believe. Believe in what? The cruelty of others? The unjustness of the universe? The pain and suffering of the innocent? Oh, I believe."

The page turned, revealing her father's writing on the back of it. "Believe in yourself."

Slapped in the face by that righteous book. "I do. How else do you think I can study a spell as intricate as annihilation?"

Another page turned. Chapter One, *Ligetraesc Scur*; Verse One, Nimoom Spell. Scribbled next to it, in a child's handwriting, was "Thunder Storm."

"The air has warped your parchment if you think I'm starting at the beginning."

The *Quodex* snorted derisively and shot open, taut, to Chapter Seven, Verse Six, Eryuth Spell.

Finally. Some respect.

Milla recited the verse with stellar pronunciation—*take that, beast*—and grabbed the handle, walking into the locked door. She pinched the book shut. "Smirk, and I'll glue your pages."

The book was right, though. Without a foundation, there was nothing to build on. Obviously she lacked the fundamentals if she could choke on a spell as simple as the Nimoom. She put her bed back together, giving herself room to pace, and began at the beginning with that idiotic spell that humiliated her in front of Parker.

Book hovering before her—it could be helpful sometimes, she had to admit—she perused the verse and spotted her mistake. "Oh. It's *forpbringan*, not *forpbryccan*. Derg."

She positioned herself by the window and recited, "*Heolstor cuman hider, ligetraesc niht; Awrecan aet se lyft, forpbringan they miht.*"

Clouds gathered low in the sky, evolving from white to gray to black. A burst of lightning shot out, followed by a shuddering boom, and rain slammed against the glass.

"Told you I knew it."

The storm dissipated as fast as it had brewed and her pushy book sealed itself until she performed it three more times, twice without looking and once, to her own amazement, telepathically. Giddy with success, she punched the air, unaware her *Quodex* was approaching, and whacked it right in the "X." The startled book hit the wall and slid to the floor with a slow hiss.

Milla ran to it, squealing apologies, and straightened the "X" as best she could. "Why didn't you tell me I could conjure silently like Father always did?"

Her *Quodex* huffed.

"No, you didn't. I'd remember. Never mind. Can we not argue for once?"

After her triumph, revisiting childhood spells was fun, but when her *Quodex* moved onto the fundamentals of altering particles, waves, and energy, she suspected it was getting back at her for knocking it silly. Perspiring more than a day of bog-hopping in the first few chapters alone, she splashed her face with water, drank a jug's worth from her hands, and got back to it. Nothing, not even hard work, could quell the happiness of performing a spell silently. When she levitated a cup and a brush synchronously, her first time ever floating two objects at once, her *Quodex* fluttered with pride, but her favorite accomplishment was modifying Walter's ugly boots to fit her like the supple metal of a soldier. She could walk without wobbling or tripping or squeaking and her feet didn't look the size of wroder talons anymore.

As the dark of night began to lighten, she belly flopped onto the bed, laughing with exhaustion and success. She wiped her wet eyes and gazed at her book, also splayed on the bed. "Can we go home now?"

Her *Quodex* opened on the Eryuth Spell and she jumped off the bed and hurried to the door. *Duru lettan min foldweg na ma, becuman hider and seo eow abidan.*

It opened.

Quodex tucked in the back of her waistband, Milla strode through the stale corridors to the vestibule. Connie abruptly stopped chatting with the nurse behind the desk and blocked Milla.

"Sweetie, how'd you get out of your room?"

"A spell."

"Get Doctor Thorn," Connie said to the other nurse, then turned to Milla. "You're not allowed out of your room unless a nurse or nurse's assistant is with you. Someone will take you around after breakfast, okay?"

"I'm going home."

"Milla, please." Connie took her by the arm and Milla spun out of her grasp, positive her feet didn't touch the floor once in the pirouette. Connie must've been shocked because she stumbled back, clearing the path, but Dr. Thorn emerged.

"What's going on?" he asked Milla.

"I'm simply trying to go home."

"I'm sorry, Milla, you can't."

"No slight, but I disagree." Milla swiped her hand magnificently through the air, throwing open the mahogany door. Well, cracking it ajar. The blasted thing was heavy. Connie closed it, unimpressed, as if Milla had nothing to do with it.

"Milla, I want you to go to your room and respect our rules here, do you understand?" Dr. Thorn said.

Milla marched past him toward the door and both he and Connie grabbed her by an arm, and the next thing she knew, two burly ogres were dragging her back toward her room. She tried to spin out of their hands like she did with Connie but only managed to fling herself from side to side in their tight grip. Cursed unreliable magic. She pulled and writhed and twisted and turned, but instead of freeing herself, she inadvertently hurled her *Quodex* from her waistband and it hit the floor with a thud and a grunt. Dr. Thorn reached for the book and Milla kicked the air, trying to keep him at bay.

"Don't touch that. It's mine."

He picked it up.

"Please." Milla stopped her fight. "Please. Give it back."

The doctor thumbed through the pages roughly and her *Quodex* winced. He snapped it shut and crammed it under his arm. "You'll get it back when you're released."

"No." Milla struggled to throw a chair at him, hoping he'd drop her *Quodex*, but she couldn't levitate it. She zeroed in on the chandelier above and remembered the verse, the one that melted the arrow at Lost

Creek. She vaporized a link in the chain and the fixture crashed to the floor inches behind him. He dropped the book in a start and the orderlies ran to his aid, releasing her. She snatched up her *Quodex* and ran but was yanked back by a strong hand as everyone yelled and screamed around her and then a sudden jab—sharp, burning—in her arm. Her head swam instantly, her body coursed with heat, she could barely stand. Her eyes were heavy, too heavy, like the mahogany doors. She couldn't keep them open. "What…"

CHAPTER EIGHT

PARKER WAS GUZZLING the sugary milk at the bottom of his cereal bowl when a thunderous crash came from downstairs. His grandparents, still clad in chest wader fishing gear, dropped the trout they were wrapping, and his grandfather wrinkled his brow. "Not again."

"Stay here," Parker said as he ran to the door leading to the shop. He took the stairs three at a time and jumped off the last ten or so, landing before an enormous figure on an enormous horse. They were both armored in a dull metal membrane that looked like carbon steel yet moved like skin. Parker nearly crumpled at the sight, but the cold tip of a blade against his neck motivated him to stand. It was true—everything—and now they found her. Almost.

"Where's the sorceress?" the metaled man asked.

Parker shook his head. "Who?"

The warrior perused the clutter, squinting as if he could see ghosts, and in a split-second, was charging out the front of the shop—Parker's neck intact—obliterating the door and surrounding wall.

"Call Hank," Parker turned and yelled up the stairs, but his grandparents were on the bottom step, immobilized with shock. He took his grandfather by the shoulder. "Grandpa, call Hank. Tell him there's an armed maniac after Milla." Parker bolted through the gaping hole, ignoring his grandmother's plea to come back, and jumped on his bike.

He gunned it down Main Street, his engine whining to catch up to the horse that galloped down the center of the paved road, effortlessly skirting the swerving cars. Parker weaved through as fast as his motorcycle could go and still couldn't catch up. He veered left and cut through the high school's parking lot and across the field, tearing up the sod. He emerged on Greene Street half a block behind the horse. *How the hell does he know where to go?*

The animal plowed through an intersection at full speed and was broadsided by a delivery truck, the crunch of metal sickening. The warrior slammed into the cement and Parker hit the brakes, thinking his troubles were over, but the mangled heap of metal leaped to his feet and pulled himself atop his steed. Parker bypassed them, taking a shortcut to Elm Crescent. He accelerated into the cul-de-sac, going too fast to hug the road, and pulverized the rose bushes on the front lawn of the hospital. He punched it up the steps and jumped off his bike, letting it slide across the landing as he tore into the lobby. He ran past Connie, who was rushing to the door to see what the commotion was, and didn't stop until he reached Milla's room. She tossed and thrashed in her bed, unconscious.

"Milla. Milla?" He shook her and she moaned but didn't awaken. He scooped her up and carried her to the lobby as fast as he could, getting the stink eye from a nurse along the way, and wasn't surprised to find Dr. Thorn waiting for him when he got there, flanked by two orderlies.

"What do you think you're doing?" the doctor said.

"Someone's after her, some guy in armor. I need to get her out of here."

"Put her down, Parker."

"She's in danger, you gotta believe me."

"The only one putting her in danger is you right now. Don't make me call security."

"Get out of the way."

The orderlies grabbed Parker's arms, wrenching them back, as the doctor took Milla from him. She panted, wrestling heavy eyelids, and labored to speak. "*Quodex*... my *Quodex*."

Parker broke free from one of the orderlies and punched him across the jaw. The orderly went down with a spurt of blood from his lip as Parker struck the other one but merely grazed his cheekbone.

"Parker, stop it, or I'll have you thrown in jail," Dr. Thorn said. The bloodied orderly got to his feet and clutched Parker's arms from behind. Parker rammed backward into him, knocking them both to the floor, but the orderly threw him facedown, kneeing him in the back to keep him there.

"Let me go."

Hailey ran in from outside, her face already twisted in fear, and she gasped at the mayhem inside. "Parker. Oh my god. What's going on?"

"Doctor Thorn." Connie hung up the phone behind the registration desk and rushed over. "Some lunatic in armor broke into Walter's Antiques. Betty says he's looking for Milla."

"I told you that," Parker said, face smashed against the cold marble.

"Hank's on his way," the nurse said.

"Please." Parker fought back tears. "Let me take her out of here."

"Bring her to my office and don't take your eyes off her," Dr. Thorn told the orderlies.

The orderly released Parker, joining the other to whisk Milla away.

Parker got to his feet, pleading with Dr. Thorn. "He's gonna find her here. He's headed this way."

Dr. Thorn ignored him. "Connie, call security, have them lock down the place until the sheriff gets here. Hailey, get patients back into their rooms." He finally addressed Parker. "She'll be safer in here than out there."

Everyone scrambled. Parker remained, his head swimming in confusion. The mahogany doors locked remotely with a loud clunk. He took off to Milla's room and ripped it apart but didn't find her *Quodex*. He screamed in frustration until he remembered where the nurses kept confiscated items. He ran back to the lobby and found the velvet-covered text tucked inside a caddy behind the reception desk. He snatched it up and sprinted to Dr. Thorn's office, and the orderly with the bloodied lip clocked him square in the eye. Parker hit the floor, completely shocked.

"Doesn't feel so good, does it, asshole?" the orderly said.

Parker got to his feet. His eye swelled instantly. "I need to give her this book."

"No can do," the other orderly said.

"Please."

They didn't budge. Parker stormed back to the lobby and watched the street through the large picture window. No sign of anything unusual, but he could hear the sheriff's siren in the distance. The book quivered in his hands, and he fumbled it, bewildered, but when he caught it, it was stock-still. He stared at the cover, contemplating—contemplating whether he was crazy enough to go all in. The cover was about as old as everything in his grandparents' shop, and as pristine, too, and the lettering was obviously done by an artist. Inside, there was no publisher. No author either. No title, no year, no anything. He skimmed through the thousands of verses packed into the book. Some were a single word, others were several pages long, and the majority of them had handwritten notes next to them, mostly in English. *Why not?*

He went to Chapter One, Verse One. The first spell had to be the easiest and the scribble of "Thunder Storm" was obviously done by a kid. He realized it was the one Milla had tried earlier, to prove she was a sorceress, and failed. He half-hoped he'd fail, too. He glanced over his shoulder and, with no one around to call him nuts, he raised his arms the way she had. Probably mispronouncing everything, he said, "*Heolstor cuman hider, ligetraesc niht; Awrecan aet se lyft, forpbryccan thy miht,*" and looked up to the sky.

"Did you just try *magic*?" Hailey gawked at him.

But the shrill, heartrending alarm blared suddenly, jolting them, and the massive mahogany doors sailed past their heads, ripped clean off the hinges. Parker swung around, the blood draining from his face as the armored figure marched in, his form too big to fit through the doorway without ducking. He pushed Hailey into motion. "Run!"

She did, and Parker took off in the opposite direction. He rounded the corner to Dr. Thorn's office and lurched in distress; the orderlies weren't standing guard. He ran in to find Milla gone, too. He turned full circle, unsure what to do next, and spied a prescription pad on the doctor's desk. He rifled through the drawers, looking for keys to the dispensary, and came across an otherworldly weapon—a bizarre white-metaled, double-edged knife. Milla's, obviously. Magical? Maybe. He pocketed the knife and rummaged until he found the keys. Adrenaline-rushed, he tore down the corridor to the dispensary and fumbled to unlock the door like he was in a horror movie. Once in, he went straight for the injectables, looking for a sedative of some sort.

Hailey ran in and slammed the door shut behind her, causing him to jump. "Could you make more noise?"

"Parker, I'm scared. We need to get out of here."

"I'm not leaving without Milla."

"You can't seriously risk your life for her. You don't even know her. Let Hank handle it."

"No one believed her and this is what happened."

"For godsakes, you don't really believe she's a sorceress. If you did, you'd let her fend for herself with magic. I'm the one who needs you right now." She tried to pull him with her, but he jerked her to his face.

"Get out while you still can, Hailey. He's not after you." He released his grasp and she stumbled back with tears in her eyes and fled from the room.

He grabbed a vial off the shelf and, steadying his hand on the table, pierced a needle through the seal and sucked the serum into the syringe. He capped the needle and pocketed it, along with a case of syringes. Muttering his new mantra—*holy crap*—he chased down the clang of the warrior's metal boots.

Hailey's curdling scream sent shockwaves through Parker's veins, and when it stopped short, the possibilities sank in. He squeezed Milla's knife in his hand and sprinted even faster, cursing Hailey for not leaving when he told her to. He skidded around the corner as Dr. Thorn was ejected from Milla's room like cannon fire, slamming into the hallway wall. The doctor's bones cracked, but he moaned, still alive.

Parker bolted into the room and was halted by a sword in his face. Hailey screamed and scrambled over the bed, which was sliced in two, but Parker said, "Hailey, don't." And she listened for once.

The warrior held the tip of his blade to Parker's eye, steady as a surgeon. "Where is she?"

"Gone. She left."

"She's here. Tell me where, or I'll kill everyone until hers is the only breath remaining."

Parker dropped and slashed, but the seven-foot mass of metal kicked him in the chest, propelling him into the wall. His knife skittered across the floor, out of reach.

"Last chance, earther," the warrior said, raising his sword.

"Freeze right there, mister." Hank stood in doorway, his gun aimed. "Drop your weapon, or I'll shoot. I swear to god, I'll shoot."

The warrior glanced at the gun, then swung his sword toward Parker. Hailey screamed and there was the blast of a firearm and, for a second, Parker had no idea if he was still alive. He realized the bullet must've addled the warrior because he missed his mark, but it didn't penetrate his armor. Hank fired again, but the maniac crushed the gun with one hand and ripped Hank off the floor with the other. Then he spun, as if catching a whiff of something, and threw Hank aside.

Dr. Thorn blocked his path. "You don't have to do this. Let us help you—"

The warrior decapitated him in a swift swipe, as if it was easier than shunting him aside, and marched down the corridor. The sheriff unloaded every bullet he had and Hailey fell to the floor, heaving. Parker ran out.

Milla's head was sand, shifting like the desert dunes at her slightest move. A throbbing, stabbing pain plagued her right temple and almost masked the terrifying vibration coursing through every breadth of her being. He was here. His essence clashed with hers, an opposing magnetic force, and always triggered her intuition. She needed her *Quodex*.

First, she needed to get to her feet. She didn't know where she was in the hospital other than a small room filled with those immodest robes and various linens along with a forgotten implement like the one Dr. Thorn used to listen to her heart. She pushed herself up off the cold floor, the world spinning, and made it to the door without falling. The unfamiliar popping noise that had awakened her had since stopped and the corridor was eerily quiet. Not much to work with, she took the heart-listening implement and left.

She trusted her *Quodex* had the foresight to return to her room and she followed the postings on the walls to find her way back. Muffled sobs reached Milla before she rounded a corner, prompting her into a run. The doctor's severed head and the acrid stench of blood hit her like a hammer.

Hailey edged back, shaking. "Stay away from me. Stay away."

"Hailey, where did he go? The man who did this?"

"He went looking for you. Where do you think? And now Parker's gone looking for him."

Milla ran off. Scrutinizing the air, she couldn't find an inkling of his presence. All her studying and not even as skilled as the army's armor.

A piercing whine broke the silence and, at the end of the hall, Parker sped through the intersecting corridor on his bike. She sprinted after, turning the corner as he rammed into Vylkrost. The captain flew back and Parker was thrown off his bike. Vylkrost got to his feet instantly, sword drawn, but Parker was back on his bike, charging, and as Vylkrost swung, Parker slid sideways under the sword. Milla pumped her fist victoriously, but Vylkrost bounded inhumanly fast—even in Earth's atmosphere—and yanked Parker from his bike, pinning him to the wall.

"Release him," she called out, and Vylkrost finally noticed her. He snorted but didn't lower his sword.

"Milla, run!" Parker said. "Run!"

"He can see my essence, Parker." She turned to the captain. "Right, Vylkrost?"

"You address me as Captain."

"Harm him and you'll spend your life chasing me," she said.

His arm, ready to plunge the sword, wavered with indecision, but he dropped Parker and reached for her.

Milla dipped back and tossed the heart-listening device toward him, saying, "*Atemian hwa geatweard.*"

The device metamorphosed into iron chains in midair and shot around Vylkrost's wrists, binding them. She couldn't help but throw a proud smile to the stunned Parker. "Chapter Four, Verse Seven."

Vylkrost raised a condescending eyebrow and, with a tug, shattered the links. "Juvenile tricks. Pitiful."

Blasted. She should've known Lucrecia wouldn't send a soldier without protection. "So you hide under the cloak of the queen. I forgot what a coward you are."

He wrenched her off the floor and, with a sharp whistle, summoned his horse from thin air, as if it breached a Shift. Milla tried to pull free, but he hauled her with him as he mounted his steed and charged through the vestibule.

The horse leaped off the steps of the entrance, clearing the sheriff and his car. Milla looked back, concerned for her *Quodex,* and saw Parker shoot out of the building on his motorcycle, also sailing over the sheriff.

"No, Parker. Stop," she called out.

Vylkrost guided his horse over a fence and through a garden, leaping onto Main Street, but Parker emerged from another path, close behind. Vylkrost kicked his horse faster and they bounded into the antique shop, rearing to a halt before the mirror. He retrieved a tome identical to Milla's *Quodex* and she choked.

"Where'd you get that?"

"A lowly warlock, where else?"

Parker burst into the shop, jumping from his bike in midair, and slammed into the floor.

"Stay back, Parker, please stay back," Milla said, but he didn't listen. He reached for her and the horse reared up, kicking to keep him at bay.

"*Leoht hwa scinan fram se sceat, onmunan eower onweald to min ingehygd,*" Vylkrost recited, aided by the faint whisper of the queen's voice under his. "*Foro mid se giedd it is min modgepanc, to gealgu on elra ge-logian.*"

A blinding whiteness shot out of the mirror in a flash and Milla was sucked into the glass with Vylkrost and his horse.

"No…" Parker screamed, but his voice faded as she rolled wildly in the vortex.

Parker lunged for the mirror to pull her out and hit solid glass. "Milla!" He slapped his palms on the surface, searching for the breach, then shook the frame desperately. "Milla!"

Hank burst in, yelling for him to get down, and Parker spun. But Hank pulled up short, gun drawn, muttering, "What the hell?"

"They went out the back," Parker said and Hank was out the door.

Parker grabbed the *Quodex* from his waistband, frantically riffling through, when, "They didn't go out the back," his grandfather said. He stood at the top of the steps next to Parker's grandmother.

"Grandpa, go back inside the apartment."

"You're crazy if you think I'm gonna pretend I didn't see what I just saw, and crazier yet, if you think I'm gonna let you go chasing that girl down a rabbit hole."

"I have to." By the time Parker found the verse, which came with a handwritten warning that non-conjurers might not survive, his grandfather snatched the book from his hands.

"Go to your room."

"Grandpa."

"Walter," his grandmother said, catching up to him.

"Don't 'Walter' me. I'm putting my foot down."

"Put it down all you want, but I've never seen him not do something he set his mind to. So unless you got a magic wand yourself, you better hug him good-bye, or else you'll regret leaving him like this." She steadied her lips. "Never miss your chance to say I love you. Right?"

Parker pulled his grandfather in and squeezed him. "I can take care of myself, Grandpa."

His grandfather sniffled and handed him the book. "You better come back."

"Promise." He hugged his grandmother. "I love you, Grandma."

"I love you, too, son." She fought tears the same way she had done when his parents were killed, with a brave face for his sake, and led his grandfather away from the mirror.

Parker turned to the book before he bawled like a baby and recited the verse. A sharp whiteness bled out and he cringed in pain as his body seemed to stretch and warp. When he thought he'd rip apart from the strain, he was sucked into the mirror in a blinding flash.

Electricity shot through his bones, his veins, his everything, and Parker grabbed his gut and wailed. He was thrown through the vortex, spinning and twisting and reaching for something to grab onto but finding nothing. His eardrums ached, his skin burned, and his eyes throbbed from the streaming, radiant lights. His head constricted excruciatingly and he wished it would implode already and be done with. The vortex jolted to a halt and Parker was thrown from the agony.

And into another.

CHAPTER NINE

PARKER FACE-PLANTED in the middle of a trodden dirt path, deafened by a sharp ringing in his ears. The good news was that he was alive. The bad news was that he felt it down to the nucleus of every cell. The ground vibrated, a million pummels to his broken body, and he looked up to see Vylkrost, on his horse, gunning toward him with Milla in his clutches. He got the brunt of the first hoof in his chest—the pressure popping his ears back to normal—but managed to grab a fallen branch and jam it between the horse's rear legs as he rolled away. The animal buckled, launching Milla in one direction, Vylkrost in another. The gargantuan soldier hit the ground with a crunch, sending up a cloud of dust, but sprung to his feet before the dust settled and roared in attack. Parker ran head on into a full charge of his own. It was official, he'd clearly lost his mind.

He swung his branch like a baseball bat across Vylkrost's chest and the branch snapped in two. Vylkrost hoisted him over his head and Parker struck again with the stub, miraculously slicing the armor. Green viscid fluid spurted from the gash and Vylkrost howled, almost dropping Parker. Parker struck again, slicing metal and flesh, and didn't stop until the behemoth collapsed, releasing his grip. Parker hit the ground and braced for another attack, but Vylkrost was out, his metal dulled even more.

Parker turned to Milla with a strained smile as he pushed himself up to a seated position. "Holy crap, right?"

She glared at him, the same expression he usually got in the dean's office. "I can't believe you followed me here."

"Well, I won't lie, that's not the welcome I was expecting."

She tugged him to his feet. "You don't understand. The army will kill you. Vylkrost isn't dead. He doesn't die that easily. He'll send his soldiers on the hunt. They must keep me alive, but you, you're marked now that you're helping me. You must go back."

"I'm not going back."

"Parker, please, you must. I can't bear the thought… Please go back."

"Forget it."

"They'll use you against me."

"They'll have to catch me first."

She sighed. "Come with me."

He followed her through a dense forest at the end of the dusty path, far away from Vylkrost. They weaved through patches of vibrant, colorful plants—leaves and fronds not flowers—and splashed across a shallow stream with a gripping current and ran some more, through thicker foliage, also unrealistically rich and multihued. Parker breathed faster than usual and still felt like he was missing a crucial element: oxygen.

Ahead, Milla leaped over a brook and took cover behind a shaggy violet-tinted shrub of spikes, and he caught up to her, greedily swallowing air. She placed her hand softly on the ground or maybe even hovered over it.

"We're safe for now, but it'll never end, Parker, not until I end it. I beg you to go back. I can't have a distraction."

"Distraction? I'm not just a pretty face, I'll have you know. I'm a straight C-student and a karate yellow belt." He raised his arm victoriously. "And I am the conqueror of the captain. Even if he's not *dead* dead."

Milla smiled, finally, and pulled his arm down. "You can thank me for being a good study lately. Even an earther should know a bough can't pierce metal."

"Sure, normally, but we're not in 'normal' right now. Besides, I thought your magic didn't work on him. The queen's cloak and all that."

"For his journey to Earth. I should've expected as much. There's no telling how many sorcerers are in other dimensions."

"Witches and warlocks in Clear Rock? Well, that explains a lot."

"True. You could be of the lineage, having survived the portal. Though probably Lucrecia's magic lingered long enough to aid your verse."

"Or maybe I'm that awesome."

"Seems unlikely."

Parker laughed. *Smartass.*

"Suffice, there's no need for a veil here. No one threatens the queen's army. Until me, I suppose. If I'm lucky, Lucrecia will continue to underestimate me."

"Ah, the bright side to being an underachiever, low expectations." He retrieved her *Quodex* from the back of his waistband. "By the way…"

"Beast." She hugged it, and the book snuggled into her.

"That's weird, right?"

"Two moons ago, maybe. Now we're the best of friends."

"Yeah, that's the part that's weird." He looked around. "Where to now?"

"I'll take you to the portal."

"You're hilarious."

"Parker, this land is unlike yours."

"I know. Purple toothpick bush," he said, motioning to the scrub. "But I took a psychedelic torture ride to get here and I did it because I want to help you. I don't care if Asper's full of evil witches and dragons and seven-foot soldiers with metal skin—which, by the way, is really cool and if there's one thing I'm bringing back with me, it's that armor—but not yet because I'm not leaving until we save the worlds as ridiculous as that sounds. And just so you know, some people would say thank you. Like… all of them."

"You talk a lot."

"It's a gift."

"For whom?"

Parker narrowed his eyes. "If the air wasn't so Mount Everest around here, I'd have a comeback to that."

"If you insist on staying, you should know we have holes in our fabric."

He turned, pretending to leave, and Milla laughed.

"Okay, maybe you should fill me in a little," he said. "Start with the holes."

"It will look like we vanish or appear from thin air, but in actuality, we've traveled into another plane. They're called Shifts and not everyone knows about them. Villagers have mistakenly gone through, never to return because they're singular in direction. But the army knows of them. They can't see them like sorcerers can, as subtle waves in the air, but they've charted thousands of them. No one knows how many Shifts have yet to be discovered, even by us. There's one behind me."

"A hole in space and time?"

"A Shift. And just space. Time is constant."

All Parker saw was forest.

"We should go," Milla said. "This path is oft traveled by the army."

She took his hand and sank into the invisible ripple, disappearing right in front of him like she had said, before she pulled him through. A sensation of warm oil embraced him inside and out, and yet somehow he also emerged instantaneously chilled, as if there was no time to feel the embrace except he did. He gasped, shocked from the transition and amazed by the vista before him. A fertile valley on one side, snowcapped ebony mountains opposite that, and a purple ocean straight ahead. Milla stepped in, blocking his view.

"You must travel quickly in Asper. The army can appear without warning and steal your life." She walked at a fast clip, toward the valley, and Parker half-ran to keep pace.

"The portal could take a lesson from the Shift. That was awesome. Right?"

"Perhaps. I don't feel them anymore. But try to stay focused on surviving. Vylkrost is vicious on a good day and worse when I'm part of the equation."

"This is personal?"

"Very much. I've escaped him many times. Death is kind in comparison to humiliation for a solider."

"Well, he must be pissed because you did it again."

"Unfortunately, my victories don't last. He's persistent."

Parker nodded. He supposed persistence was what got the captain to Clear Rock. Drawn to the undulant mountains, soft as syrup, and devoid of flora and fauna, Parker didn't realize he was walking toward them until Milla caught his arm.

"Don't be enticed," she said. "The Black Mountains are as hungry as they are inviting. The Marman Sea, however, is friendly."

He nodded. Mountains bad, sea good. "So where are we?"

"In the hinterland of the north North."

"The north north?"

"No, north North."

"Isn't that what I said?"

"You said 'north north' not 'north North.'"

"Do I have to know the difference?"

"Let us hope not."

"Great. Off to a good start."

The bottom curve of a full moon rested on the horizon, its silvery surface flickering like candlelight. Next to it, a half-moon hovered just slightly higher than it and not as big, though it appeared to be in motion as if it was farther away and moving in, extremely slowly. Beyond the half-moon, smaller or farther away, it was hard to tell, the hint of a crescent moon teased the sky with its presence.

"That's a lot of moons," Parker said.

"Moons," she corrected.

"Moons. That's what I—okay, now you're messing with me."

She laughed but gazed at them the way someone reveres art in a museum. "The Rising is rare, perhaps once in a lifetime. It's symbolic of our lineage." She lost her wistful smile. "I don't know if my father ever saw one."

"Sorry."

"I shouldn't act privileged. The crescent hasn't risen yet. The half hasn't settled. I hope to be able to say I saw one."

"Good goal."

"We should keep moving."

Parker lost pace with her down the pebbled path leading to the bottom of the valley.

"There," she called over her shoulder, and vanished into thin air with her next step.

"Uh..." He stared at the vista. "We're gonna have to have a talk about this." He managed to trace her footsteps into the Shift.

Milla chose the fastest way home, through the Desert of Riftinad and the Hinterland Marsh, even though the army often used those routes. When she emerged outside the forest surrounding her shack, she stopped, feet rooted in the ground as firmly as the cluster of tall pines before her.

"What's wrong?" Parker asked.

"I haven't been home since..." She panted to curtail any tears. "I left him here and ran off to kill the queen."

"We'll do something now."

Milla took the path she had taken countless times before when returning from Lost Creek. The shack, the grounds, everything looked the same, except for one thing.

"He's gone." Her father's body. "Those fiends! They took him to the 'mongers." She bolted only to be grabbed around the waist and hoisted up by Parker.

"Whoa, whoa, whoa," he said.

"They've no souls, those barbarians." She kicked her feet, trying to free herself. "Let me go."

"Where?"

Where, indeed? She stopped squirming and he put her down. "I hate them."

She strode into her shack, longing to kill someone. The cots were still strewn, the table still on its side, and broken shelves and pottery everywhere. Parker righted the table.

"We're not staying," Milla said. She sifted through the shards of pottery, looking for potions that might remain, but they were dry. She scoured through her father's destroyed paraphernalia in the study area, hoping to lift any lingering spells, but they felt as dead as her heart. She scanned her home, bereft of its warmth, and took out her anger on an innocent jug of water, bursting it with the flick of her hand. Parker leaped back but was splashed with water and clay fragments.

"Apologies," she said.

"That was impressive."

"At a party for children, perhaps." She sorted through some loose parchments scattered about but found nothing of interest. "My father had a brother. Queldar. I remembered him once my memories began surfacing."

"You have family? That's great."

"Oh, Parker, nothing's that simple. He used to visit us but stopped for some reason. I've spotted him many times since, following me, but I didn't know who he was. Just an odd man with a white crow."

"You think he had a falling out with your dad?"

"Only he can answer that now. I have to find him. I need to know what happened. And he might know the truth about the queen."

"What do you mean?"

"She might be my mother."

"Spoiler alert."

"She abducted me when I was a child and raised me for several years; she said I was her daughter. I don't know what's true anymore. Until my father's death, I had no memories of the castle, or Queldar, I had only what my father deemed acceptable. I love him, Parker, but he was so protective he didn't let me know who I was."

Vibrations underfoot alerted her to the encroaching trot of a horse. "Vylkrost," she said, peering out the window. "I wish I could say he lacked imagination, but here I am."

She grabbed Parker, motioning for him to be quiet, and brushed her hand along the earthen wall, releasing the hidden door. She slipped inside the secret passageway, taking Parker with her, and closed the door behind them, then led him deeper into the tunnel until she reached her old study room. Forgotten powders and potions littered the dilapidated wooden table, and the naked cot was eaten through in many places. Jungle squirrels, most likely.

"When we first built this home, we lived here, in hiding. After we decided the army had forgotten about us, we abandoned this room." She bit her lip. "If I had stayed home and studied that day instead of running off to play, we would've hidden here and been safe. My father's dead because of me, Parker. Because of my selfishness."

"No. He's dead because someone killed him, Milla. You can't blame yourself."

She wiped her nose and nodded. Right. Stay fixed on the root of evil—Lucrecia.

Parker pointed to the far side, where several tunnels branched off. "Escape routes?"

"To different forests."

"Maybe we shouldn't press our luck. If the captain's as persistent as you say, he might find that secret door."

Her *Quodex* concurred, but Milla settled the fidgety book with the back of her hand.

"Soon." She assessed the dried twigs, the powders, and even tasted the potions, but none had retained any sort of potency to do any good. She opened the drawer of the table and found her father's journal. The size of her palm, it must've held a hundred pages, counting front and back, filled with handwritten verses, a few in English but most in Old Asperian with mathematical calculations or diagrams. They were clearly added to over time, written in any space available; some scribbled sideways, others upside down, and some interspersed between other spells with arrows directing the order of things. Ink covered every possible part of each page and none of it made sense. Not to mention the strange repetition peppered throughout. "*Leodscipe*" was on every other page. In the middle of the journal, the phrase "*mid ors*" circled an entire page, spiraling from the center outward. "*Seo ymele*," "*peawfaest hyge*," and "*asparest ureu friou*" showed up twenty or more times.

"Your dad's?"

"He was clever. Too clever for me."

"He didn't think so. Why else would he put it here for you to find?"

"I understand none of it."

"Yet."

Milla smiled. *No pressure.* She tucked the book in her waist, but her *Quodex* kicked it out. She handed it to Parker. "Would you mind?"

"Mind holding a book with secret spells? I'll manage." He put it in his back pocket.

Milla considered going to Lost Creek, but if Vylkrost came here to look for her, he'd go there next. She decided on the tunnel that exited farthest from her shack. By the time they emerged, deep in Aelderoy Forest, the glow of the crescent moon shone brighter.

"How many moons are—" Milla threw her hand over Parker's mouth before he could finish and motioned to the white crow circling above. She ducked beneath a giant leaf for cover, pulling Parker with her.

"That's Queldar's crow."

She scanned the area. The bald man was wrestling with a blockade of vines and leaves, then disappeared through an opening. She ran full speed and breached the barrier before it sealed, finding the backside of Queldar inelegantly sticking up in the air with one foot braced on a wall of shrub and his head and torso deep inside it. She and Parker exchanged looks as she held back a giggle. She nosed around. Braided twine encircled the towering trees and isolated this vast section of the grove from the rest of the jungle. Several awnings made of twigs and fronds protected potions and elixirs, roots and herbs. His cauldrons and crystals, staffs and stones were arranged neatly throughout. A collection of swords and daggers, white-handled and black-handled, was displayed along a verdant wall. His cot lay beneath an ornate canopy at the farthest end. Seemingly everything he needed was in this secluded wilderness. How lonely.

With a grunt, Queldar heaved a milky crystal from its den, losing his balance and landing on the floor. It was scarcely the size of his head, but in fairness, Crystal Beholders were heavier than they looked as they carried the weight of their history. And his head was quite large. He rubbed his cloak over the stone to cleanse it from visions past and colorful auras escaped, some peacefully, others with moans and screams, until the Beholder was foggy but translucent. He still didn't notice them, so Milla cleared her throat. Queldar shot upright and spun midair without touching the ground. A look of fright turned to shock when he saw her.

"How did you get in here?" Queldar said.

"That's a peculiar welcome from someone who's been following me."

He shook his head. "If we crossed paths, it was merely coincidence."

"I suppose living near to us is coincidence as well?"

"Must be, for I know not where you live."

Milla gave him the 'come now' look and he chewed his lower lip as he rubbed his bald head where he bore the mark of a sorcerer above his left ear.

"I know who you are, Queldar."

He sank.

"In fact, I remember many things now."

"But not all?"

"What happened? Why were you and Father estranged?"

"Please. You cannot be here. It's too dangerous."

"He's dead. Did you know?"

The sorcerer had no reaction or perhaps no love. "Milla, I beg of you, go. The army is pillaging the land for you."

"So? I don't fear them anymore."

"You should. Your father hexed the scroll. The verse for the Unification is undetectable until after the Rising."

"Ingenious," she said with a smile. "We have nothing to worry about."

"On the contrary. He created the hex before you were born. The spell is inherent in your blood. Only you can remove it now that he's gone."

"He's not gone. He's dead. Slain by the army."

Queldar's sagging cheeks quivered with emotion. "Please, don't get caught up in your anger. With the third moon approaching, you're in grave danger. You must hide until it passes."

"I'm done hiding."

"The queen will force your hand or take your life. She won't stand idle for failure."

"Is she my mother?"

The poor man nearly crumpled to the ground. "Why would you ask such a thing?"

"It's my right to know."

"Jovia is your mother. She carried you in her womb, gave birth to you."

"Are we playing with words now, Queldar?"

Queldar looked from Milla to Parker, suddenly uncomfortable. "Who is this?"

Parker held a hand up, introducing himself. "Parker."

"He came from Earth, to help."

"How in the name of the Omniscient can an earther help?"

"No, really, pleasure's mine," Parker said.

"Honestly, Queldar," Milla said. "He deserves esteem not insults."

"My apologies," he threw to Parker before pleading with Milla. "But he'll lose his life here. As will you if you don't heed my advice. The queen will not forego her one chance to unify the worlds."

"I'll take her down, whether or not she's my mother."

Queldar clenched his jaw, speaking through gritted teeth. "You're as stubborn as your father."

"Thank you."

The sorcerer huffed in frustration. "I share your admiration, Milla. Your father was a smart man, an honorable wizard, but it's only a spell. And you know as well as I, a spell can be broken. You must hide. They'll do unspeakable things to bend your will."

"Maybe we should hide," Parker said.

"Alas," Queldar said, "the boy is more astute than he looks."

"Queldar," Milla said, unwittingly in unison with a tiny voice. Everyone swung their gaze up, surprised. Even her *Quodex*, concealed beneath her shirt, stiffened with attention. The white crow was perched on the canopy over Queldar's cot.

"Aloysius, mind your tongue," the old wizard scolded.

"Mind yours," the bird said.

Queldar flung a root berry, but Aloysius fluttered out of the way.

"How did Lucrecia know Father had the scroll?" Milla asked.

Queldar's face tensed. "Do you not recognize the power she wields? She has usurped generations of sorcery. She's not bound by our tangible limitations. She has mastered the craft. She can materialize, shift, consume one's soul. She's unstoppable."

"I know her might, Queldar. I lived with her."

"Then you're an arrogant fool."

"Hey," Parker said, but Milla quieted him with a hand on his shoulder.

Queldar thrust his arm sharply, producing an opening in the blockade. "Leave my home at once and never return. You're not welcome here."

Milla spun on her feet and marched out, Parker on her heels. *Blasted wizard.* No wonder her father had nothing to do with him.

CHAPTER TEN

ZANUB LEFT HIS HORSE on the border of Aelderoy Forest and traveled by foot. He had gone to Milla's home to collect trinkets and instead spotted the captain snooping around. He was disconsolate the bloodthirsty savage had survived his journey through the portal but thrilled Milla must have escaped him. *For the fortieth time.* He chuckled and raised his eyeshield for a clearer view, thankful to be rid of the murky tint.

As he neared the old warlock's abode, he choked on his own surprise. Milla stormed away from it, sporting that same determined, furrowed brow she wore as a child, and he nearly laughed out loud. But when a boy followed after her, Zanub's smile vanished. He ducked behind a tree until they faded into the distance. *Did that troll just take her hand?*

Zanub burst into Queldar's hovel without the courtesy of their usual bird call. "Who was that?"

Queldar threw up his hands in defeat. "By all means, come in unannounced."

"Who was that clod with Milla?"

"He's an earther. No concern to anyone. She would no sooner wed him than a soldier."

"Your mouth is faster than your intellect, warlock."

"Oh, calm down. I've had a day and a half already. And I have no time for Lucrecia."

"I'm not here on behalf of the queen."

"Then what?"

"Your spell is fading. Her Beholder practically gleams."

"Spells are not permanent, Zanub."

"I know. That's why I'm here. You must reenchant the crystal."

The warlock shook his head. "Under what pretense might I go to the castle? The last time I went uninvited, she stole my *Quodex*."

"Rather dim-witted to bring it, Queldar. But for that ancient tome of yours, the queen would never have remembered the portals."

"Thank you for your insight. I shall cherish it two moons ago."

Zanub gritted his teeth. "What do you propose?"

"Has it occurred to you to simply hide her Beholder?"

"A blatant act of treason would have me dead, and as pleasant as that sounds to you, it would leave Milla without an ally inside the queen's court. Do you want that on your head?"

"No, he does not," the small voice said. Zanub rolled his eyes along with Queldar as they both turned to Aloysius.

"Have you no social etiquette?" Queldar said.

"I'm in no mood for your trite platitudes, bird."

"Aloysius, if you please."

"I don't," Zanub said to the nosey crow and turned to Queldar. "I gave you fair warning, warlock. I'll take matters into my own hands unless you curse that Beholder before the new day rises." He pivoted to leave, but the feisty warlock sealed the exit with braided vines. Zanub swung back, his hand on the hilt of his sword.

"Careful now, Zanub. The soldier in you is showing."

Zanub refrained from slicing the warlock in two—he had an oath to upkeep—but his blood coursed with an evil that was getting harder to resist. "Open the passage."

"Lest you forget we are on the same side you ill-mannered child, you will find me to be the worst enemy you've ever imagined." The warlock swiped his hand in the air and the opening appeared. Zanub about-faced and marched out, his lips pursed tighter than his grip on his sword.

Ill-mannered child? Child? Zanub hewed a reedy hedge to its roots, wishing it was Queldar, and ran back to his horse. That warlock didn't know who he was dealing with. Zanub had some wiles of his own. He knew what Queldar was up to, sneaking off to the Nameless Village with his precious basket of berries. That imbecile never even noticed he was being followed. Zanub didn't need him; he'd take matters into his own hands.

Child?

He traveled the Shifts carelessly, ruminating ideas, ways to broach the news, and came up with a satisfactory script by the time he entered the hold outside Castle Hill. He pushed his horse faster up the mountain, leaping onto the drawbridge before it had fully lowered, and rode up the stairwell and into the Grand Hall without pause. He reared to a precise halt in front of the queen, who was on her throne in the center of the room, forcing the captain to step aside.

"My, my, Zanub," the queen said, though her arched brow would have sufficed. She closed the book hovering before her, Queldar's *Quodex*, and rose, fingers strumming the air, itching for something, someone, to destroy. "You're either fearless or foolish. Let us see which."

"I've found another… that is, I *may* have found one…" Perhaps he didn't think this through. A bead of sweat tickled his cheek, and he glanced at the captain, who smirked. Swine. "There's another who holds the verse to unhex the scroll," Zanub blurted, and his heart plunged into the chasm that was once his soul.

"Who?"

"There have been words she is the sorceress Jovia."

The queen paled, and even the pandering Inferno waned. "Words? Whose words? The forest chatter? Gossiping soldiers? I've no time for words, Zanub. I need truth."

"With your favor, I shall investigate the veracity of these rumors."

"Majestic Ruler rid our land of the sorceress Jovia years ago," the captain said.

Zanub addressed the queen. "In a world where much is beyond our understanding, perhaps a magic we've yet to encounter, we must seize every advantage. Should Milla elude capture or escape as she has done before," he said with a cutting glance to the captain, "you might lose your chance for omnipotence."

Inferno flapped in the wake of the queen's exhale. "Fetch this woman, if for no reason but to quell the rumors."

She ripped open the book, manually, and Zanub had a rush of guilt as the *Quodex* winced under the queen's hard hands.

"You fool no one with your attempts," the captain said to Zanub. "I'll find the girl whether or not Jovia exists."

"You do well finding her," the queen said, not looking up from the book. "Holding onto her seems to be difficult for you, however."

Zanub chuckled quietly, until the queen said, "If either of you fail, Inferno will snack on your sizzling corpses." She brushed her hand toward Zanub, flinging him and his horse out of the Grand Hall. The captain landed beside him in the corridor a moment later.

"How do you enjoy your cleverness now, Zanub?" the captain said as he picked himself up off the ground. "You've given me the freedom to snap the girl's neck."

"And the queen will have yours."

"After the heroic efforts I took to try and save the wench from such a tragic accident?" He snorted his derision. "You don't merit the armor that shields you, imbecile."

The captain stormed off, leaving Zanub to wonder what on Asper he started.

"How dare he make me doubt myself? The coward. A grown man with nothing to lose, hiding from the queen. As if I should do the same. As if I might be the cause of ruination if I don't. And his reaction to Father's death? Not a blink of his baggy red eyes. Heartless sack of dung. I'm ashamed to call him family. Oh, and his offensive efforts to get rid of me. Not just rude; suspicious. That wizard is up to something. I have a good mind to nick his loudmouth bird and squeeze the truth out of his feathery brain."

"Don't hold back on my account," Parker said.

Milla stopped, spinning around and narrowly avoiding a collision with Parker, who sidestepped in time. "Parker. Apologies. Please, speak up when I'm rattling off in a rage. I'm not unreasonable."

Her *Quodex* snorted and Milla snatched the book from her waistband. "Really, beast? You want to test our boundaries now?" The book ruffled sheepishly and Milla placed it back inside her waistband. "It's like training a bush possum. Requires constant reinforcement."

Parker threw his hands up. "Books."

"As I was saying, I do appreciate the input of others."

"Except Queldar."

"Were you not listening? That wizard is heartless and rude and—"

"He has a valid point."

"About what?"

"Staying low until this third moon passes. I mean, if that's the only time in the whole wide universe that the queen can do this spell that's going to ruin everything, it seems stupid not to wait it out."

"Stupid?"

He took a second to reconsider. "Yeah. I'm sticking with stupid."

Milla folded her arms. Why was she always alone in her views?

"Look, Milla, I'm all for stopping a reign of terror. But what's the rush? How long does this third moon thing take, another day or two?"

"It's called the Rising, not a 'third moon thing.' It's the birth of our lineage, it warrants respect."

"Sorry."

She exhaled with enough force to shake the surrounding leaves. "But you're right. Without the scroll unhexed, she can't do the Unification. I'll kill her after the Rising."

"Sweet."

"I know how it sounds, Parker. The longer I wait, the harder it is to say. But I owe Father that. The world is unjust without it and I simply wouldn't be able to go on in such a world."

He nodded like someone whose arm was twisted behind him, but it would have to suffice. She wove her fingers through his and led him through a Shift, emerging on the fringe of the slum. The stench brought forth an involuntary gag from the both of them, and Parker folded, hand over mouth.

"Wow. That hits you hard," he said.

"The pong of the Hinterland Marsh is nothing compared to the Nameless Village."

"I can think of a name for it."

Milla lowered her eyes to avoid the glut of sadly grotesque anomalies as she weaved through the muddy paths, passing filthy falling-down homes constructed mostly of rusted metal pieces and broken furniture parts with rags and bed-stuffing to fill the gaps—essentially garbage. The array of creatures residing here, people once upon a time, were afflicted with goiters and moles, matted tufts and clumps suited to feral beasts, and either too many or no limbs at all. Milla and Parker skirted around a three-walled tent overrun by a pustule family, and the youngest girl, three or four years old, reached out to them with one hand while wiping green mucus from her eyes with the other. Milla nodded congenially and ushered Parker ahead before he could come in contact with her.

"Best not to touch anyone here."

"Yeah, it would take a lot to get me to. But are you saying they're contagious?"

"Not exactly. Cursed."

"By who?"

"No one knows. Witches? Warlocks? The Omniscient? The cursed don't tell. An admission of guilt, some say. I say a desperation to avoid madness. Regardless, magic can be alive and glom onto prodding hands."

"Neat-o."

"Perhaps I shouldn't have brought you here. I only thought it would be a good place to hide."

"It is. I don't think anyone would come here voluntarily."

Milla scanned the village, sizing up their options. "We should build a shelter and stay indoors. We're obvious among the others."

"You flatter me."

She smiled, letting her guard down, and got kicked in the palate with a putrid waft of sewage. Worth it. Because he smiled back and overrode everything that was bad about this village.

"We can use those fallen logs and perhaps that jumble of vines. Create a lean-to."

Parker slapped his hands together victoriously. "Finally. My Eagle Scout training pays off." He jogged over to the branches in a playful zigzag fashion and Milla couldn't hold in her laughter, stink or not. His muscular arms, bronzed from the Asperian sky, gleamed with exertion, accentuating each curve. His shirt (a T-shirt he called it, she didn't know why) clung to his broad shoulders, and his back tapered in symmetrical perfection to his waist. And don't get her started on his—she blushed—his buttocks. There, she said it. Until Parker, she had no idea the beauty of buttocks on a boy. A horse, yes. Strong, fast, a boast of strapping power to travel the land swiftly. But a boy? She couldn't stop staring. She had the urge to tackle him to the ground and—goodness! She threw her hands over her mouth as if to stop her thoughts from spewing out. Her body tingled with goosebumps, even her toes. She cleared an area, pushing aside leaves and twigs and unsavory yearnings.

They constructed a shelter worthy of a merit badge according to Parker, but Milla was just glad they needed to huddle closely to both fit inside.

He pointed to a tiny glint on her wrist. "Did you scrape yourself?"

"No, no, no..." Milla pressed her palm onto the glint, shocked. "I don't understand. Why is this happening? Everything's tranquil."

"Tell your voice that."

She peeked under her palm and gasped. Her entire forearm glistened with the waning spell. "Parker, you mustn't let me out of here. Do you understand?"

"You're kinda freaking me out right now."

"My father's spell is fading. I can't control it. That's how I ended up on the roof. Don't let me leave."

His voice was nothing but a garble of noise and his face twisted into a horrid blob. Milla grabbed her throat, unable to swallow the viscid saliva. She couldn't breathe. The twigs and branches closed in on her shivering body and she flew forward as the world stopped and time streaked past in a trail of lights.

CHAPTER ELEVEN

DRESSED IN ONE OF LUCRECIA'S diaphanous gowns made of gold—the front folded so she wouldn't trip over it and the back trailing behind like a train—Milla ran across the Grand Hall. Zanub raced in after her.

"My queen," he said in a formal tone, then groaned. "Why are you not on the throne? A slug could run faster than you."

Inferno swept in and scooped her up, letting her slide down its fiery back onto the throne. "Thank you, Sparky." Inferno curled its lip in distaste.

"My queen," Zanub began again. "The ogres attack. I must defend our castle." He drew his pretend sword and Milla jumped to her feet dramatically.

"No, my king. We will send our army to protect us."

"But I must lead them."

"Alas. I will perish without you." She flung herself back against the marble with her hand on her forehead. "Do what you must."

Zanub laughed and Milla laughed harder. He ran up the steps and sat on the arm of the throne. "We will rule together one day, will we not?"

"We will. And we'll be kind and generous."

"And we'll have parties and games every night."

"Sounds dreadful," Lucrecia said, appearing before them. Milla and Zanub moaned simultaneously. "But now, Zanub, you must tend to your training."

"A king needn't train," Milla said. "He'll have an army for such things."

"He's not a king yet, my sweet. And he must study harder to

match the skill of a true soldier. You wouldn't want him unprepared, would you?"

"No."

"I brought him here for you, but he's not your pet. He must excel, as must you. Have you studied your lessons today?"

"Oh, how did it come to this?"

"As I thought. Zanub, fetch your sword and go to class. Milla, acquaint yourself with the talent inside you."

"I've met my talent. I don't care for it."

"Learn to."

She furled both her lips. "Very well. But he will be king one day, will he not?"

"That's up to you, my princess."

Milla giggled. "He shall be king when he slays the dragon."

Zanub bowed to one knee. "A dragon for my queen."

"Oh my," Lucrecia said as she ushered him off with a gust of wind from the wave of her hand. "Channel your determination, dear boy."

Zanub made a funny face to Milla and ran out.

"He's my favorite boy," Milla said.

"I'm pleased to hear that. Now study."

Milla pouted. "I'll study, but I won't like it."

"Your choice." Lucrecia burst into an ethereal mist, scattering into oblivion. Milla crinkled her nose.

"That would be fun to do."

Milla practiced her funny faces in front of the hovering mirror while Lucrecia wound her hair with silver strands into a braided bun.

"You fidget like a jungle squirrel."

Milla crossed her eyes and stuck her tongue out sideways at her.

"That suits you well. Perhaps I shall cast a spell to keep you that way."

Milla quickly uncrossed her eyes. "You dare not."

Lucrecia squeezed Milla's cheeks affectionately. "Indeed. To spoil such beauty would be indecent."

Zanub peeked in from the corridor and Milla spun from the mirror to greet him, but Lucrecia spun her back. "She'll see you at dinner, Zanub."

"But I have a gift." He entered with his hands behind his back. "I've slain the dragon."

Milla curtsied, until he presented her with the limp body of a wild hare, and she shrieked in horror. "What is that?"

"Your dragon, my queen."

"You fiend. You killed it?"

"You asked me to slay the dragon."

"I was playing. How could you do this to a living creature?"

"It's nothing more than dinner fare."

Milla held her stomach. "Undo it. Undo it this instant."

"How?"

Milla turned to Lucrecia. "Please."

"Please, what?"

"Please, Mother, heal this poor animal."

The queen took Milla's hands. "You misunderstand, my child, some things cannot be undone."

Milla pulled free. "What's the good of magic then? Life is the only thing of value." She glared at Zanub. "I never want to see you. Ever. Leave."

Zanub ran out of her room, crying, and Milla hurled herself into her pillow.

Lucrecia rubbed her back. "For someone who values life, you were quick to dismiss his."

"At least I didn't kill him."

"He merely wished to please you, Milla. He was mistaken, nothing more."

Milla stayed buried in her pillow until the queen vanished. She cried herself to sleep, skipping dinner, and didn't awaken until the rapping on her bedroom door in the middle of the night. The torches on her wall lit up and swung their nosey gazes over. She opened the door to find Zanub, his eyes reddened from crying.

"Don't hate me, Milla, I beg you. I'll never kill again." He presented a plump rat with an unwieldy tail. "A gift, along with my sorrow. See? It's alive."

The beady-eyed, scraggy-furred rodent twitched its whiskered snout and Milla melted. "Your oath, you'll never kill again?"

"My oath."

"What shall we name him?"

"Furry."

"No, no. Be clever."

"Love."

"Ew." Milla shoved Zanub. "I know. Promise. For our oaths to each other. To be kind and generous, to rule the kingdom together, and to never kill."

"Never."

The rat was plucked out of Milla's hands. "Hey!"

Lucrecia, interfering as usual, dangled it by its tail, out of reach.

"That's mine. Give it back."

"My castle, my rules."

Milla stomped her foot. "You're mean and evil and I hate you."

"Behave like a princess, not an imp."

"Very well. I demand my pet back."

Lucrecia smiled, impressed, but still held the rat by its tail. "Zanub, if you dedicate as much to your training as you do to Milla, you might become captain of the army one day."

Zanub turned to Milla, eyes as wide as his open-mouth. "Captain <u>and</u> king."

"I have ears, Zanub." What she lacked was patience. *That innocent rat swinging upside down.*

Lucrecia about-faced Zanub toward the door. "No more visits this night."

Zanub left and Milla stared down the queen with folded arms. "My pet if you please."

Lucrecia tossed the rat to her. "Keep it in your chamber, or it will suffer the fate of the hare." She dispersed in a sparkling mist, spraying the room with vibrant twinkles of color that evaporated midair.

Milla growled intentionally loud so the irrational queen would hear her.

Milla stood on a pedestal, leaning out her window, when Zanub clutched her leg. She screamed.

"You ogre. I might've splattered all over the bridge. And you'd have to sweep off my guts."

"I had your ankle." He peered out, next to her. "What are you doing—teasing the 'mongers?"

"Look at that funny man." In the forest outside Castle Hill, a short figure in ill-fitting armor tripped and stumbled his way toward the gates.

"He's not a soldier," Zanub said.

"Clearly. Where did he get their metal skin?"

"Perhaps he's a suitor."

"Gutter mind."

"Who else would brave the 'mongers? The queen is beautiful. You look very much like her."

"That's not a compliment."

"Fine. You look like a three-toothed desert eel."

"I'd rather, than look like her."

"Not true. I see you in her gowns."

"Stop. Please."

"And what do I look like?" He tried to pose as handsomely as he could and Milla laughed. "Cruel," he said.

"You look like a boy, Zanub. A kind boy."

He furled his lip. "That's worse."

Milla whacked his arm several times in excitement and motioned out the window. "They're lowering the bridge. Hurry."

She ran out of her room and through the corridor, into the labyrinth of stairwells. Traversing them was more fun than any game she and Zanub played. Every stairwell emerged into the atrium at some point, with many of them crisscrossing each other, and there was nothing but caution or skill to prevent travelers from falling off; there were no rails, just steps going up and down and sideways. But the view—the wide-open, spectacular view down to the dungeon and up to the top of the castle—was the best part. When Milla was feeling especially adventurous, she'd leap from one stairwell to another, much to Zanub's dismay, but he always followed. Like now.

"Slow down, Milla."

Pssh. She waved him on and crouched low on one of the stairwells in time to see the armored stranger enter in the vestibule ten stories below. She held a finger to her lips.

"He can't hear us up here," Zanub said.

Inferno shot out from the dungeon and snaked through the corridors to greet the visitor with a custodial roar and Milla giggled when he leaped with fright. The fire remained on his heels, encouraging his run, as he scrambled into one of the stairwells off the vestibule.

"Where to?" Zanub asked.

"The Grand Hall."

They jumped to their feet and, slamming into each other, flew back. Zanub squealed higher than a boy should, but Milla had him by the wrist. He was nowhere near the edge. "Goodness. What do they teach you in soldier studies?"

"Har har. Even you couldn't survive that drop."

"Perhaps I can fly."

"Perhaps donkeys can talk."

"Perhaps they can."

He mocked her tone with nonsense mumbles, which meant she won this argument. She led the way to the corridor outside the Grand Hall and was blocked by the blazing heat of a feisty torch. She swatted furiously with both hands, nearly extinguishing the flame, and it retreated with snide pops and flickers to its gossipy klatch. Milla peeked into the Hall with one eye and gasped in shock.

"What is it?" Zanub pushed her aside and looked in. She climbed onto his back and watched.

"It's Queldar, the brother of my father."

The bald wizard stood before the queen, his armor pooled by his feet. Milla jumped off Zanub and spun him into a hug. "I'm going home." She didn't get a step inside the Hall when he pulled her back into the corridor.

"You act faster than your wit," he said. "You cannot barge in on the queen."

"And you think too much."

"Would you prefer a brainless king?"

"Oh, Zanub. I won't be queen and you won't be king. You're just a boy. And I'm just girl."

"Is that what you believe?"

"Yes."

"Go then. Go home." He marched off, arms folded, and didn't look back, not even once.

Milla slumped against the cold craggy stone. Leave it to him to ruin a perfectly fun day. The flames tittered and Milla swung at them all, closed fisted. If she had a bucket of water, she'd squelch them permanently. She gathered her courage, took an exaggerated moment to think—*happy, Zanub?*— and stepped into the Hall. Lucrecia and Queldar didn't notice.

"The scroll holds the key," Queldar said to Lucrecia. "I can find it for you."

"Before the Rising?"

"Of course. It's of no use otherwise."

"Bring me the scroll and you have my word."

"Give me your word and I'll bring you the scroll."

"Such a clever little man." Lucrecia said. "No."

"No?"

"I don't bargain on the hearsay of a feckless wizard."

"You need time to think. I understand." As he reached for his armor to suit up, Lucrecia caught Milla's stare and was upon her in sorceress speed.

"You little witch." Lucrecia's eyes hollowed to the back of her skull and the moisture drained from her supple skin, tightening leather over her angular bones.

Milla trembled. "Please. Don't be angry."

The ugly queen grabbed her by the arm and flung her into the atrium. Milla screamed for her life as she plummeted, until Inferno swept under and caught her.

"Thank you, Inferno, thank you." Inferno trailed through the castle and deposited her inside a cage in the prison. "No! No!"

She screamed and screamed, pleading to be released, begging forgiveness, until the snarl of a 'monger snapped her quiet. She scuttled to the back of her cage and covered her eyes. The 'monger devoured a boy-like creature in the cell next to hers, specks of flesh and bone landing on her bare arms and legs. She choked her last breath and shot open her eyes.

CHAPTER TWELVE

"TRAITOR! FIEND! WARLOCK!" Milla ran but was hoisted off the ground by a pair of arms wrapped around her from behind. She kicked and twisted and elbowed her way to utter exhaustion and slumped in defeat. She looked over her shoulder to see who was holding her. "Parker."

His face lit up and he released her to the ground. "You're back."

She was tethered to him with twine around both their waists. "What's this?"

"Crazy day. You took off like a bat outta hell. Lucky for you, I was junior varsity track, and caught up as you dove through a Shift. This seemed easier."

Milla untied the twine. "Where are we now?"

"Well, if you don't know…"

She tested the weight of the silvery fronds swooping up from the ground and fanning out overhead. Heavy. The thicket masked everything in every direction.

"This isn't Aelderoy. I would've expected to be at Queldar's hovel if anywhere. That two-faced swine conspired with Lucrecia. She never would've known about the scroll but for him."

"Are you sure?"

"I heard them with my own ears. That's why he rushed us off. Not because he feared for our safety, he feared I'd uncover his traitorous ways and slice his cowardly neck." A frond snaked up her shoulder and flopped over her head, sticking to her. She whacked it away. "Stop that."

"Did that plant try to eat you?"

"They're salt-lickers. Harmless. Nonetheless, we should seek a Shift out of here."

Seeing none, she took his hand and sprinted through the jungle, letting the occasional frond steal a lick. She emerged from the thicket and was blocked by a fortification of tall leafless silvery trees with intertwining limbs. No Shift.

"Blasted."

Parker pried at the branches, but they didn't budge. "I want to go on record saying your trees are really weird."

"Noted." Milla's *Quodex* nudged her in the small of her back. "Derg." She pulled out the book, which fell open to the Eryuth Spell. It had gotten her out of the Royal Suite, why not here? She recited the verse expertly, but nothing happened.

"Odd. That was eloquent and exact. It should've worked." Her *Quodex* fluttered in agreement.

"I got this," Parker said, his tone playful as he stretched his arms and neck.

Milla stepped back, gesturing for him to proceed.

"Abracadab—no wait, that's not it. Open Sesame," he said in a low, commanding voice.

Her *Quodex* shuddered. Milla laughed. "Goodness."

He bowed. "Thank you. Now all we need is a chainsaw."

With a creak and a snuffle, a gnarled twig unfurled itself from a bough. The lianas underneath followed suit and unraveled until they draped off the branch like a set of curtains, dancing in the still air. Milla gaped.

"How'd you do that?"

Parker shrugged. "You must've loosened it for me."

She passed through the curtains, entering Ravaenwood Forest, greeted by foliage as dark as everything else surrounding the queen's empire.

"Whoa," Parker said, on her heels.

In plain view, the black stone castle stood, but not quite still, at the peak of the mountain—borne out of it—impossible to discern where the mountain ended and the castle began. Expansive, it spanned the length of the range and rose higher than the foreboding clouds, its tower lost completely within. It would take a day's trek by foot to reach the gates, but evil permeated the air around them like a menacing fog.

"Is that castle moving?"

"Just breathing. It appears to be asleep."

Milla's bones rumbled and she dropped to one knee, hand on the soil. "The army."

She jumped to her feet, grabbing Parker by the arm, and ran. The metal soldiers crashed through the air atop their metal steeds and Milla pulled Parker to the ground behind a tree for cover. The army continued toward the outer gates of Castle Hill, stirring the crazed scentmongers into a mania of howls.

"That sounds like a pack of hyenas strangling another pack of hyenas," Parker said.

"Scentmongers." Milla squeezed his arm and pointed to a soldier transporting an armored box like the one she'd been thrown in when she was abducted. "Parker, that's not good. They're bringing someone into the castle, alive. There's only one reason Lucrecia would do that. They have something she needs."

"Like what?"

"Worst case? A verse to unhex the scroll."

Frenetic, wild movement surged by the gates of Castle Hill. The army, not yet inside the hold, scrambled to protect their catch from the invisible attack. Shouts rang out and the soldiers parted, allowing three scentmongers to bolt into the leafy woodlands. Each 'monger was chained with four leads and each lead was gripped by two soldiers, and even under the restraint of eight soldiers apiece, the sinewy beasts were hard to control. They weaved through trees and shrubs, over creeks and bogs, whipping the soldiers along for the ride, as they chased the scent of flesh. Half the army followed, some on foot, some on horseback.

"Squeeds," Milla said. Perhaps Tobly. But she couldn't stay to see him, not when the hunt was on. She grabbed Parker's hand and charged through brush, away from Castle Hill. Bays and yowls ricocheted around them, spurring her to zigzag as much as the 'mongers. A soldier screamed and she looked back to see him ambushed from his horse by a pack of Squeeds. A scentmonger caught a whiff and about-faced in pursuit, hoisting the eight soldiers into the air. It pounced on the pack, pinning two of the Squeeds under its claws. Milla turned away, running faster. Once it finished its feast, she and Parker would be next. She tripped and fell and cursed herself, only to be tugged to her feet by Tobly. *Tobly!*

Derg.

Holding her hand, he ran in the opposite direction and she reached out for Parker. He clutched onto her fingers and kept pace.

Tobly pulled her through a turbulent stream, into a wall of handsy greenness, and penetrated three successive Shifts in three successive bounds so quickly she hadn't the chance to see where she was before careening head over foot down an earthen tunnel and losing her grip on Parker. Tobly took the steep descent on his heels and somersaulted into a nimble landing at the bottom. *Show-off.* Milla hit with a thud and grunted unglamorously when Parker bounced off her chest and knocked the breath out of her. At least that was all he knocked out of her.

The air—humid, dim, stifling—spoke volumes: they were in a Squeed hovel. Oh, her father would have a fit. The enormity of it, too. Thousands, perhaps more, of tiny dwellings were dug into the subterranean walls which wound and twisted out of view, probably covering the breadth of Asper.

Teams of boy-like beings went about their business in effortless choreography, doing who knew what, but they never stopped moving. In a nearby alcove, several boys fashioned spikes from a pile of lifeless armor. Others tended to bonfires throughout the cavern, roasting flesh.

Rattles and clanks echoed as a pack of Squeeds riding an armored soldier shot into the colony from one of the many tunnels. They scurried to a darkened corner, prying the hardware from their latest conquest before rigor mortis set into the magicked metal. All but two, who did a double take and tackled Parker to the ground, prompting others to swarm Milla. Tobly demanded an immediate retreat, but the Squeed straddling Parker plunged his spike toward Parker's eye. Milla screamed. Tobly rammed his brother, causing him to narrowly miss his target and pierce the ground next to Parker's ear. Parker jumped to his feet and pulled Milla close to him.

Tobly gave the Squeed a scolding, with plenty of finger pointing and gesticulating, but Milla couldn't hear any of it. The reprimanded Squeed dashed off with trembling lips and Tobly glared authoritatively at the others until they returned to their chores.

"Tobly." Milla swooped him in for a hug and he was helpless in her grasp.

This is my reward for sparing you the ugly words? Next time, I'll let you listen. And you know my temper has a temper of its own.

"I missed you." She released him and Tobly gasped for air melodramatically. Some things never changed.

We'll discuss this later. He retrieved a skewered anthropoid limb from one of the many fires and offered it to Parker.

"Uh... nope," Parker said.

Tobly looked to Milla. *How can he refuse? He has a stomach louder than mine.*

"Don't be insulted, Tobly. He's unaccustomed to your fare."

Tobly shrugged and gnawed at the flesh.

Milla leaned in closer to Parker. "This will be a good place for you to stay until I return from the castle."

"Wrong. For one thing, you're not going to the castle alone. And B, I don't know where you were a second ago, but they tried to shish-kabob my brain."

"Only because they didn't know we're Tobly's friends."

"We're not splitting up. Either we go together or we hide out together. But not here."

"Why not here?"

The cave rumbled—showering pebbles and sediment—as an aged earthen woman emerged, grown from and still one with the wall, embracing a wrinkled brood of newborns.

Parker threw his hands up. "For starters."

Milla hurried toward the woman, but Parker yanked her back. "Are you crazy?"

"Don't panic, mortal, I won't bite," the woman said. "Unless you ask nicely." She smiled, and like Tobly, it was a sight. Ear to ear.

"Funny. A wall with a sense of humor," Parker said.

"And an appetite." She pinched his flesh, then frowned. "Not as brawny as the soldiers. Yet irresistible." She patted his head like a pet, leaving behind grainy residue and an irritated Parker.

"Thanks. I was thinking I could use more dirt in my hair."

Enamored, the wall tore herself from Parker and addressed Milla. "So you're the sorceress Tobly speaks of."

She nodded. "Milla."

"I'm Mirth."

"I'm honored to meet you."

"And I, you. Tobly has labored to keep you safe." She motioned to a complex map etched onto one of the walls. "He has forbidden the hunt near your home or the surrounds you visit and has received a number of taunts from his siblings for his devotion."

Mooothhheerrrr, Tobly groused with pursed lips.

"Tobly, you never told me you did this," Milla said.

A friend doesn't boast their kindness. A lesson in there for you, perhaps?

"I hardly think I'm the one who needs schooling in humility."

Spoken like a braggart, Mill.

"Takes one to know one."

So you admit it?

"Is he talking to you?" Parker asked.

"You can't hear him?"

"Just his raspy breathing. He might have a deviated septum."

"Tobly, do you keep your thoughts from Parker?"

He smells of human.

"Derg."

Word thief.

"Settle down," Mirth said, and when Tobly folded his arms and snorted, she continued. "Why are you going to the castle? You must know soldiers are our main source of sustenance. If you kill them, we'll perish as well."

"We don't want your food," Parker said. "We just need to stop the queen from destroying the world."

Mirth brightened to a light shade of ocher. "A noble human."

"Right, 'cause everyone here is peaches and cream."

She laughed, shaking the ground, and stroked Parker's face affectionately. "I'll permit you to leave. However, if I've misjudged you, I'll have you for dinner and the girl for dessert."

"That's fair," Milla said, but Parker thought otherwise because Tobly shot him a look that could flatten a desert vole. "Parker, they're telepathic."

"I was joking," he said to Tobly. "You all seem super sweet."

Tobly glared at him, hurtling insults, and Mirth grinned.

"Don't be so serious, Tobly. He has a right to be wary." She shifted toward a crevice behind the pile of armor. "This path will take you to the castle. Journey safely. Especially you, human," she said with a wink. "I enjoy your demeanor."

"Yeah, I have a crush on you, too," Parker said.

Mirth receded into her cavern, fading from view, along with her brood.

Milla and Parker headed to the crevice and Tobly fell in step behind them.

"Apologies, Tobly, but you can't come with us," Milla said.

Who says I'm going with you, conceited? I was already planning to go there on my own.

"To what end?"

Tobly shrugged. *To peruse the menu.*

"Please, you'll be a distraction."

You're the distraction.

Milla gave him the look he usually gave her; the one that challenged his wisdom.

You can't defeat the queen on your own.

"I'm not on my own."

"I'm gonna take that as a compliment," Parker said.

You don't even have a weapon. Where's your blade?

"I have my craft."

It's worse than I thought.

Milla pinched his cheeks, because she knew it would drive him mad. He batted her hands away and she pulled him in for a tight hug, squeezing a squeal out of him. *I'll be prudent. My oath.*

She entered the path, taking Parker by the hand, and leaving Tobly behind. Without light from the bonfires or the squabbles of Squeeds—abounding in silence and darkness—Milla was suddenly self-conscious about holding Parker's hand. Should she let go? Oh, but the tornado of sensations sweeping through her from the touch of his skin. It hardly seemed possible, not even with magic. But her heart pounded and squeezed, racing from her belly to her throat. And the urges, deep, where she never knew she existed, to the surface of her skin, flushing her face with desire. No, not desire. *Need*. A desperate, indisputable *need* essential to life, drowning her in the fog of her hunger. She moaned, and Parker turned to her.

"You okay?"

She dropped his hand—*blasted, that was an overreaction*—and fanned her face to cover. "Hot… in here… the passage."

"I'll say." He flapped his shirt for ventilation, revealing glimpses of his perfect abdomen, and Milla shuddered on weak legs.

"So is that who you were talking about, back in Clear Rock?" Parker said. "The boy who wouldn't let you live with him."

"Yes, he's my boy friend, Tobly."

"Your boyfriend? Or your friend who's a boy?"

"Boyfriend, boy friend, my friend who's a boy. Are they not the same?"

"Not even close."

Fascinating.

They arrived at a stone wall with nowhere else to go and Milla said, "There must be a secret entrance." She pointed to a rock protruding more than the rest. "Too obvious?"

"One way to find out." Parker kicked the rock and the ground dropped. They fell onto a gravelly slide, tumbling over each other. As the bottom raced up toward them, they covered their heads for impact but instead breached a veiled cavity, and plummeted ten feet that felt like fifty, before landing in a puddle of fetid albeit cushioning mud near a group of rats gnawing on the remains of a carcass.

They were in the castle.

CHAPTER THIRTEEN

ZANUB STOOD BY THE ENTRANCE of the Grand Hall, dripping in shame. Thanks to him, the queen's posture was unbefitting her usual temperament. Reclined on her black marble throne, relaxed, with one leg crossed over the other like a commoner, she smiled serenely. Inferno purred by her side, making Zanub eager to smack it back to the dungeon. After agonizing silence, the queen slithered her torso through the air until she was face to face with Jovia, who stood before the steps of the throne. Their features were identical except Jovia's azure eyes shone with brightness whereas the queen's black irises sucked the light out of the universe.

"My, my. After all these years." The queen stroked Jovia's cheek lovingly. "My sweet, beautiful, kindhearted, pathetic little sister. I had forgotten about you."

"I think of you every day, Lucrecia."

The queen stood erect, her smug smile gone. "Don't rely on sentiment, Jovia. I have none."

"You've lost your way. Your anger with me has led you to this."

"You credit yourself for my success? What vanity you have. If Mother could hear you now."

"She wouldn't approve of your quest."

"I'm the ruler of our world. You're a useless witch decaying in the Nameless Village. Who would she approve of more? You? The favored daughter? You never studied, you never cherished your lineage. No, she would see. You're nothing because you deserve nothing. I'm almighty for I've earned it."

"Your passion leads you astray. Power needn't be evil—"

"Evil? You think I'm evil?" The queen roared with laughter and her pandering fire joined in. "Is it because I don't skip around the pond anymore and pick flowers? Is it because I defend my land? Because I want to unite the worlds? Tell me, my sister, what makes me evil? I know. It's because I don't agree with you."

"You've killed innocent people."

"I've protected my throne. It's my right. My duty."

"You've stolen the studies of many conjurers."

"Conjurers who wish to see me fail."

"There's no reasoning with you, you believe your own nonsense. No one challenges you because they're afraid and you're left with your own delusions."

The queen slapped Jovia to the floor. "You will remove that hex from the scroll, Jovia."

Jovia pushed herself back to her feet. "How? I've no powers. What little I had have waned."

"Don't treat me as a fool."

"Thieve any spell you like," Jovia said with open arms.

The queen erupted in a spectral mist and swept through Jovia with fervor. She returned to her physical form, angrier. "The hex is from the *Book*?"

"If you say so. I cannot remember a single word."

Lucrecia sucked in a breath. "Where is it?"

"The *Book*? If I had it, I would've ended your reign. Clearly, I don't have it."

"Then you'll unearth that verse from your stale mind before the settling of our third moon, or Milla will pay for your failure."

"Please, Lucrecia." Jovia reached out. "I kept our pact. I remained in hiding. I never saw my beloved or my daughter. I beg of you, please, keep yours."

The queen sat back in her throne. "Zanub. Remove this crone from my presence."

Jovia cried plaintively, still reaching for her sister as Zanub hauled her out. He didn't speak until they were in the atrium, where crosswinds masked many clandestine conversations. "Forgive me. I meant you no harm. I'm doing this for Milla."

Jovia stopped. "Doing what for Milla?"

He pushed her ahead. "Keep walking. If you unhex the scroll, the queen will let her be."

"If I unhex the scroll, the worlds will end. You do Milla no favors."

"She'll be hunted and captured, I assure you. Perhaps Queldar has not shared the stories, but she's headstrong. Her capture will be the death of her."

"What do you know of Queldar? Who are you?"

"I'm a friend."

"Of whom? Not me. Not Milla. Nor Queldar. No friend would force us to choose death, for that is what we'll do. We will not allow Lucrecia to prevail."

He deposited her back in the musty chamber. "I implore you to make the right decision."

"You're asking a mother to choose between her daughter and the fate of the worlds. Without one, the other is meaningless."

Zanub closed and locked the door and fell against the stone wall, holding back the itch to skin Queldar alive. If that obtuse bag of bones hadn't bartered with the queen to begin with, Milla never would've left the castle and none of this would be happening.

Flat on her back, covered in ample mud to make a shack, Milla spit a worm out of her mouth and sat up. Parker looked like a creature from the Hinterland Marsh, caked in sludge and moss, and she snorted a laugh, inadvertently swallowing some muck.

"Serves you right," he said, wiping gunk off his face.

"Shh." She motioned to Inferno in the center of the dungeon, looming from the depths of the planet and soaring out of view. "We don't want that busybody to hear us."

"At some point I'll stop asking stupid questions, but… the fire's alive?"

"Alive, extremely egotistical as far as fires go, and very protective of Lucrecia."

They pulled themselves out of the gelatinous puddle when an ear-splitting avalanche of armor, whining and groaning, startled them into each other's arms. The vociferous metal liquefied to silence inside the flames of Inferno, draining into a grated channel in the floor which flowed into cauldrons.

"I remember now," Milla said. "The metal must be cleansed and hexed anew so it'll mold to the next soldier like skin."

"That's pretty awesome."

"One doesn't become ruler of the world without being as clever as they are powerful." She eyed the myriad of stairwells leading up into the castle, none more inviting than the other, and headed to the closest one. Parker hit a patch of slime and his feet flew out from under him. Milla stifled a laugh and helped him up.

"I'm usually really good at walking," he said.

"So you say."

They climbed the uneven stairs, leaving the warmth of Inferno's blaze. Flames of the occasional torch on the wall wafted lazily, casting shadows that held no interest in them, thankfully.

"The torches are simpleminded," Milla said, "but be wary of their gaze. Should they realize we're intruders, they'll warn Lucrecia."

"Got it. Torches, evil."

The watery muck gelled to a thicker sludge without the heat of the dungeon and their feet slurped with each step. Parker skidded on a rotted carcass and, in catching himself against the wall, latched onto the crusty head of a meaty cockroach (the kind that ogres snacked on) and its dexterous antennae wrapped around his fingers. He shrieked, trying to shake it off and Milla shot her palm over his mouth and stilled his hand, pinning the roach.

"Please," she whispered. "Sound carries in the enclosed stairwells."

When she was sure they hadn't been heard, she released her hand over Parker's mouth, gently unwrapped the cockroach's antennae, and placed it back on the wall.

"Honestly, you two."

"He started it."

The cockroach hissed its retort. Milla urged it away with a pat on the rear—she had no time for unforgiving roaches—and continued her ascent. Parker jogged after.

"I had a dog smaller than that."

Milla took Parker to the cleaning quarters for the soldiers and their horses two levels above the dungeon. The wall was lined with large stalls and buckets of icy water. She had to pour three buckets over Parker to get rid of his sludge. He doused her with two. Soaking wet and freezing, she led the way up the stairwell, in search of a heated chamber. Horses' trots rebounded off the stones and crazed snarls rang out. Milla slowed, pressing Parker back against the wall.

"They're transporting a 'monger to the prison." She climbed another flight and pointed to the landing above. "Stay in the shadows and move quickly as we pass."

"Shouldn't we wait till they leave?"

"There's no end. They'll leave, more will come."

The prison looked the same as when she had lived in the castle—a wide expanse filled with a maze of metal cages imprisoning Squeeds. Against the far wall, empty cages stacked side by side and ceiling high, were newly magicked like the soldiers' armor and ready for use. The army would transport 'mongers in, sidle the cells together, release the bars to allow the carnage, and seal the Squeed cell to transport the beast back to the grounds. Modular.

A pair of mounted soldiers waited for a 'monger to finish feasting on chunks of gore—all that was left of a Squeed—as rats fought for splattering flecks. Covering their noses from the gamy rot in the air, Milla and Parker passed behind, unseen.

Four or five stories later, Parker began to lag, so Milla took the next corridor. A few pools of light from sparse torches dotted the vastness enough to reveal the curve of the hallway.

"The army has no reason to come here." She entered the first chamber, which was empty and torchless, but the floor radiated heat from the far wall. "Inferno rises from the center of the castle, beyond that wall. You can lean on the stones for warmth but don't fidget much. No sense in alerting that tattler to our presence. I'll return shortly."

"Where're you going?"

"You have to eat."

"I don't think so."

"Nothing anthropoid."

"Thanks, even though it had to be said. But I'll go with you."

"You'd be more helpful if you remained here."

"Did you just call me a wimp?"

"If that's akin to a jungle squirrel, yes. But it's no slight to you. Our air is different than yours."

"Yeah, like being in the stratosphere."

"You'll acclimate soon and this is a good place to rest."

"All right. But be careful, okay?"

Milla nodded. "I know no other way." She closed the door gently behind her.

Milla traveled expediently. She knew where the food was stored; three levels above the prison, two levels above the soldiers' quarters, one level above the stables, but on the easternmost side. As a child, the kitchen had become a refuge when she was barred from the stables as punishment. Most everyone, even the soldiers, couldn't stomach the cooks, but Milla held no prejudices. After all, kindness was in the heart not on the face. Lucrecia proved that.

She crouched lower than a full-grown rat and peered in from the hallway. As expected, the same three cooks were still there, chopping slabs of meat and bones and tossing them in boiling cauldrons of liquid. They were neither soldiers nor part of the army but a rare breed of Asperian ogre found in the badlands. Ghastly, by most accounts. With hairy fingers that dragged on the ground and necks bigger than their dainty ovoid heads, their stocky forms were freckled with goiters that hissed and popped like the badlands geyser. Milla gushed at seeing them. It had been too long since they cradled her in their hirsute arms.

She pulled her gaze away and opened her *Quodex*. She pondered an immobilization spell in Chapter Eight but rejected it, not because there were several words she couldn't pronounce, but because the ogres would be able to see her and her only advantage was that no one knew she was in the castle. Her *Quodex* flipped its pages to the last chapter where various annihilation spells were, offering a chance to practice before her encounter with Lucrecia, but Milla gave her book a good glaring to. As if she would ever annihilate a kitchen ogre. Yes, they worked for the queen, but they weren't evil. They suffered with the intellect of an ant, as her father would say, and knew no better.

She turned to an earlier chapter and briefed herself on an incantation to render them sightless. Perhaps sightless and immobile, combining two spells in one. She came to her senses, deciding now wasn't the time to experiment, and landed on Chapter Four, Verse Nine, *Swefecung*. Slumber. Like old times. They had often lulled her to sleep with the bouquet of lemon and rose biscuits baking in the fire oven; she would return the favor.

She recited the verse silently, employing some hand gestures for good measure, but the ogres cleaved more meat and threw the slabs in the pulpy broth, unaffected by her magic. She scooted closer—proximity was everything she told herself to save face—and tried again, this time whispering out loud (silent spells were finicky). In midcleave, the creatures slouched, their eyes wide open, and Milla slapped her forehead. Derg. How could she forget the badlands ogres had no eyelids? A ploy to trick scavengers. Well, she'd know soon enough if it worked.

She entered the kitchen, ready to flee, but the ogres, wide-eyed and oozing, didn't flinch. She hurried to the containers of food, gathering as many as she could carry. She couldn't resist; she dashed to the cook by the cutting board and kissed him on his pustule cheek, tickled by his fuzzy mole, and exited just as he awakened and cleaved the massive haunch before him.

Milla sprinted up the serpentine stairwell, emboldened with success. She rounded the curve, entering the atrium, and slammed into a metal-clad soldier. The collision occurred in an instant that took forever to unfold in her mind. *Zanub*. Her friend, her confidante, her king. That was her first thought. Her second was to slice his jugular. His heart. His soul. The imposter. The fiend. The backstabbing soldier. But really it all happened at once. The impact punched the breath out of her with a wheeze, her stomach twisted in agony, and she instinctively reached for her knife that wasn't there; but she was already flailing, having lost her footing, and slipped off the precipice, the rush of her heart in her throat. The soldier's crushing grip squeezed her wrist and she crashed face-first into the side of the stair, saved from the fall. He pulled her onto the steps.

Milla's head and chest stung from the impact, but nothing compared to the pain of him, in his metaled-flesh, standing before her as if it was six years ago, except the last time she saw him was at her shack when her father was slain. She swung her fists at his head, but he caught them with one hand.

"You monster!" she screamed.

He slapped his hand over her mouth, hoisted her up in the air, and slammed her on her back, pinning her there. "Quiet," he sharply whispered.

She struggled to free herself, but he was too strong.

"Milla. It's me. Zanub," he said as if it would please her. She bit into his gloved hand, trying to tear his armor, and he jerked it away from her mouth. "Stop it. I'm trying to help you."

Help her? His malleable face stiffened and froze suddenly, scaring her into a tremble, and he yanked her to her feet and threw her into a corridor. In good time, too, because Vylkrost emerged into the atrium from one of the stairwells above.

"Contemplating a jump, Zanub?" Vylkrost said. "Perhaps I can persuade you."

Zanub surreptitiously slid his eyes to Milla, who stayed ducked in hiding, her mind throbbing as fast as her heart, then he sprinted up the stairs without a response to his captain. Bold.

When the atrium cleared, Milla gathered the single container of food that remained on the steps and raced up, disappearing into the next enclosed corridor, desperate to reach Parker before anyone else. She ran all the way to the room, foregoing the shadows, and rushed in, relieved to find him there. More to the point, alive. She brushed her hair aside casually, as if nothing was wrong.

"Roasted with aromatics, none of it human," she said as she deposited the food before him.

"Or soldier?"

"Or soldier."

"Good. Don't want to get on Mirth's bad side." He grabbed a fleshy haunch and bit into it as rapaciously as a Squeed. "Mmm. Harsh and bitter with a nice bristly texture."

He mocked it but cleaned the bone of meat and moved onto the next slab. Again, like a Squeed. When she was satisfied he'd had plenty, she said, "I was seen."

He stopped eating. "By who?"

"Zanub, a soldier, once a friend."

"You're friends with a soldier?"

"Not anymore. When we were children, when I lived here. I hate him now. But he hid me from Vylkrost and let me leave."

"Why?"

"I don't know." She went to the door. "We need to move on. He and I played on this floor when we didn't want to study. He'll come looking for me here."

Milla stayed to the interior stairwells, avoiding the atrium for as long as she could, until arriving near the top of the castle when she had no choice. All the stairs crisscrossing the open expanse were below them, except the one they were about to take. "We have to move quickly. Every stairwell leads to the atrium sooner or later and a soldier can emerge at any time."

Parker peered over her shoulder. "How big is this place?"

"Endless, unless you wish to hide. We only need to go one flight, to that corridor. I'll go first. Give me a few seconds, then follow. But don't look down, look up. The stairs will hypnotize you. Ready?"

"Sure. Wait. Like, literally hypnotize me, or just make me dizzy?"

"Either way, you're plummeting to your death."

"Kinda taking the fun out of it."

She had the impulse to grab his hand and flee the castle to live out the rest her life staring into his mesmerizing brown eyes. But he said, "After you, m'lady."

She scanned the atrium—all clear—and bolted up the steps and into the corridor safely. Parker flew in next to her, skidding to a stop, panting and laughing. "Serious adrenaline rush."

"Shh," she said, trying not to laugh along with him and failing. "This is Vylkrost's floor," she managed to get out.

"What?" he whispered.

"Best to hide where no one would think to look for us, especially Zanub. Lucrecia's chamber is on the level above."

She sprinted to the first door about a hundred paces from the stairwell, grasped the iron handle, and hesitated. She shook off the doubt and twisted the handle, releasing a frigid gust of wind as she opened the door. Empty. They entered, only fortuitously, as Vylkrost exited from the stairwell into the corridor, his long shadow falling by their doorway. Milla swung the door closed, cushioning it into the jamb. Vylkrost rattled and clanged, each step heavier than the last, and stopped midstride outside their room. He sniffed the air louder than a feral boar and Milla motioned with the tilt of her head for Parker to hide behind the door for safety. Her fingers were still wrapped around the handle, having had no time to let the latch click in, and Parker steadied her hand with his, staying by her side. Vylkrost grunted and continued down the hall. A heavy door slammed shut and Milla and Parker breathed again. They released the handle as gently as possible, letting it click in place.

Their chamber was freezing and bare with a window opening that invited the squawks and screeches of wroders to filter in.

"And I thought I was gonna impress you with a ride on my bike. Who knew?"

"Perhaps one day. Though I enjoyed our travels in the ugly metal beast."

"Ah, the Gremlin. I think that was their motto. Ugly metal beast." He leaned against the wall, crossing his arms for warmth. "So is this what your life is like here? Nonstop crazy?"

"No, it was mostly uneventful. Father and I argued over lessons, chores, whether I could go outside. He was quite the worrier. Rather, quite the father. For years we lived like any family, but I think he knew we couldn't escape their hunt. Why else would he hex the scroll? I don't know if I'll ever acquire the skill to defeat Lucrecia, but I'll give my life trying, Parker. I must and you mustn't stop me. Do you understand?"

Parker nodded. "I get it."

Milla slid to the floor and opened her *Quodex*. "Whoever Lucrecia abducted is probably a sorcerer, so I should study, and you should sleep."

Parker sat next to her. "What kind of spell you gonna do?"

"Turn him to stone, I think."

"Kill him?"

"Stone merely suspends one in the seventh dimension."

"There's no such—you know what, never mind."

"It's only until the Rising has passed."

"Hey, why not turn the soldiers to stone?"

"A verse doesn't penetrate armor easily, not to mention an army of armor. Also, I've never done it before."

"Well, you know what they say. 'There's a first time for everything.'"

"Who say that?"

"They. People. Everyone."

"I've never heard it."

"I guess we like our clichés back home."

"Curious."

Parker closed his eyes and leaned into her, shoulder to shoulder. "Right, I'm the curious one. Not the freaky tree-boys or their made-of-a-wall mother."

Milla laughed. "Now you understand."

He was asleep, breathing heavily but relaxed.

Finally. She could stare without shame. She followed every contour of his face—more breathtaking than any magic—from his brow, furrowed in contemplation, to his perfect straight-edged nose, past his irresistible tender lips, down to his strong angular jaw. She kept going. How could she stop? His lean, muscular frame begged her to ogle, covered but not masked, perhaps even accentuated, by his soft shirt. She placed her hand in his open palm and he wrapped his fingers around hers, causing her heart to pound rapidly, her breath to increase, her face to flush with heat. *Goodness!*

Her *Quodex* fluttered, and she jolted upright, abashed to find herself nearly touching his lips with her own. Oh, but they were parted slightly, beckoning. She ached to feel them against hers. Her entire body throbbed with wonderful pain.

Her *Quodex* shuffled robustly, blowing her hair into a mess fit for wroder hatchlings, and didn't stop until strands whipped her eyes, stinging them shut.

"All right," she hissed.

She studied the verse until she fell asleep, but her true focus was on the rousing sensation overtaking her body, mind, and soul.

A slamming door startled Milla out of her sleep, and she found herself curled in a ball, head on Parker's lap, their hands intertwined. Vylkrost's passing footsteps stole her joyful moment, and she sat up, releasing Parker's hand. He awoke.

"Are you rested?" she asked.

"Yeah. You?"

"I slept like a desert vole during the high winds."

"I was gonna say the same thing."

She went to the window to check the sky. The majesty of the full moon lit the world with a silver tint. The half-moon, smaller but no less majestic, rested below the curvature of the full moon, dangling like a charm. The crescent moon, faintly aglow, would soon shine in its final position, its outer arch gracing the bottom cusp of the half-moon, like their markings.

Milla turned to Parker, who stood and stretched and looked at her with that tantalizing smile of his.

"Parker, why did you follow me?"

He shrugged cavalierly. "I couldn't let some maniac kidnap you."

"Why?"

"That's a weird question. Because."

"'Because' is not an answer, we established that. You might never see your world again. You might lose your life here."

"Well, the joke's on you. I wouldn't be losing much."

"Don't say such things."

"Milla, I think it's pretty obvious I don't have a plan for my life. Truthfully, when my parents died, I sort of died, too. I lost interest in everything. My teachers kept telling my grandparents I was an underachiever, had lots of potential, needed discipline. They didn't understand, nothing mattered anymore."

Milla understood.

"I look for excitement. It's the only thing that makes me feel alive."

"And that's what you're looking for here?"

"Well, of course I didn't want anything to happen to you, but sometimes you just want to be abducted by aliens, know what I mean?"

Milla nodded. Not that she knew exactly, but enough to surmise the intense longing in her heart, among other blush-worthy areas, was hers alone. "Is it because of Hailey?"

"No," he said with too much protest. "I mean, we went out for a few years, but we broke up months ago."

"She wishes otherwise."

"Yeah."

"You don't?"

"It's complicated. We were close, really close, then things weren't good anymore. We'd break up and make up and, well, somewhere in there, she got pregnant."

"She's with child?"

"She lost the baby. Before it was born."

"That's sad, Parker." She crossed the room to him now.

"The thing is, I don't know if she really was pregnant. Hailey lies to get what she wants. She always did. But she knew me better than anyone. Knew I needed something, or I'd take off on some adventure."

"Such as this?"

"You keep skipping over the part where I didn't want anything bad to happen to you."

"Apologies. Thank you."

"Ahh, don't mention it."

Milla melted, amused.

"Anyway, I was kind of a jerk. When she told me she was pregnant,

I got mad because I thought she did it on purpose. But it didn't matter after a while. We were talking about a baby. My baby. I actually felt like I had a purpose in life. I know it sounds crazy, but I already loved the baby."

It didn't sound crazy at all and Milla fought the well of tears building.

"Hailey was mad that I was mad and she slept with my friend to get back at me, and that's never a good solution. But eventually I got past it so we could raise our baby." Parker steadied his lip. "But even that was taken away from me. So you see, I don't have all that much back home. I'd prefer to see what else there is."

Milla nodded, tears spilling over her lashes, and Parker wiped her face.

"It's not that bad. Look at me now. I'm in a whole other universe."

She laughed and sniffled at the same time. "Dimension. We're still in the same universe."

"Tomato, tomahto."

Milla wanted to lose herself in his… everything. His body, his essence, his thoughts, his touch; perhaps his touch most of all. She wanted him to lose himself in her. To forget his pain, their pain, together, and bury themselves in each other. But somewhere, somehow, she had acquired a nagging sense of responsibility. Righteousness, perhaps. Vengeance? She wasn't sure anymore.

She collected her *Quodex* from the floor, awakening it. That book could sleep through a maelstrom. She let it yawn and ruffle its pages before tucking it in the back of her waistband, then put her ear to the door. Satisfied no one was out there, she opened it. Only to close it and spin to Parker.

"Maybe Hailey wasn't lying. She shouldn't suffer the loss of a child alone, Parker."

"I know, Milla. Believe me. She's kept me on a string because I don't know what's what anymore. But with Hailey, it's the boy who cried wolf."

"How does one cry a wolf?"

"No, it's a parable, a story. If you lie a lot, then no one knows when you're telling the truth."

"I see. If she had never lied, would you still be with her?"

The time he took to respond was the answer she needed, but he said, "I told you, it's complicated."

Isn't everything?

She turned to leave, but Parker stopped her by the shoulder, pointing to her arms. "Here we go again."

Her skin glinted with beads of the waning spell.

"Not now, oh, please, not now."

The last thing she heard was Parker say, "Milla, don't!"

CHAPTER FOURTEEN

WIND WHIPPING AGAINST HER CHEEKS, nose dripping like a leaky well-bucket, Milla soared high above the Ebony Tower, dotting in and out of the cumulus clouds. They were nothing like she expected; she expected to feel the cushion of the puffiness when she entered, but they felt no different than the sky, just cooler. She wiped her nose and banked into a layer of billow clouds, parting them down the center, and swooped up acrobatically into an inside loop. She squealed with delight and rolled onto her back as her mother glided in next to her, effortless and ever beautiful, so much so, the wind dared not move a strand on the tight bun braided with gold threads.

"Careful, my sweet."

Her mother had conjured an airstream countering the gravitational pull above the tower, allowing Milla to play in the clouds. It would be years before she could learn to shapeshift at all, let alone into a creature that could fly, but she had spent enough time trying in earnest that her mother surprised her with the gift of flight for her eighth birthday. But there were boundaries—sorcerers could only create a finite area of lift—and if Milla went past that, she'd plummet.

She spent the morning airborne while her mother supervised, mostly from the tower as if flying wasn't a big deal, and protested when it was time to come down. The others would be waiting for her soon and there would be cake and she could wear her gold gown, her mother bribed, and while cake alone was normally an effective lure, it wouldn't come close today. Milla pretended she didn't hear her, and shot straight up, aiming for an outside loop this time, arching back elegantly. As she crested the top of the loop, the airstream disappeared, and Milla dropped. She screamed, her heart beating in a constant thrum. As the darkness of the ground rushed up to teach her a lesson, a featherless wing swooped in with the ease and plushness she had expected from the clouds. She opened her eyes to see her mother's head on the craggy neck of a wroder.

"What did I say, Milla?"

"Good princesses listen to their mothers."

Her mother landed gracefully, transmorphing back to her majestic self, and deposited Milla on the tower with an affectionate cheek-pinch. "Now go feed Promise."

Milla ran off.

"He fled again."

Milla looked up from her books—three opened at once—sure the bags under her eyes matched the folds of an ogre's chin. She didn't have time for this. She was cramming for her quiz, having gotten up well before the sunbirds, thanks to Zanub's day-long game of 'find the ruby scarab' yesterday. It was in his pocket the whole time. Cheater.

"Mother," Milla groaned, flopping back on the black marble throne, rag doll fashion. "What did you do to him?"

Her mother folded her arms and shook her head. "Not I. You."

"What did *I* do?"

"You filled his head with grandeur. He's simply a boy, Milla. He can achieve only what is humanly possible."

"Then why does he take soldier studies?"

"To become adequate. You cannot expect a rat to swim like a fish, can you? His chance for competence is patience, of which he has none. He falters a move and storms off like a petulant child, rather than trying harder. I shall miss him, but I have no use for a boy in my castle, even for you. He must be a soldier or he must be gone."

Her mother vaporized in a shimmering mist to coalesce directly in front of her. "My sweet. Your eyes. They're practically amphibian. Put your magic to use. Or do you want Zanub to see you as a frog?"

Milla stuck out her tongue, but her mother was a spectral of vanishing light. She sent her books back to their pedestal with a wave of her hand and an infuriatingly prolonged grunt. *Talk about patience*—when would hers pay off? It had been months since she achieved object levitation and still the objects hadn't lost their heft.

She found Zanub in the rear of the stables, flinging his sword in a high arc so that it rotated in the air toward a bale of hay. It struck, hilt first, and bounced off. He fetched it and went again, this time piercing the stack with a wobble. He yanked it out and flung again, missing. When he bent down to snatch it up, he finally noticed Milla.

"How long have you been here?"

"Long enough to see you succeed."

"One of seven is not success." He jammed the blade into the top of the bale and sat next to it. Milla sat next to him.

"She's harder on me than anyone," Zanub said. "Saradmin scarcely survived the jabs of his spars, but because he is three phases older and two heads taller, he moves on."

"Because you're her favorite."

"That makes no sense."

"How can you be the captain if you're not better than everyone else?"

"I'm not a fool. I know my shortcomings."

"You *are* a fool, for the opposite reason. Blind to your own potential and believing the taunts of others simply because you don't excel at the speed of a soldier, and yet you hold your own among them. A lesser boy would've perished by now. So what if you're not as fast in the lessons? You'll get there, and when you do, you'll be better than all of them."

"Why do you care?"

"Because I do. I'd be lost without you, Zanub. You're my friend. My best friend."

"I see you less and less. With my lessons and your lessons, not to mention the time you spend with your mother lately, fussing over gowns, of all things."

"Do you not want me to be pretty for you?"

"You already are. Prettier than anything I've ever seen. Even the moonstar."

Milla blushed, and pushed him hard enough that he almost tipped over.

"Besides, I prefer you like this, in your long pants, rolled up and ready for adventure, not strangled in jewels and gold."

"Please, stay here for me and I promise to wear nothing but long pants and ugly study shirts."

He kissed her on the cheek and ran out.

"Zanub. Your sword."

He ran back in and plucked the blade from the bale and fled.

Milla wore her most extravagant silver gown, the one with iridescent crystals splashed across it in the shape of flower petals and straps delicate enough to expose her moons. She paced, her feet barely touching the floor, as she went over the impending ceremony in her head. Shelves carved into the stone wall, from floor to ceiling, held potions and elixirs too numerous to count. Another wall of shelves, ten times higher than she could reach on her own, housed books of magic. Rows of cauldrons stood at the ready, some brimming with mixtures, others awaiting their brew. Then there was the Crystal Beholder—clear, sparkling, translucent, everything a Beholder should be. Her stomach fluttered even though she had aced every lesson in this session. A natural once she put her mind to it, her mother had said many times, but one mistake today and she wouldn't graduate to Beholding.

"You look stupid."

Milla didn't bother to face him. "I'm busy, Zanub."

"Busy looking stupid."

She turned. "Would you prefer I never grow?"

He folded his arms and leaned against a cauldron which, luckily for him, brimmed with a cool elixir since he hadn't earned his armor yet. "I thought I was your friend."

"You are. But I've no time to play right now. Mother says I'm to be the youngest queen ever, and I can't rule if I have to rely on my scribbles, now can I? I must know my spells."

"And forget me in the process."

"How can you say that?"

"Because I buried Promise without you today."

"It was just a rat, Zanub."

"You loved him once. As you did me."

She ran to him and hugged him. "I'll always love you, Zanub. Always."

"Your oath?"

"My oath. Besides, if I graduate, I can finally ride. Can you imagine? Once you merit your steed, we can take the countryside together."

"I need my armor first."

"Then go. You'll not earn it watching me."

He smiled and whistled for Inferno. "To the arena!" Inferno swooped in, taking Zanub in its embrace, and snaked out of the Hall of Magic.

Milla giggled. With her tenth birthday approaching and her impending graduation (Omniscient willing) her mother would assuredly permit Zanub to dine with them from now on, and he could have no complaints about missing her. In fact, she could take the head and he the tail of the table, in preparation for their reign.

Her mother entered, filling the air with melody from her gown woven of gold strands, but she had no joy for such a joyous occasion.

"Worry not, Mother. I'm practiced."

"Milla, my sweet." She knelt, face to face. "You must return to your father."

The jolt hit every pore of her being. Milla stumbled back. "What?"

"Please, don't take it hard. It's merely until you're grown. Do you understand? A scant few years. Then you may return to me of your own accord. I'll count the days. No, the seconds."

Milla trembled, her body alive with anger. She pushed her away. "I knew it! I knew you weren't my mother. No mother would give up her child."

"Only a mother would make such a sacrifice, Milla. The fate of the worlds is at stake."

"But this is my home. I'm to be queen. You said so! And Zanub. What of Zanub? I cannot leave him." Tears began to well. "Please, Mother. Please!"

"If there was any other way, Milla, I would take it. Alas, we must both suffer now so we can be rewarded in time."

Vylkrost hoisted Milla off the floor and she kicked and squirmed. "Release me, you barbarian! *Faran o' onweald fracod...*"

Her mother, that witch, snatched her verse out of the air and quelled it in an instant. "Do not test me, child. I'm still your mother and you'll do as I say."

Vylkrost deposited Milla in the metal cage inside the metal box. She didn't want to cry, but her tears were stronger than her will.

"Don't make such a fuss," the backstabbing witch said, now inside the box with her, wiping her tears.

"Why do you not love me anymore? What did I do?"

"I love you with all my heart, Milla. But you must trust me. We'll join forces again and be unstoppable. First, I need you to be strong. Can you do that?"

Milla nodded through quivering lips and her mother kissed her cheek, then vanished in a radiant burst as the box sealed. Milla yelled and screamed and called for Zanub, flung about on the move, but he never came to say good-bye. She curled into herself and sobbed.

CHAPTER FIFTEEN

MILLA GASPED AND CHOKED, shooting open her eyes. Zanub was kneeling before her as she lay in the fetal position on the floor, chilled by her own sweat. *Zanub?* She sprung into his arms, hugging him. "Oh, Zanub."

She snapped out of the emotion from her memory. Hate mushroomed inside her blood and she shoved him back like the monster he was now. Mind swirling with spells to bash his head, she poised her arms to attack, but they were grabbed from behind and pinned to her sides.

"Milla, no," Parker said.

She writhed out of his grasp and spun around. "What is going on?"

"He's on our side. You ran off calling for Inferno and I could hear it coming for us like a fireball, but Zanub pulled us in here just in time."

"He's a loyalist to the queen. A liar. A soldier."

"And you're still obstinate," Zanub said.

She raised her arm again, but Parker jumped in front of her, blocking her aim.

"Milla, give him a chance."

"He had plenty. And now my father's dead and Lucrecia has the scroll."

"I was there to protect you," Zanub said.

"Hogswaddle!"

"You must believe me, Milla. The captain has worn such fury in his eyes of late, I thought he would slay you and welcome the consequences."

"What consequences?"

"Surely you know the queen has forbidden us to harm you or your father."

"Then why is my father dead?"

"Because the captain has a hatred for you that overrules his judgment, but not so much that he can't fabricate a tale to save himself."

"As you're doing now?"

"What would be my motive? You're alive and no one knows of your presence here but me. Inferno would've tossed you before the queen."

"Perhaps that's where I wish to be."

"So go."

Milla grumbled and turned her back to him, arms folded.

"Yes, there she is. The petulant princess."

She spun on her heels, teeth gritted. "Don't call me a princess."

"Don't behave as one."

She punched the air, making him flinch. "What'd you do with my father? And so help me if you fed him to the 'mongers."

"I laid him at the Creek. Beneath your tree."

Her eyes welled instantly. "You did?"

"Yes."

She cried, everything in her burning with sadness and relief. "Thank you, Zanub." She hugged him and he held her close, no longer the scrawny boy she had left behind.

Parker cleared his throat and she pulled free.

"Where's the scroll?" she asked Zanub.

"I expect somewhere impenetrable. Somewhere safe. The queen is not one to take chances."

"Will you help me kill her?"

Zanub's armor paled at the very question.

Milla shook her head. "As I said. Loyalist."

"I took an oath, my friend. Perhaps you've forgotten."

She had. "We were children. Things have changed."

"Possibly for you. For me, an oath is for life."

"Then stay out of my way."

"Milla, you're alive only because the queen forbade your death. She has known your whereabouts since the day you left. As have I, for I was given the task to watch over you. You're not practiced. You spent your years reading earther books and playing outdoors like a child and lost all that you learned. Your limitations outweigh your skills now—you cannot win. Much as she loves you, she won't perish for you. Lest you forget, she's not one to forgive betrayal, even from her own blood. Please. Allow me to help. I can transport you out of the castle so you can hide until the passing of the third moon. You can return when there's no threat, and finally, we can have everything we dreamed. We can rule together, as queen and king."

"Wait, what?" Parker said.

"I'm not leaving," Milla said.

"I beg you."

"Forget it."

"Milla—"

"No."

Zanub turned to Parker. "Have you any influence on her decision?"

"What do you think?"

Zanub sighed.

"Seriously, though, the queen and king thing," Parker said. "What're you talking about?"

"He's talking about a game we used to play."

"A game?" Zanub said. "You take the portal, befriend an earther, and suddenly our aspirations mean nothing to you?"

"You can't be king, Zanub. You can never be king. Why won't you understand that? You're just a soldier. Not even a captain."

Zanub's armor shifted and tensed. "For one who decries evil, you speak venomously." He left, his words stabbing.

"Think he's going to cool off or to rat us out?" Parker asked.

"He's contemplating both, I suppose. He's loyal to me and Lucrecia. All the more reason to silence the captive." She listened at the door, then faced Parker. "Where are we?"

He shook his head. "You have to stop asking me that."

There were no windows, no furnishing, and one torch, which slept, its flame drooped over.

"What does it matter, anyway?" Milla said. "I've no idea where the captive is. We simply need to start searching."

She cracked open the door and peeked out. The corridor curved immediately—the worst kind to sneak about in. She waved Parker to follow and they crept along the wall until they came to an enclosed stairwell too narrow for an ogre to use, let alone the horses. Perfect. She ducked in and ascended the steep steps, assuming the queen would want the captive nearer to her than the dungeon. A hint of wind whistled through, undoubtedly coming from the atrium.

"So, Zanub, huh? Seems like a nice guy, as far as soldiers go."

"Zanub was brought to the castle for me. He wasn't born a soldier, he was a boy. Taken from his parents I suspect. He had to work harder to earn his metal, but he's not evil. He's kind and generous, in fact. I wish he would abandon his armor and flee this horrid place."

"He's staying here for you."

"What do you imply?"

"Only the obvious."

"You speak in riddles now."

"He's in love with you."

"Is not. I was his best friend. If anything, perhaps he regards me as a sister."

"Nope."

"You know nothing about him."

"I know that look. Not even his metal skin can hide it. I'm only bringing it up because I think he does have your best interests in mind. Maybe we should listen to him."

"His only interest is in our union as king and—Oh."

"Derg," Parker said.

"Derg, indeed. But he's still a loyalist, and that defies everything else. Even love."

She quieted him with a hand motion as they approached the landing of the next story. A long straight corridor, with no soldiers standing guard, Milla continued the ascent. She knew she should focus on her upcoming spell, but Zanub overshadowed her common sense. Of course she loved him, but they were children. He didn't truly believe they'd wed and rule the land, did he? Still? After not seeing each other for years? She hated herself for giving him false hope. Though she couldn't help wonder if she hadn't met Parker, would it have been false? Perhaps she would love Zanub that way if she had the chance.

Eleven flights later, feeling like the traitor she accused Zanub of being, she spied a metal-clad figure outside a chamber door. "I believe we found our captive."

"That's a long way to go without being seen."

Milla nodded and leafed through the pages of her *Quodex* but closed the book. "Being seen is not the problem."

"Pretty sure it is."

"A soldier would covet my capture. In fact, he'd think himself lucky to be alone for such a coup. He'll let us approach."

"And what?"

"We use the Patty-Cake Spell. It requires two of us but the verse is simple and no soldier has seen it." She demonstrated the spell for Parker and he grabbed her hands mid-patty-cake, looking amused.

"You're kidding, right?"

"No, I saw it work."

"When?"

"At the hospital. On the Crystal Beholder."

"There's no crystal anything at Rose Garden except the chandelier."

"Trust me, Parker. It confounds one into submission, allowing a surprise attack."

She stepped into the corridor and a chamber door flew open, missing her nose by a fluke it was that close. She whirled Parker into an about-face and they fled down the stairs. As they veered into the atrium, she was yanked off the ground by her hair. She shrieked and Parker turned, prepared to charge, but the soldier—now gripping her by the wrists—swung her over the drop to the dungeon.

"Attack and I'll release her."

"I'm sure the queen will love that," Parker said, sounding cavalier, considering. The soldier snarled and pulled her back.

"I'll bring you both to Majestic Ruler." He pushed Milla and Parker up the atrium steps. Her *Quodex* pressed into the small of her back, struggling to open to a verse, but she had a better idea.

She glanced at Parker. "Patty-cake?"

He shook his head, but she began.

"Patty-cake, patty-cake, baker's man." She clapped her hands together, then against Parker's palms, and the soldier's helmet contorted with the same befuddlement on Parker's face.

"Bake a cake as fast as you caaaaannnn." Milla shoved the unsuspecting soldier off the stairwell, thrilled, until he grabbed her leg as he flailed back. She hit the stone step, belly first then face, and was dragged over. Parker latched onto her arms, above the elbows, but she was sliding down his grasp fast. She thrashed, trying to get the weight of the soldier off.

"Milla, don't. I can't hold on."

She managed to free a leg, but one of her wrists slipped from Parker's hands and she screamed as the sudden release spun her away from him. She swung back, reaching up, and clutched onto his hands, which still clutched her other arm. With her free leg, she stepped on the soldier's head, pushing him down until he dangled from her ankle. Then, with everything she had, she jammed her heel into his wrist, cracking it, and he lost his grip. His roars bounced throughout the atrium as Parker hoisted her up like she was a bag of feathers.

She held onto his hand and ran down the winding path, taking the staircase that led out of the atrium and into the next level, ducking inside the first entranceway she came upon. With a gasp, she slammed Parker back against the wall.

"Blasted! Of all the rooms."

A mountainous heap of faded metal rippled before them, reeking of pungent, sour blood.

They were on a ledge that bordered a vast circular room, separated from the massive mound of armor by a white-hot grate about three feet wide. Inferno's flames rose from the dungeon, dusting the grate and lighting the darkened room periodically, unaware of their presence.

"What is this place?"

"The incinerator."

Parker reached across the grate and pinched a piece of armor with his first two fingers.

"Parker, please. You don't want to leave this ledge. That pile ends up in Inferno."

"If we blend in, we could get around easier." He put the glove on and the metal molded around his hand, a living, breathing membrane, but didn't fit as snugly as it did to the soldiers. "Did you see that?" He waved his hand around. "It's so light, I can barely feel it."

Milla ripped the armor off him and threw it back in the pile. "Did you not hear me? We can't go in there for scraps. The bottom will open—"

"I heard you."

"I've seen a soldier incinerated when I was punished to the dungeon. He fell from this pit, by accident I assure you. I heard his skin bubble and pop as Inferno gorged on his metal shell, knowing full well he was in there."

"Milla, this is a gold mine. We've been lucky so far, we shoulda been killed ten times over. We can't walk away from our good luck now."

She eyed the armor. Freedom to travel the castle would be a gift. She sighed. "When the doors close after the next drop, we go. But be quick and don't tangle yourself with the armor or there will be no escape. Luck or not."

The labored creak of iron stung her ears as the trap opened and pieces of armor funneled into the pit. When it closed, they jumped over the searing grate and onto the pile, involuntarily sliding partway down and causing a mini-avalanche, but they managed to stay on the mound. They collected pieces until they heard the strained groan from the trap.

"Hurry." Milla said.

They jumped back onto the ledge as the bottom opened and more scraps fell into the fiery pit. Milla and Parker shared their stash, wrapping pieces around them—Milla was shy a helmet, boot and chestplate, and Parker needed cover for his left arm and leg—and like before, the supple armor shaped to their forms loosely. Which was fortunate, Milla realized; they might be able to pass as young soldiers entering the ranks.

She connected her armor seamlessly, like liquid, and turned to

Parker, whose pieces were still separated. "The armor's intuitive. You have to will it together."

He scrunched his forehead intensely, staring at the metal, and Milla burst into laughter. "You look like a desert vole stalking a sand eel."

"Mission accomplished."

"Relax your brow. Simply… seal your armor," she said with a gentle flow of her hands.

"Oh, is that all? Seal my armor." He mimicked her gesture jokingly, but the metal melded together, leaving him agape. "Did you see that?"

"Mind your thoughts, that's your true protection. Many soldiers have let fear steal their focus and paid with their heads."

Parker sealed and unsealed his metal glove a dozen times, trading off exaggerated looks of shock with joy.

"Honestly. Boys—" She stopped, in alarm. "Someone's coming."

"Hide."

"Where?"

"Where else?" Parker laced his fingers through hers, and when the footsteps were near, he squeezed her hand in signal.

She jumped with him over the grate at the worst time possible; the trap door creaked and moaned open, sending metal pieces around them as the center of the pile sank into the funnel. Milla's leg was wrenched in a mess of armor, ripping her from Parker's grip. They reached for each other, brushing fingertips as she was sucked in with the fervor of a hinterland bog. She clawed for the surface, attacked by metal edges scraping every inch of her, pushing her farther and lower, head over foot, into the tangle, disorienting her. Suffocating. And the blistering heat. She was on fire; if she wasn't, she might as well have been. The armor—the perfect conductor of Inferno's fiery blaze—burned her skin like a sizzling iron. When she thought she'd pass out from the torture, the trap closed and the pull stopped, leaving her buried in total darkness. A heap of scraps clanked onto the pile and footsteps retreated. Pinned, not knowing which way was up, Milla struggled but couldn't move. And then salvation.

"Milla? *Milla?*" He sounded so far away, and desperate, but there.

"I'm here." A ruckus of metal flew everywhere and she couldn't tell if he was getting closer or farther until her arm was tugged. "That's me."

Parker uncovered her enough to hoist her to her feet with one hand clenching her biceps like a soldier might, just as the iron trap groaned in warning, and they jumped across the grate in clumsy haste. Safe, but shaken, they erupted in stifled laughter. When they settled down and the trap closed, they gathered the rest of their armor.

"I keep seeing flashes on the side of my helmet," Parker said. "Like numbers or something, but they disappear before I can read them."

"Lingering magic. The helmets provide coordinates so the army can orient themselves and locate their charted Shifts. And so Lucrecia can track her soldiers."

"She can track us?"

"Discarded armor is removed from her inventory until it's refashioned and remagicked. We needn't fret."

"Fret. You're so cute."

No, you are!

They did their best to walk naturally in their unnatural armor as they entered the corridor, and the soldier guarding the chamber door paid zero attention to them. Apparently a little metal went a long way.

When they reached him, Parker deepened his voice and said, "Captain ordered us to replace you in watch."

The soldier didn't respond. Milla waved her hand in front of his eyeshield and he didn't budge. She snorted. "The swine's asleep."

She slipped into the chamber, Parker following, and closed the door silently. Gusty winds and wroder squeals outside the window worked in their favor because the captive, tucked beneath a worn blanket in the corner, didn't stir when they entered. Milla knelt by the blanket and took a moment to concentrate and another to encourage herself.

"*Beon gan o bodig and gemynd*," she whispered and looked for a transition of some sort. A clue that it had worked. Parker questioned her with a shrug and she shook her head, unsure. With a light touch, she lifted the corner of the blanket, and choked down a gasp.

"What's wrong?" Parker asked.

The spell failed— the captive wasn't frozen in stone, just sleeping—but that wasn't her shock. It was the captive. The woman. Around her neck, an amber amulet peeked out from the ratty cloak, but Milla didn't need to see the gem to know who this was. Even in tatters, imprisoned and bruised, this woman looked like Lucrecia.

Parker leaned over Milla's shoulder and choked down his own gasp. "Is that your mother?"

"It can't be."

"But the necklace—"

"She's dead," Milla said in a sharp whisper. "The army killed her. Lucrecia told me so. My own father told me." She hurried to the farthest side of the room and Parker followed.

"Obviously, they were wrong," he said.

"Don't say that."

"I don't get it. Isn't this good news?"

"If that's her, then where has she been? Why did she never come home? With every memory, I search for a flaw in Lucrecia's stories to free myself from her, but this fits into her tale—the gift of child from one sister to another. Lucrecia gave her fate unto Jovia, *her* fate. Jovia never loved me as her own; how could she? I only exist but for the grace of Lucrecia. My poor father never had the heart to tell me."

"That's a lot of speculation."

"It's the boy who never cried wolf, Parker. Lucrecia never lied to me. She's evil and cruel, but I can't find one lie. Why should I doubt her about this?"

Jovia shifted and Milla fled, panicked, slamming the door behind her and leaving Parker in the room. The soldier bolted upright with a start and seized her by the shoulder, spinning her into the wall as Parker exited the room.

"It's fine time you arrived," the soldier said. "Did the captain think I was to guard her all day?" He pushed Parker ahead of him as he marched off. "Faster, neophyte. Have you no pride?"

Milla shook off the shock and hurried after but Parker motioned for her to stay.

Stay? Was he insane?

She rocked in her own confusion, sorting through millions of thoughts. Could she let him disappear, possibly forever, for the sake of saving the worlds? Shouldn't she? Of course she should. What was she thinking? But a life without Parker seemed… lifeless. Blasted! Her heart was her downfall. She ran after him, not two steps in, when a frigid chill stopped her in her tracks as particles of light mingling into a vibrant blend of color settled into beauty incarnate—Lucrecia. *Mother.*

Draped in steel mesh, the queen's lissome figure jingled melodically. Milla jumped to attention, on instinct, as a soldier is required to do. Her body palpitated with hatred, fear, and worst of all, lost love. An anthology of memories flooded her at once—storytelling, tea parties, rat races, food fights, mending scrapes with kisses. True or not, it was true in its own right; Lucrecia was her mother. Milla surged with hope. Surely, she could reason with her. Surely, a mother would embrace her daughter over the ruling of two worlds? Surely, it needn't come to death. *Death.* The thought of her father's death hit her mouth like bile. Sharp. Burning. Unforgiveable. Her pulse quickened with hatred.

"Is the prisoner awake?" Lucrecia asked.

Milla gave a curt nod and Lucrecia materialized in her face, drowning Milla with her steaming breath, but all Milla could wonder was whether the malleable metal favored the previous soldier's features or hers.

"Next time you fail to respond properly you'll be silenced for eternity."

The previous soldier's.

"Yes, Majestic Ruler." Milla spoke from the pit of her stomach, mustering a low timber.

Lucrecia shot open the door with a finger flick and Milla followed into the chamber as a soldier would. Jovia didn't rise and the queen's cheek twitched in offense, but she didn't miss a step, taking a seat next to her prisoner, like sisters might when visiting one another.

"Have we not played this game long enough, Jovia? Let us be the family we are, not enemies," Lucrecia said.

"I'm not your enemy, but I won't allow you to rule the worlds, Lucrecia." She sounded so fragile, as if her essence had been beaten from her. As if her soul had been smothered.

"You cannot win."

"I'm not afraid to die."

"My sweet. Death would be the kindest thing I'd do to you."

Jovia looked at her, a sadness compared to none. "I miss my sister."

Lucrecia shot to her feet. "Don't put this on me, Jovia. *You* abandoned *me*."

"I did no such thing."

"Revisionist! I did everything in my power to keep our family together. You shunned me, denied me my rights, my daughter. Still, I reach out. I invite you into my home and you show me contempt. I offer you greatness and you refuse. I have no more sympathy for you."

"I have sympathy for you. I always have."

Lucrecia snarled, her bony ugliness flickering. "Find your senses, Jovia. If not for me, if not for Milla, for Mother." She stormed out of the chamber, her three moons angry on her swaying hips, and the door magically slammed after her.

Milla waited, making sure a nosy rat didn't surface, and turned to Jovia. "Where did you get that amulet?"

"It's of no use to you."

"It's of great use to me." She removed her helmet and Jovia's azure eyes pooled with tears.

"It can't be. My daughter…"

"Daughter? You say it so easily. I want the truth."

Jovia wiped her face with her cloak, stalling no doubt, but she had no escape; Milla stared her down. "The truth is complicated," Jovia said.

"The answer when one doesn't care to answer."

"You have the candor of your father."

"How would you know?"

"The years may have passed, but I still remember my beloved."

"Apologies. But I have a right to know the full truth, not half-truths."

"So Lucrecia has told you."

"Is she lying?"

The pause said enough, but Jovia began. "We had great plans to raise a family, your father and I, but after years of trying, we weren't favored with child. Lucrecia knew our pain and offered to help. She was powerful, even then. I didn't know she wanted a child of her own, Milla. She told me after your birth that she had tried many times but never carried to term." Jovia's lips trembled. "She wanted to take you from us, said you were hers, but she was mad with grief. It's true, I couldn't conceive without her. But I carried you, I gave birth to you, I raised you until the army found us, and because I loved you more than life itself, I—" Jovia broke off, unable to finish. Milla put a comforting arm on her shoulder and Jovia pulled her in, hugging her, metal and all. "Forgive me. I made a pact with her."

Milla pushed out of Jovia's arms. "What pact?"

"She promised you would be spared if I lived in exile. I couldn't risk your life. Sorcerers were being hunted and killed."

"By her."

"Yes. And she gave her word that you would remain safe, as long as everyone believed I was dead."

"Did you ever think to look for us? That together we might escape her evil?"

"Every day, my daughter. Every day I thought of you and my beloved, and every day my heart broke anew. But how could I chance your life, just for my own happiness?"

"Not just yours." Milla paced and exhaled deeply, the sting of tears threatening her. *Complicated* didn't begin to describe this. She put her helmet back on. "Are you fit to travel?"

"Yes."

Two horses cantered across the drawbridge, and Parker, to his dismay, was on one of them. His horse seemed oblivious to the treachery of the steep, uneven descent down the mountain, slipping on occasion, and Parker bobbled atop with gasps and grunts, his hand fighting a cramp from holding onto the reins so tightly. Halfway down the snaky path, he caught sight of the rolling swarm of fur and fangs at the base of the mountain. Scentmongers. Hundreds of them. Uncaged and looking for food.

Alerted to the movement, the feral beasts bounded up with greedy cries and Parker tensed every muscle, unintentionally spurring his careless horse into a gallop. The soldier urged his horse faster, as if it was a contest, and Parker was glad to see him pass. But it made no difference who got there first; 'mongers were everywhere. Parker prayed his improvised suit of armor was seamless and remembered that was up to him. He prayed for that kind of focus.

A 'monger made a bipedal run for him, like a mugger in a dark alley, shoving its face in his, snout pressed up against his helmet. Parker's stomach turned at the malodorous gray mucus in its nostrils and rancid meat wedged in its yellow fangs. *Sealed armor. Sealed armor. Sealed armor.* The beast was gone in a flash, uninterested, and Parker felt faint with relief.

Somehow he made it into the hold and out of Castle Hill without any recollection of it, only realizing he was safe, at least from the 'mongers, when he heard the gate lock behind him.

"Take the south, I'll take the north. Return when you've slain five."

The soldier disappeared into the deep mist of the forest, leaving Parker to guess five of what? Bunny rabbits? That he could do. Maybe. Here, a rabbit might be five feet tall and fire-breathing.

He headed in the opposite direction of the soldier, hoping to pass a respectable amount of time staying alive until he could return to the castle. To Milla. He regretted not telling her that *she* made him feel alive, not this stupid adventure. Excitement was the last thing on his mind when she had disappeared in that mirror. He shook his head. When would he get it right?

He discovered his horse was as responsive as his motorcycle—the slightest shift, lean, or flick of the wrist was sufficient to guide it—and he settled into his ride with more confidence. Zigzagging his new best friend through the lofty trees, his serenity was quashed by a sudden chill, as if he was being watched. He stopped his horse and scanned the area but didn't see any living creature, just a black-leafed forest of stillness. A twig cracked behind him, spiking his heartrate, and he kicked his horse into a gallop. Incomprehensibly, he was airborne, knocked off by an invisible force, and he hit the ground with a crunch. The forest sprung to life as tiny camouflaged figures darted back and forth, and Parker was covered with Squeeds. *Squeeds*!

"It's me," he said. The dogged Squeeds converged on his armored frame, pinning him down. "I'm not a soldier. It's me. Parker." One of the wily beings raised his spike overhead as he flipped up Parker's eyeshield.

"Agh!" Parker realized how easy it was to lose focus on his protection, but his alarm worked in his favor because he thrashed violently enough to throw the Squeed clean across the brush, lowering his eyeshield before they could puncture his brain via his eyeball. More Squeeds clambered aboard, tugging at his arms, and luck, if he could call it that, intervened. Barks and howls echoed all around as soldiers set out on the hunt for Squeeds.

The bush-creatures fled, but not empty-handed; a pack dragged Parker while others rode atop his shell, awaiting their opportunity to pierce his skull. Before he knew it, he was sliding down a bumpy tunnel, the clatter of metal reverberating inside his brain, until his head slammed against his helmet and everything went black.

CHAPTER SIXTEEN

MILLA SUITED JOVIA IN ARMOR from the incinerator, ensuring the lightly magicked metal formed somewhat to her frame and sealed itself. She led the way down one of the lesser traveled stairwells to the stables, one level above the soldiers' quarters. The floor teemed with horses, some armored, some not, but it also teemed with soldiers, so she took Jovia to a barren chamber several flights up to wait. They removed their helmets.

"How do you know your way around this castle?" Jovia asked.

"I lived here for years."

"With your father?"

"Of course not. The army took me from him."

"That can't be. Lucrecia promised your safety if I kept my oath. She's a woman of her word, if nothing else. That much I know."

"A reflection of her cunning mind. I was safe."

Jovia furrowed her brow like any mother filled with regret, but Milla looked away. "How did you escape?" she asked.

"I didn't. She sent me off one day and told me to return on my own accord."

"And here you are. Though I suspect she didn't imagine it would be to save me."

"I came to kill her."

"Milla!" Jovia's shock was expected.

"She killed Father. At least her army did. Forgive me for being so blunt, but better you know sooner than later."

Jovia nodded. "Queldar told me."

"Queldar? That rat knew you were alive?"

"It was serendipitous that we met, and I swore him to secrecy."

"Serendipitous or planned? He's betrayed our family in many ways, I wouldn't trust a word from his wicked mouth."

"Don't fault him for respecting my wishes."

"Is it your wish that he align himself with Lucrecia?"

"Why, the old sorcerer is as honorable as your father."

Milla flared her nostrils, inhaling not enough air to quell her anger. "Queldar is a fake and a fraud. A warlock. I saw him with Lucrecia when I lived here. No doubt, his visits to you were a means of spying."

"I assure you, his heart is not evil. But for him, I'd have no stories of you or my beloved. He alone kept my spirit from dying."

"Then how did Lucrecia know we had the scroll?"

Jovia shrugged. "Not from Queldar. He didn't know. No one knew we had it."

Milla pounded her fist on the floor, splitting her glove. She sucked in a deep breath to calm herself and willed her metal back together. "Why did we have it?" she asked Jovia. "Why us?"

"Oh Milla, I suppose only the *Book* and the Omniscient know why your father was chosen. He was collecting berries one morn when a dove flew overhead, and since he had never seen one before, he was piqued. He followed the regal bird until it met with another as resplendent, and what happened may sound incredible, but your father wasn't one for exaggeration, not much. The doves joined wings and without witnessing precisely when, a parchment was gently carried by the breeze in their stead."

"The birds became the scroll?"

"It drifted to his feet, and the fate of Asper and the worlds was placed in his virtuous care."

"He should've torn it to shreds," Milla said softly.

"Destroy the scroll and the worlds will be destroyed in its wake."

"So what? The worlds are nothing but evil."

"Your actions belie your words, my dear."

Milla grumbled. "Well, hexed or not, no one's safe with Lucrecia holding the scroll."

"Pity we can't return it to its pure form."

"Are you saying it can be done?"

"The doves would take flight and go in search of their next keeper, taking the verse with them."

"Why didn't Father do that?"

"He tried. He never stopped trying. His journal was indecipherable for all his attempts."

Milla leaped to her feet. "I have his journal—" She remembered. "Blasted. I gave it to Parker."

"Who?"

"A boy from Earth."

"Earth?"

"Yes, it's in another dimension."

"I know where it is, Milla. You speak the curses well. But how did you meet a boy from Earth?"

"I took the portal. Before you make a deal of it, you should know the captain also took it, as did Parker, who followed me here. Apparently, if there's a hint of magic remaining, anyone can travel it."

"You're too modest."

"That, I've never been accused of."

Jovia smiled. "Where is this boy now?"

"If he has any sense at all, he's on his way back home, so probably somewhere in Asper."

"I see."

"You see nothing. I barely know him."

"Yet your eyes sparkle."

"Please, I've no room for distractions. I have to save the worlds, in case you didn't know."

"I'm delighted to see your father taught you discipline, a lesson that escaped me."

Milla curled her lip. "It's a new trait. Revenge is motivating. It pains me to say I took advantage of Father's compassion to avoid most of my studies. I regret it. The anguish I caused him, that is."

"I'm familiar with such tactics. Even Lucrecia didn't covet what few spells I had. Or perhaps she spared me out of love."

"Her heart is buried too deep in evil to find love."

"I hope not. I hope to have the sister I once had. We were happy, inseparable, as children. I watched her pride swell in tandem with her talent over the years, and rightfully so, for she was practiced like no other. My, she was brilliant. And kind. My reverence blinded me to her pain. I didn't know she had ventured spell after spell in an effort to carry a child of her own. When I shared my news, I thought she would rejoice. I thought she had gifted me with her mastery because she wanted my happiness. But the unfairness of it—I, unskilled, and she all-powerful—filled her with madness. I don't know why she was cursed with such suffering."

"Maybe it's so evil will end with her."

"Perhaps you never saw the beauty in her, but I did."

"I've seen all sides of her. I loved her as a mother once. I may still."

Jovia looked up with hurt in her eyes.

"No disrespect to you."

"I understand. We had little time, Milla. I can't expect you to love me."

"But I did. Father told me stories every day, I felt like you were with us. But when he died, a spell he cast to bury my memories died with him and things are coming back to me now. Not just events, but emotions I never knew I had, emotions that are real. I lived with Lucrecia for four years, longer than you. She raised me as her daughter. She taught me. She loved me. I fought it at first, but it began to make sense, to feel right. Honestly, when she sent me back to Father, I was heartbroken and angry. How could my own mother abandon me?"

Jovia dropped her head.

"I don't mean to hurt you, I'm simply confused as to who is my real mother right now."

"You owe me nothing, Milla. No apologies and certainly no love. But perhaps we can get to know one another, not through stories from others, but together."

The clamor of horses trotted past as the stables emptied, and Milla slipped her helmet over her head. Jovia donned hers as well.

Parker stirred, groaned, and opened his eyes to a metal spike plunging toward his retina. He jumped up, swinging, and once again sent a Squeed flying off his armored body. Five others grabbed ahold of him, but Parker threw off his helmet before they could skewer his brain. "It's me, damn it!"

The boy-like beings squeezed their small hands tighter around his wrists and legs, turning to their mother for instruction. Mirth's earthen form emerged from the wall with an amused smile on her face.

"You shouldn't travel the forest in such dress."

"I wasn't given much choice."

She nodded to her children and they released him, kicking and swiping the air as they trudged off.

"Any of those guys Tobly?" Parker asked Mirth.

"Tobly would have succeeded."

"What? I thought we were friends. Never mind."

"So you haven't completed your mission."

"Good guess. You seem to know what's what around here. You know where the *Book of Knowing* is?"

The woman's eyes thinned. "Why do you seek the great *Book*?"

"I'm not clear on the details. Something about all hell breaking loose that only the *Book* can stop."

"The *Book of Knowing* protects the distinction of our two worlds. Many have sought it in the hope of abolishing that distinction."

"That's not why I want it. I think it's the complete opposite."

"Why should I trust a human of the world that once strove to destroy our beliefs—our lineage—would choose to keep our world autonomous?"

"I don't know. I don't know why you should trust me. All I know is that I have to find that book. I have to do something. I can't let Milla sacrifice herself to save us. Me, you, everyone. I have to find that book."

Mirth pierced his soul with her sandy eyes, and he let her. Protruding farther from the wall, she spoke quietly. "In a cave, deep beneath a reef in the Marman Sea, the ferocious Dragon guards the *Book of Knowing*."

"Marman Sea. I've been there."

She smiled sympathetically. "Having been there is rarely helpful in this land unless you know how to travel the realm. Our paths are not linear."

"Shifts. Been there, too."

"The visibility of which is exclusive to those with the power of sorcery."

"Oh, right, forgot that part."

"Is your helmet magicked with coordinates?"

"Mostly flickering. You know, to make it really annoying."

She receded into the wall until she disappeared completely, and reemerged, handing him a rolled up parchment—rough, prickly, like chapped hands, snagging on his own fingers, but incongruously soft and pliable.

"What's this?"

She moved up to his face and spoke in a whisper. "A map of every Shift in Asper."

"There's a *map*?"

Mirth covered his mouth with her rocky hand. "You might rather keep it to yourself. The map is highly coveted." She retreated and Parker spit out grit and wiped his tongue.

"Considering everything, this seems a bit too easy."

"Easy?" Mirth howled with laughter. "*Easy?*" She laughed again, shaking the cavern and causing Parker to stumble for balance.

"All right, I get it. Not easy."

"You do brighten my day." She settled and wiped the amusement from her face.

He opened the parchment, finding a jumble of indecipherable overlapping nonsense etched, or maybe burned, into the tawny hide. "Okay, this is a joke."

"You're in Asper. Release the constraints you put on your mind."

"Those constraints keep my armor sealed, just so you know."

"The freedom to believe is what seals your armor."

No truer words. For a skeptic, he believed whole lot of unbelievable stuff lately, landing himself in another world wearing magic-ish armor and seeking a dragon. Why start doubting now? He looked at the jumble—*ready when you are*—and the symbols flashed into a three-dimensional atlas, intermittently, but enough to give him hope. Mirth closed his mouth, which had fallen open in shock.

"Don't be fooled," she said. "Reaching in the cave beneath the reef is the least challenging part of your task."

"Right, ferocious dragon."

"Not dragon; Dragon."

"Why does everyone do that here? We're saying the same thing."

"A dragon is not the same as Dragon. You'll see. Magic is not a weapon. Strength is not a weapon. Honor is not—"

"I get it already. But I'm going." He parted his armor, like a pro, and retrieved the journal Milla had asked him to carry. "In case Milla shows up before I return, this is hers." The wall brushed the cover, intrigued by the journal. "No peeksies."

Mirth chuckled.

Parker motioned to packs of Squeeds as far as the eye could see. "I don't suppose one of them wants to go with me?"

"They all do, but only for the feast."

"Solo it is."

"One more thing."

"Let me guess. It's not easy."

She smiled. "Shed your armor before you enter the sea or you'll spend your last days with an army of metaled corpses on the bottom. My thoughts are with you, human, as is hope." Mirth withdrew into the cavernous wall, disappearing completely.

Parker set out on his expedition across Asper, in search of the *Book of Knowing* and the ferocious dragon that guarded it.

CHAPTER SEVENTEEN

THE STABLES HAD CLEARED except for a few horses deep inside the maze of stalls. Milla followed the snorts and whinnies, looking for candidates, as Jovia stayed by her side.

"Have you ridden?" Jovia asked.

Funny thing—she didn't know. How many memories floated in limbo, awaiting their place in her history? "Not to my recollection. But if a soldier can do it, it can't be difficult."

She grabbed a few carrots from a feed bag and went down the next aisle. "Why hasn't Lucrecia taken the verse from you to remove the hex? Isn't that her strength—stealing other conjurers' hard work?"

"Your father acquired the spell from the *Book of Knowing*."

Milla grabbed Jovia's arm, stopping her. "He had the *Book*? Since when? Where is it? And why is this the first I'm hearing of it?"

"I suspect he didn't want to give you any ideas. I hear the desert vole has nothing on your stubbornness."

"Queldar's a gossiper, I see."

"His favorite pastime," Jovia said fondly. "But this happened before you were born. To keep you from danger, your father wanted to release the scroll to another guardian. He had the *Book* but hadn't found the spell to free the doves when, in his words, the most beautifully ferocious creature he had ever seen emerged, spitting fire and hate and honor. He lost his grip on the *Book* and it was gone, in a flash. But not before he had seen a verse to hex the scroll, and you know how quick a study he is."

"Was."

"Yes. Was," Jovia said, the glimmer paling in her crystalline eyes. "I lived without him for so long, I suppose I haven't distinguished the loss."

Blasted. Milla's mouth outran her sensitivity, but Jovia continued, no admonishments.

"I watched him hex and unhex the scroll until he was certain of its efficacy. We never expected I would retain the knowledge, I was such a poor study, but somehow I did. The puzzling humor of the Omniscient, I suppose."

"But no one, not even Lucrecia, can steal a spell that was taken from the *Book of Knowing*. She can't win."

"She needn't steal the spell, Milla. She'll coerce it from me because she knows I can't bear the thought of harm coming to you."

"You said she was a woman of her word. You made a pact."

"Which became moot once Zanub found me."

"Zanub? Zanub, the soldier, brought you here? That fiend, that monster, that liar?" Milla hurled the carrots through the air and pummeled an innocent bale of hay into pulp and didn't stop until she slipped and fell to her knees. She dropped her head in her arms to stop from screaming at the top of her lungs and groaned until her throat burned. How could he? How many times could he hurt her and still profess his love? He was no better than Lucrecia.

Jovia rubbed her back in comfort. "Milla, I've never met a soldier I liked, but he thought bringing me here would stop Lucrecia from looking for you."

Milla wiped her face angrily, distorting her metal. "How? Thanks to him, she has no reason to honor her agreement now."

"He knew nothing of that. No one did. That was the point. I'm the one who broke our agreement by being found."

"Don't you dare take the blame." She got to her feet and fixed her armor, sealing gaps she created from her hissy fit, and walked off, but Jovia took her by the arm.

"If you have a friend in the army, I suggest you use him."

"Do you? Because he was no friend when they came for the scroll. When Father was killed. His friendship is self-serving." Milla marched off in search of a horse.

Naturally, the pickings were paltry. Why should she expect any better? She eyed a tan-colored foal with a white mane, too young to be armored. Useless. She spotted another foal, tall enough to rest its chin on her head, but also too young to suit up. A nudge from behind pushed her into the stall and she spun around, thinking Jovia had done it. "Seriously?"

But Jovia was stock-still, maybe trembling, because Lucrecia's horse, fully armor, flared its nostrils and snorted. Milla squealed in delight, then shot her hand over her mouth. "This is Malefactor. My one true friend in the castle. Isn't that right, Malefactor?"

The horse lowered its nose and nudged her again, and even though she braced herself, she was pushed off balance.

"Still a brat." She hugged its leg tightly. "This may work out."

She sized up the horse in the next stall—older and larger than the foals but not as broad or tall as Malefactor—already armored and ready for the ride. Perfect. She filled Jovia in on the essentials. "Never approach a horse unseen, keep a hand on them when leaving their line of sight, relax when riding, use a light touch with the reins, and carrots and apples are indispensable." After feeding plenty of both, they mounted their steeds.

Milla unsealed her chestplate and retrieved her *Quodex*, holding it out for Jovia. "This is beast."

"Milla, I can't take your *Quodex*."

"No slight, but you need it more than I. If only you make it out of the castle, I want your oath you'll take the portal."

"Provided you make the same oath," Jovia said as she tucked the book inside her armor.

The horses ascended the stairwell to the main floor without prompting and began the long trek across the massive foyer toward the drawbridge. The soldier keeping guard lowered the chain and lifted the bars, bringing a smile to Milla's dull helmet, but the onslaught of approaching hooves wiped it off. He wasn't opening the gate for them but for those returning—Vylkrost and his army—and Milla instantly regretted taking Malefactor. She kept her gaze straight ahead and, as soldiers dispersed into the various stairwells leading down to their quarters, she and Jovia passed Vylkrost in the center of the enormous vestibule without incident. And then, "Close the gates!" the captain yelled.

Milla whacked Jovia's horse on the rear, sending it into a run, and kicked Malefactor into a gallop. The gate groaned and creaked, crashing toward the ground like a heartless guillotine and Milla ducked under the jagged edges, glancing over her shoulder. Jovia's horse whinnied and bucked as the barrier slammed down, blocking their exit.

The drawbridge was already angled at forty-five degrees, closing upright, and Milla held on, stomach muscles straining to keep from sliding off her horse as it ran up the wooden planks, the sky as her view. They were airborne, sailing off the drawbridge toward the ground. Malefactor barely cleared the fizzing moat, its hind leg slipping into the muddy channel, but it righted itself and ran down the steep hill at breakneck speed.

But Milla couldn't. She just couldn't. She pulled back, pleading for Malefactor to stop, and finally halted the massive animal halfway down the mountain. Chest heaving, she turned toward the castle in time to see the drawbridge slam back down over the moat. If she hadn't seen it, she'd have felt it, it hit so solidly. Vylkrost sprung out of the castle atop his steed, and over the drawbridge in two bounds, charging in attack—so arrogant, his sword remained sheathed. Milla kicked her heels into Malefactor's belly, charging right back. As their steeds converged, Milla launched herself off Malefactor, toward Vylkrost, and he had the same idea, diving for her. They collided in midair and Milla took the brunt of the impact, hitting the ground breathless, with the monster on top of her.

Vylkrost went for her helmet, trying to rip it off, but she held it on, sealed tightly like an abled soldier, and escaped his fumbling grasp. She lost her footing and tumbled down the rocky slope, head over foot, front over back, faster and faster, uncontrollably, until she was stopped by a jagged rock slamming into her back, ending her descent with the same force of plummeting off a cliff. She moaned, and flopped onto her stomach, bruised and injured. Arms shaking with pain, she pushed herself to wobbly legs as Vylkrost loped toward her like a rabid 'monger, lunging for her neck. She'd barely gotten to her feet and couldn't think to move, when Malefactor reared up before him, protecting her. Vylkrost dove out of the way of the horse, but rolled to his feet without pause and snatched Milla off hers, his armored glove squeezing her neck so she couldn't breathe. She silently recited the spell to convert his hand to stone, but he dropped her, as if scorched by fire, and the spell didn't take. She scrambled to her feet, readied for battle, but he stepped back in retreat and Milla knew.

Encased in mercurial armor, from head to toe, Lucrecia stood on the edge of the drawbridge, her black eyes pinned on Milla. She shot a spectral radiance down the hillside that swept over Milla, exposing her aura from inside the armor. Lucrecia's mercurial face softened with a gentle smile. "Welcome home, my daughter."

Milla collapsed to her knees in defeat.

CHAPTER EIGHTEEN

HELMET UNDER HIS ARM, Parker emerged from the Squeed hovel into a lush forest like one he might find on Earth, except for the umbrella-sized pastel leaves dotting the trees. The air was calm and fairly quiet, some distant chittering that sounded harmless, and a hint of breeze. He consulted his map, taking longer than expected to free his mind and let go of distractions—maybe the chittering wasn't harmless; maybe he taunted death to cover his survivor's guilt; maybe he was as stupid as they came; maybe his grandparents wouldn't be alive by the time he returned, if he returned—before the lines of the diagram shifted into their positions, upward and outward, creating a small holographic world emanating from the parchment.

There was no simple north, south, east, and west in Asper because many of the lands existed in the same space but on different planes, and Shifts weren't shortcuts, like Parker had thought, but were the only way to reach many of these places. They existed, independent yet interwoven, with the rest of Asper.

Seeing it in its three-dimensional form, he understood it better; not just the geography, but the differentness. Entire lands—mini-worlds— had no idea that others existed, other people. In the blink of an eye, in a single footstep, everything they knew, everyone they loved, could be gone; forever. Unfathomably. But that was life, wasn't it?

Parker began plotting a course to the Marman Sea. If he could discern north from north, he'd be golden. He laughed; north from north, but he knew what he meant—a northern direction from a north plane.

After studying the map from different angles, he noticed a subtle variance in the weight of the lines between directions and planes and it became easy to read. But not to lay out a trail. He started over seven times before he charted a course that didn't result in a dead end. Helmet on, he raced off.

About a mile from the Squeed hovel, he approached the first Shift at the base of a mountain and looked for the ripple in the air, as if having the map might give him magical powers. It didn't. He reached out, searching for the breach, and kept reaching until the rocky wall stopped him. *Bogus.*

Parker referred to the map and concluded he was in the right place. So what was wrong? He flipped the parchment every which way, seeking a new perspective, but the holographic image righted itself gyroscopically. *Not helping.*

Rather than tilting the map, he tilted his head. The other way. *Oh.* He smiled, finally picking up the slight curvature of the line.

The Shift was perpendicular, not parallel, to the mountain. He pivoted a quarter turn to his left, stuck his arm out in front of him and it disappeared into the soothing warmth. Stoked, he sank into the Shift.

Parker emerged with an involuntary gasp, dripping with sweat that had nowhere to go but to pool in the boots of his armor. Dark, scorching nothingness surrounded him. Berated him. He spun full circle, or at least he thought he did because everything looked the same. The land had been charred lifeless. Fissures the size of whales mottled the cracked, ashy ground. The sky was gray and low, so low, the weight of it pushed on his back. And the heat. Suffocating.

A vicious wind snatched the map from his hands, no warning, and Parker jolted in a start, stunned motionless for a millisecond. He took off after the parchment, but it whipped up and out of reach. Dehydrated, mouth like sand, he chased it, sloshing in his sweat—he couldn't lose his guide.

The paper drifted toward a fire-spitting chasm and Parker dove, catching the tip between his first two fingers before crashing to the ground and skidding out of control. He flipped and rolled, his torso careening over the ledge—death by magma—but somehow found the strength mothers had when their babies were trapped under cars and stopped himself from going farther. The parchment ignited from a flurry of sparks and Parker instinctively dropped it only to snatch it back quickly from the wafting air.

Face on fire from the molten lava, flicking and lashing, he growled from the pit of his quaking abdomen and slithered back to safety with one thing on his mind: save the map. He shoved the fiery parchment deep into the ashy powder and tamped it down a hundred times to smolder the flames before extinguishing his own burning helmet with handfuls of dust. Panicked, he brushed away the slag, uncovering parchment, and freed a flurry of cinders that scattered into oblivion. Miraculously—magically?—the hide was unscathed; the map emerged three-dimensionally.

Parker sprung to his feet and sprinted, anxious to leave this hellhole. No, this hell. He breached the Shift right into a jumble of vines, snagged, a fly in the web, but didn't fight it, relieved to be out of purgatory. Also, there weren't any giant spiders looming. After catching his breath, he peeled the vines, which were rife with suckers, off his suit, squeezed through a small gap in a tight cluster of saplings and entered a mesh of woven branches. He pushed through the tangled twigs, unsnarled more vines that deliberately clung to him, and crawled beneath a low canopy of monstrous leaves until he found open ground.

A narrow stream flowed downwind a few paces ahead, and he hurried over. Tired, Parker sat by the almost-blue, almost-clear, almost-Earthly water and slid his helmet up, listening for bays of scentmongers. Quietness. He dropped his helmet to the ground, welcoming the freedom. He hadn't realized how oppressive the lightweight armor was. Without it, his head was a helium balloon, ready to float away.

He glanced at his reflection dancing in the ripples, afraid to know if the magma had scarred his face, and was pleased to find it merely sun kissed. He removed his gloves and splashed his neck, relishing the crisp, cool wetness on his hot skin. He thirsted for a mouthful but resisted. Everything was bigger, bolder, badder in Asper and he wasn't about to invite an unfriendly microbe into his gut. Or brain.

Parker checked his coordinates for the next Shift, collected his armor, and followed the stream, arriving in a clearing where the gentle flow matured into an earsplitting, churning cascade over a mile-high cliff. He eased away from the dizzying edge, perplexed, and consulted the map. Supposedly, the Shift was *in* the waterfall.

"Come *on*." Was anything easy here?

He stuffed the map in his glove and, legs spread for balance—one behind, one in front—carefully peered over the cliff. Ridiculous. He backed away. How was he supposed to find a Shift *inside* a torrent of water? He'd have to jump at exactly the right place, hit exactly the right spot (like that wasn't absurd in itself; too high, too low, left, right?) and get shoved under in exactly the right trajectory. And that was assuming the two hundred metric tons of water per second didn't shred him into ground meat.

He was scared, he admitted. Petrified, in fact, as long as no one was listening. But how would he face a dragon if he couldn't face a waterfall? Damn it; whose side was he on? He slipped the helmet over his head and sealed, sealed it good. Then he told himself to jump. *Just jump. Jump already.*

Jump!

Parker ran full speed and dove into the shimmering curtain with a scream. He hit the rush and was forced under, hard, roiling with the angry foam. Caught in the undertow and dragged, he knew he had missed the Shift. And then utter relief—the warm aura enveloped him—but short-lived. Unlike the other times when he had instantaneously emerged elsewhere, here, he swirled in the residuum of the falls, disoriented, aching for a breath. Dying for it. His body jerked spastically as instincts fought reason and Parker gasped involuntarily, stabbing his lungs with water. He convulsed in a hacking fit, not realizing when he had surfaced, but he had.

Being ushered away by the heavy current below the falls, Parker was disappointed he had missed the Shift after all, but giddy to be alive. He swam to shore, wondering how he'd get to the top of the cliff to try again, when he deduced from the thickness of the air that he was, in fact, in a different land.

He checked his map for orientation and scrambled through the dense jungle, ducking low branches and leaping over shrubbery until the vegetation thinned and he sprinted at full speed. His run ended at a rocky wall that rose into the clouds and spanned to infinity in both directions. The end of Asper.

Parker climbed, using crevices and cracks as his footings and handholds, and never looked down. When he reached the peak, he was rewarded with a path no wider than the stairs in the atrium but was glad to see the world continued on the other side.

Arms out for balance, he walked the path like it was three inches, not three feet, over to a conspicuous clump of willowy palm trees fanning out from an exposed bulbous root in the dusty ground. Parker tested the sturdiness of the trees—perfect, for an imperfect, unbelievable quest—so he held onto one of them for stability and reached up. His fingertips disappeared into the fluid air above him, but he couldn't breach the Shift entirely. He counterpoised himself against the trees and edged his way up, reaching into the warmth and finding an anchor to hold onto. With a grunt, he pulled himself through, surfacing from beneath the green sands of the beach. He collapsed next to the rock he had used to hoist himself up and soaked in a moment of rest. He was in the land of ebony mountains and purple water. He was by the Marman Sea. One step closer to the *Book of Knowing*. No more Shifts to travel, only a lagoon to conquer. And a dragon.

Stripped of armor, Milla was thrown into a dank chamber so violently, she stumbled and fell to her face, splitting her lip on the floor. A hand touched her cheek and she scrambled to her knees, swinging. But it was Jovia. Milla pulled her in for a hug. "I didn't know what they might've done to you."

"I'm safe. Lucrecia can't bargain without both of us." Jovia wiped Milla's bloodied lip.

"She knows I'm weak."

"A loving heart is strength not weakness."

"How can you say that when Father's dead only because he came back for me? When you've had to live in hiding? When I handed over the scroll? All for the sake of love. And here we are."

"Yes, here we are. I thought I would never see you again. But here we are. There's still hope, Milla, because here we are. You mustn't give up now."

"She'll torture you."

"Nothing will hurt more than the time I spent without you."

"Please. Don't say such things. It only makes it worse."

"Do you remember when you were three years old and you wanted to learn the Zaephyr Spell?"

"Three? No, I don't remember."

"Your father and I joked you would rule the world one day, for all your confidence. You insisted you were grown up—you had taken to wearing my clothes—and as such, deserved a grown-up spell to enchant."

"Sounds disastrous."

"On the contrary. Many joys can be lost in too much caution."

A wash of regret swallowed Milla. That was her father; cautious, joyless.

"But we didn't know that then. We agonized for a full day. The things that could ensue if it went awry, but the thrill if it went well. There was no right choice—either might fail or succeed—which meant there was no wrong choice. So we did what any good parents would, we tossed a stone and let fate decide."

Milla smiled. "And I suppose it landed in my favor."

"You be the judge. You spoke the verse brilliantly, impressing us with your enunciation, and called forth the preliminary breeze in an instant. Your father lit like the summer sun over the desert."

"Uh huh, and what did I destroy?"

Jovia laughed. "Not too much. We knew the impending bluster could get away from you, so we held the lesson in the forest. Once the breeze swelled into its full whirlwind, it twisted on direct route for our shack."

"Oh no."

"Oh yes. Your father never ran so swiftly. And you, you roared with laughter as he was plucked up once, perhaps twice by the cyclone, on his scramble for home. He halted the spell, of course, but he wasn't as spry as the days of his youth and, suffice to say, the damage to the shack took nine short moons to repair."

"I toppled our home?"

"It was worth the labor to see the delight on his face when you performed that spell, and the delight on your face when he raced the storm."

"And on yours. You see it as clearly now as the day it happened."

"I do. I see every second of your life as vividly today as yesterday and the day before. So while my heart broke anew every morning I woke in exile, I also had the indescribable happiness that I was able to secure your safety. Can you imagine the comfort that would bring any mother? I know not one who would pass up that offer."

Milla's face burned with the rise of tears. "And now I must choose between your life and the rest of the worlds."

"As before, as so often, there's no right or wrong choice, Milla, only a choice. But know this: I don't fear death." She took Milla's hands and squeezed them to her heart. "And you must believe me, no matter the outcome, no matter the path you take, I'll always love you. You cannot fail me. Do you understand? I will always love you."

The tears spilled over and stung the gash in Milla's lip. "She's diabolical. She put me here for this very reason. To play on my emotions." Jovia wrapped her arms around Milla and Milla wept.

Zanub didn't leave his horse on the outskirts of Aelderoy Forest this time, for the first time; he rode all the way to Queldar's hovel and would've entered on horseback if Queldar hadn't rushed out and barricaded his approach with a netting of lianas. His horse bucked, breaking the vines, but Zanub dismounted anyway and shoved the old warlock into the leafy walls of his hovel. "The queen has Milla."

Queldar swatted the air between them as if Zanub could be fended off like a gnat.

Aloysius swooped down and said, "Behave yourselves. We are allies."

Zanub snatched the bird and threw it hard enough to hit the thatched overhang before its wings took effect.

"Aloysius!" Queldar reached for his friend, but Zanub yanked the old man by the collar of his cloak.

"Clean your ears, warlock."

"I heard you, Zanub." Queldar entered his hovel and Zanub followed. "Your temper does no one any good."

"Your magic does no one any good."

"Hurling insults is not a solution."

"You're the sorcerer, yet you have no spells to protect your own blood. You're nothing but a coward and a weakling."

Queldar shot his arm out and Zanub flew into the wall, then fell to the floor beside the cot.

"Mind your tongue, soldier, or I'll mind it for you. I've given my soul to protect my blood. The queen is no fool. I must be clever."

"Far from your specialty," Zanub said as he picked himself up and checked his armor for dents. The puerile crow snickered, making him think there was damage somewhere, but he couldn't find it. "The queen has your *Quodex*. She has your soul. Is there anything of you she does not possess?"

"His might," Aloysius said.

"Anything of value?"

Aloysius hovered before Zanub's face. "You walk a thin line with your loyalties."

"Control your pet, warlock."

"Pet? *Pet?*" The bird squawked irately, feathers rising on the scruff of its neck.

"Ignore him, Aloysius." Queldar scooped the bird from midair, tucking it under his arm, then turned to Zanub. "Where's the earther?"

"Perhaps in a bucket for 'monger feedings."

"He was captured?"

"I hardly think he could evade the queen if Milla couldn't."

Queldar ran to a wall of shrub, the bird forgotten—dropped to the ground like dinner fare—as he dove inside. Zanub grabbed his feet before he could escape, but the old warlock returned with his Crystal Beholder. Jagged, murky, inelegant, the rock was nothing like the queen's.

Queldar wiped it down with his sleeve and his aura was sucked out of his physical being and into the rock. Zanub sighed. *Sorcerers and their crystals*. But the faint image that arose on that ragged stone quashed his repugnance. It was the earther.

Queldar's aura shot back inside his scrawny frame, knocking him into a somersault, but he jumped to his feet with excitement. "Luck has been bestowed upon us." He wiped his crystal rock for a clearer view before the images faded.

"I saw," said Zanub. "He's alive. So what?"

"Look closer. He has a map. *The* map."

"Your reason for joy escapes me, Queldar."

"Welcome to my world," Aloysius said.

"This map charts every Shift across Asper. They were part of our studies until the divide when all maps were destroyed by order of the Omniscient. But now, now there's someone who holds this most valuable map, a map surely stolen from Mother Nature herself."

"And you wish to return it. How grand," Aloysius said.

"Oh, Aloysius. Do you not know me at all?" Queldar turned to Zanub. "I can barter this priceless map for the freedom of Jovia and Milla."

"Is it wise to give evil a map of every Shift in Asper?" the bird asked.

Queldar kicked the dirt. "Can we solve one issue at a time?"

"Where does he go with this map?" Zanub asked.

"The Marman Sea. If the forest chatter is to be believed, dragons reside beneath the reef. I suspect the earther searches for the *Book of Knowing*."

Zanub's stomach rose to this throat. He steadied himself. "He has the courage you lack, Queldar."

"You as well," Queldar said.

"A quarrel between lovers?" the captain said from behind Zanub, giving him a fright. The arrogant leader was standing next to his steed by the entrance, twirling his sword. How long had he been there?

"Captain," Zanub said.

"Second." The captain strolled in, eyeshield raised, and surveyed Queldar's habitat. The books, potions, knives. The Crystal Beholder. Zanub darted his eyes to the stone. The images were gone.

"Beholding?" the captain said.

"What's your business here?" Queldar asked. "I'm tired of soldiers barging in. If the queen requests my presence, I shall go. Otherwise, both of you, leave my home at once."

The captain ran his sword gently up and down Zanub's armor. "Perhaps you'd like to tell me what *your* business is here, Zanub."

"He came to find the boy for Lucrecia," Queldar said. "For assurance."

At least the warlock was fast at lies.

The captain swung his sword over to Queldar's chin, teasing the loose skin but not drawing blood. "Unless you wish to rid the burden of your enormous head upon your neck, stop blathering and tell me what you beheld."

"You need only ask, Captain. The earther is after the *Book of Knowing*."

The captain laughed. "A futile journey."

"Not for him. He knows where to find it."

"How?"

"Seems Mother Nature has taken a liking to him."

The captain withdrew his sword, his brow pressed tighter than his armor. "Where is it?"

"The Marman Sea. Beneath the coral reef."

"If you lie, warlock, I'll remove your tongue with my bare hands."

"May the Omniscient strike me dead," Queldar said with inviting arms.

The captain glanced to Zanub as he mounted his horse. "Take this information to Majestic Ruler and tell her I'll return with the *Book* before the Unification." He kicked his horse into a gallop, destroying half the foliage around Queldar's habitat as he rode off.

Queldar smiled. "Problem solved." Aloysius alit on his head and the warlock shoved him off, his glory stolen. "Must you do that?"

"Are you mad?" Zanub said. "Why did you tell him where to find it?"

"Because that self-important fool will be killed. No one can retrieve the *Book*."

"Then what of the earther?"

"Small price to pay, is it not?"

"You truly did sell your soul to the queen."

"I don't pull the strings, soldier. That earther took it upon himself to seek the *Book*. Now you're to tell nothing of this to Lucrecia. Understood?"

Zanub about-faced and hurried out.

CHAPTER NINETEEN

FLANKED BY THE TWO SOLDIERS who had escorted her, Milla stood in the doorway of Lucrecia's chamber. Nothing had changed. Even her precious brush with the exquisite crystal handle lay atop the satin pillow, as if the witch planned to pick up where they had left off. Lucrecia was looking out the window, her back to the door, prominently displaying her three moons. An obvious power play. Milla had the urge to shove her out, but she'd only fly back in.

Lucrecia shifted, her three moons swaying, and turned toward Milla. Her face lit with genuine sentiment. "Milla. Come in, my child."

Milla entered and the door closed behind her—a subtle flick of Lucrecia's finger.

"Give me back my *Quodex*."

Lucrecia smiled as if no time had passed and Milla was merely testing her boundaries, ever the rebellious daughter. "We've much to discuss before you make demands." Lucrecia's gown, knitted of soft metal, chimed delicately in song—a lullaby she used to sing—as she approached. She stroked Milla's hair. "Sit with me. Let us reminisce."

Milla pushed her hand away. "I'm not the youngster you abducted, Lucrecia."

"There was a time you called me Mother."

"I know better now, I've grown."

"You have. You've traveled portals and added a lesson or two."

"Yes."

"Don't sound defiant about it, Milla. Was I not the one who fought with you to study? I had your best interests."

"You ruined my life. I lost my childhood. I was so broken, my father had to bury my memories so I could go on."

Lucrecia shook her head. "Your father buried your desire to return and be heir to the throne."

"Liar! You couldn't possibly know his intentions."

"Do you not recall the day you left? You cried and pleaded to stay."

"Because you brainwashed me."

"I loved you."

Milla slapped her fast and hard, catching her off guard and giving her no time to deflect. Inferno charged in a fiery blaze, its blistering heat popping, but Lucrecia halted her pet before the flames swept over Milla.

"Don't you dare hide behind love in the name of your cruelty," Milla said.

Lucrecia touched the handprint on her pallid face, openly heartbroken. "You doubt my love?"

"You killed my father."

"My orders were to spare you both, forever." Her eyes flooded with tears. "I failed you. Worse, in a way I cannot make right. I'd give my life to bring his back if it would mend your heart."

"You're demented. You act like you're not holding me hostage right now. Like you're not using my own mother to manipulate me."

"I'm your mother."

"You're not my mother!"

Tears fell over Lucrecia's lashes. She conjured a sword from the crystal brush and held it out for Milla, hilt first. "Pierce my heart for it would pain me less than your words."

"Gladly." She snatched it, thrusting the tip of the blade against Lucrecia's chest without hesitation, but no farther. Blasted, of all the times for cowardice to strike. She could solve everything if she just plunged it through.

"You do still care for me," Lucrecia said after Milla stood immobile for too long.

Milla dropped the sword and it reverted back to the brush, the crystal shattering as it hit the floor.

Lucrecia lifted Milla's chin. "My sweet, is it not obvious we're mother and daughter?" She summoned the mirror over. "Look at your face. Your skin, your cheeks, your hair."

Milla shut her eyes.

"Closing your eyes doesn't make it untrue."

"I know we're of the same blood."

Lucrecia shot the mirror back to the wall. "So I didn't carry you in my belly, I hadn't the fortune of bringing you into this world, but I gave my fate unto Jovia. *My* fate."

"What gives you the right to take it back?"

"It was the only way to have you in my life. I favored her, trusting we would raise you together, but she denied me fair time. She insisted you live in that shack and be raised like a commoner. She was jealous of my power. Afraid you would love me more, that I could offer you more. After unbearable torture watching my baby grow with another family, unable to hold you, kiss you, share bedtime stories with you, I had to do something. I was desperate, Milla. Only a mother can know such desperation. I told the army where you were, knowing Jovia would leave you with your father; he was the most practiced, after all. I found her and tried to reason with her—we were so close once, we shared everything—but she would have none of it when it came to you. Alas, I made her choice simple. You must believe me, my intent was to visit at will, that's all. I would've freed her once you and I bonded. I thought your father would welcome my involvement if he didn't have her to help raise you, but he refused me any visitation. And he was more clever than I knew. I lost track of you for years, but then my efforts paid off. I found you that day at Lost Creek."

Milla panted, pained. "You tell the truth by omission. Isn't that lying?"

"I told you what was important."

"*Important?* You thought it unimportant that my mother was alive?"

"*I* am your mother!" she screamed, jolting Milla stiff. "And lest you forget, I raised you longer than she."

"Because you exiled her."

"I had to."

"You didn't have to keep her there, keep her from her beloved. You could've released her from the pact once I was at the castle. Surely, the years we spent together were enough."

"The curse of motherhood, Milla. It's never enough time. I had planned to release her, my oath, when you returned of your own volition. But you never did."

"I'm here now."

"Against your will."

"It doesn't have to be that way. Release her. Let the Rising lapse and I'll remain at the castle. That's what you want, isn't it?"

"I want us to rule the worlds together."

"I can't let the Unification take place."

"I cannot allow you to prevent it."

"You have no choice, Lucrecia. Even with your power, what happens next is up to me."

A flash of ugliness—veins pulsating beneath paper-thin skin stretched over her skeletal face—turned lovely, she stroked Milla's cheek. "Still obdurate."

"Until the day I die."

"Don't tempt me."

"You don't scare me anymore, Lucrecia."

"Anymore? If you were ever frightened of me, child, that dissipated day one. I hope all your memories surface one day so you can abandon your righteous indignation. But you're correct about one thing. I don't have the power to rip the spell you inherited from the *Book*; however, I have the collateral to break your will. Recant the hex on the scroll, or Jovia will not see the sun rise."

"Are you so wretched you would rid the universe of your only family? Is it not sad and lonely?"

"It's quite sad and lonely, Milla. Quite."

Lucrecia called for her soldiers and the two metaled brutes raced in. "My daughter is to be confined to the prison unless she chooses to take her rightful place by my side."

"No. *Please*. Lucrecia, *please!*" Milla screamed for mercy as the soldiers carted her off, but Lucrecia never came to her aide.

Zanub rode halfway to the Marman Sea, juggling schemes in his head—ambush the captain before he reaches the reef; lie in wait and ambush him afterwards, stealing the *Book*; beat him to the reef and partner with the earther—before his senses kicked in. None of them were equipped to slay a dragon; the *Book* was safe.

He pulled the reins, rearing his horse into a U-turn, heading back toward the castle in full gallop. Leaned forward in a jumping position, he crested shrubs and brooks, bogs and bubbling fissures. He broke out of Ravaenwood Forest, his horse snorting with exertion, and he let the animal slow to a walk over to the hold. Eyeshield raised and forgotten until the sentry told him to lower it, he cursed the warlock; the captain; the Omniscient. He closed his eyeshield and did a mental check to make sure all seams were sealed. His thoughts had been everywhere but on his armor. Satisfied, he motioned to the sentry, who opened the interior gate leading into Castle Hill, and Zanub kicked his tired steed into a gallop up the mountainside. He crossed the drawbridge, scraping under the rising gate, and continued up the stairwell to the chamber where Jovia and Milla were being held. He left his horse with the guards standing watch and entered the room. Jovia looked up, the hope on her face stolen by his presence.

"Where's Milla?" he asked.

"They took her."

Zanub closed the door and approached her. "Has she her *Quodex*?"

"Lucrecia has it."

Zanub punched the air and growled from his throat in an attempt to stay quiet. "I should let her suffer the consequences for being pigheaded."

"You were close when she lived here. You saw their bond. Will Lucrecia harm her?"

"The queen is mad with love for Milla. But she has already lost her, has she not? She may take solace in ruling the worlds."

Zanub left, closing the door on her sobs. He returned his horse to the stables and took the stairs on foot. He wasn't seen until he entered the atrium where two soldiers descended a parallel staircase in the opposite direction. They exchanged passing nods, and once in the clear, Zanub broke into a sprint and ducked into the next corridor. He hurried into the Grand Hall, tripping a step in surprise, to find the queen slumped on her throne, twirling Milla's brush reverently. She looked up wistfully.

Zanub sighed in spite of himself. *Here we go.*

"Am I so vile, Zanub, that my own flesh and blood cannot love me?"

"No, my queen." He continued toward her, hiding his frustration.

"You love me. Are you not grateful that I brought you into my castle? That I raised you to be a notable soldier? Where would you be without me? A lost boy in a jungle shack picking greens to survive."

"Yes, my queen."

"Then why? Why does she despise me so?"

"She lost her way. Now that she's in the castle, she'll remember the joy in time."

"I have no time."

Zanub shifted, fighting his own instinct, and blurted out, "Perhaps you have more than you know."

The queen perked up. "Another rumor, Zanub? You're quite the chatterer outside these walls."

He arrived at the foot of her throne and stood at attention. "The captain is en route to the *Book of Knowing*."

The queen sat fully erect, the vulnerability gone from her face and tone. "How does he know where to find it?"

"The warlock."

She smirked and, with her finger, summoned a book off one of the pedestals in the corner and over to Zanub, letting it float in front of him. Queldar's *Quodex*. The pages fanned furiously, giving glimpses of handwritten notes in the margins and next to the titles, most of them smudged and illegible, half of them crossed out or written over with new calculations and verses, until settling on a particularly unreadable scrawl.

"Is that the scribbling of an informed sorcerer?" she said. "I've yet to find anything of import."

"Useless indeed," Zanub said even though he couldn't read Old

Asperian. "But the warlock beheld the vision on his crystal. I was there, as was the captain. The earther, the one who was with Milla, is after the *Book*."

She snorted. "The earther? Good riddance. The night will devour him whole."

"But for the grace of Mother Nature."

Lucrecia's gown chimed with tension. "He's being aided by that crone?"

"Apparently, for he knows where the guardian resides. But what he doesn't know is that the captain is on his tail."

She reclined on her throne and Zanub continued, "With the *Book of Knowing*, you can have both the Unification and your daughter. You needn't force her to remove the hex. As before, she'll grow to love you."

"And you as well, Zanub? Do you still fancy your fabled future?"

"My loyalty is steadfast, my queen. I'm a soldier, first and foremost."

She stroked his chin affectionately. "You've always been my favorite. Not like the others born of the lineage. You earned your metal. Thank you, Zanub."

"My pleasu—"

She erupted in an ethereal mist before he finished. Zanub wiped his face of the clammy residue and sighed. *Drama queen.* She made herself increasingly difficult to revere. He sprinted to the pedestal across the room and grabbed Milla's *Quodex*. The book tensed in his grip.

"Not a word," Zanub whispered. "Or we'll both see the incinerator." He tucked the *Quodex* inside his metal.

Milla picked at her jeans, which were now as tattered as her old burlap pants. Rats gnawed on fleshy scraps that had splattered across the floor, some alongside her feet, but she kept her eyes on Braulgar. That sadistic swine worked the prison more often than any other sentry. She wanted to hex him to the nether-realm, but the prison was cloaked, preventing her from using magic. If he came close, though, she'd gouge his eyes out with her fingers. Unable to stomach his smirk anymore, she turned away and spotted Tobly in the corner of a cage two cells down, across from her. She fell back against the bars and covered her mouth to stop the sickness from rising.

Like the rest of his clan, he was as gray as the surrounding stones but not entirely camouflaged. Why hadn't he said something? How long had he been here? She called to him telepathically, but he didn't respond. She'd never seen him despondent, never. He was spirited and tenacious and downright arrogant. He was invincible. She reached out again and, in a sudden rush, the Squeeds scuttled to the rear of their cells, including Tobly. Vicious barks rang from the stairwell and two mounted soldiers entered with a caged scentmonger.

Braulgar retrieved the key from his sheath and palmed it, his armored glove melding seamlessly around it. It was a woven piece of bronze that looked like the bow of an ancient skeleton key. In here, it was the key to life and death.

"Who shall be the feast?" Braulgar strolled past cages, holding up his palm threateningly as he sized up one Squeed after another. "No volunteers?"

He stopped before Milla. "One day my patience will be rewarded and you'll be fed to the 'monger." She stared him down, eliciting a snarl from him. "Such bravery you have knowing your fate is out of my hands." He motioned to Tobly. "You'll do."

Milla gasped and Braulgar swung his eyes to her, lips curved in a grin. "Excellent choice, I agree." He nodded to the soldiers and they dropped the caged beast before Tobly.

"No, please," Milla said.

"No, please," Braulgar mocked, and the soldiers laughed.

"Please! I'll be indebted to you. Anything."

Braulgar made a show of slamming his keyed glove onto the scentmonger's cage, which was now butted up against Tobly's, and a row of bars evaporated, leaving a single set of bars between them.

Tobly finally looked over to Milla. *Turn away.*

Milla shook her cell. "No, Braulgar. Stop, stop! I beg you!"

"Ah, there she is. The whiny princess." Braulgar reached for Tobly's cell and Milla felt faint, nauseated. Her hands slid down the bars as she folded to her knees, unable to breathe when, from out of nowhere, Zanub grabbed Braulgar's arm, stopping him. A bolt to her heart, reviving her. Braulgar spun and Zanub released his grip to show no confrontation.

"Start at the rear," Zanub said.

"Are you now captain of the army?"

"I bring orders from Majestic Ruler. Shall I tell her you refuse?"

Braulgar glared at Milla as she pulled herself to her feet, still trembling. He slammed his palmed key onto the scentmonger's cage and the bars shot up securely in place. "We'll get to all of them sooner or later."

He motioned to the soldiers and they lugged the cell to the end of the long chamber where Braulgar released the barriers on both pens and the animal pounced on the Squeed, puncturing his skull with its monstrous fangs. The crunch of bone, the pop of flesh, sickening. Milla turned away as Braulgar sealed the bars, leaving the 'monger to devour the lifeless body.

Braulgar salivated. "Does it not make you hungry to see an animal enjoy his food?"

"Perhaps when you're the meal," Milla said.

Braulgar growled.

"I'm to continue the watch," Zanub said quickly, to intervene.

The sentry gave him a surly glare, removed the key from his gloved hand, and flung it recklessly, but Zanub snatched it midair. The soldiers hauled away the cell that now housed the 'monger and not a fleck of the Squeed. When everyone departed, Zanub rushed to Milla's cell, a broad smile crossing his face.

"There were no such orders from the queen."

"You expect my gratitude?"

"I saved your friend."

"And killed another."

"The 'mongers need to be fed, Milla. That I couldn't change."

"Congratulations, Zanub. You've grown into a mindless minion. You should be proud."

"And you've not grown at all."

Milla lunged for him, reaching through the bars, but he stepped back. "I hate you."

"And I still love you. Perhaps that's your failing. You don't recognize the love of others. I've cherished our friendship. I've done my best to bring you happiness. Lived my life watching over your shoulder to be certain the captain didn't secretly seek you out. But I can only do so much. Please cooperate with the queen. Not only will she spare you, she'll spare Jovia. You can stay in the castle and we can spend time together. The queen won't live forever, Milla, and we can rule with a kinder heart. Save yourself and Jovia now, and protect the worlds in time."

"Oh, don't confuse me, Zanub. I can't let her unite the worlds. No one will win if she succeeds. We'll all perish."

"Milla—"

"Please," she said before he could continue. "Unlock my cell and fight with me not against me."

"I've never been against you."

"If you're loyal to Lucrecia, you're against me, Zanub. It's fact. She seeks power at the expense of everyone else, even her own flesh and blood. How can you dedicate your life to one as wicked as that?"

"I'm nothing without my metal, Milla."

"You're everything without it. It's your metal that ruins you."

"I fought to be a soldier for you, lest you forgot."

"We were children. We didn't know better."

"Don't dismiss my love as youthful ignorance, Milla. It's undeserving." He turned from her, his shoulders uncharacteristically slumped. "Will we never be king and queen?"

"Zanub." Milla quelled her tears. "There was a time I truly wanted it. Truly. You saved me when I wanted to die. You made me live, and laugh. I loved you. I do love you. But we'll never be king and queen. Not in this world, not in this life."

He nodded, closing his eyeshield to hide his emotion, but she could hear his pain. After he composed himself, he turned back to her. "I have your *Quodex*." He removed the book from his armor and slipped it through the bars.

"Beast." Milla hugged her book and it rippled affectionately.

Zanub raised his eyeshield and stared into her eyes with a depth that scared her. "I cannot go with you, Milla. But I'll free you. From this prison and from my heart."

"Don't say that."

"I must. How can I go on dreaming of a life that will never be?" He retrieved the key when a sharp, gleaming talon pierced through his chest, speared from behind. "Milla…"

Lucrecia reverted from a rat to her anthropomorphic form, her nail still impaling Zanub, before Milla grasped what had happened. Her *Quodex* slipped from her hands, bouncing off the cell, as she went into shock, unable to scream. *No, no, no!* Her blood ran cold, so cold, it burned. Paralyzed, she watched helpless as Lucrecia sucked the *Quodex* from the cell and shot it out of the prison while it screeched in futile protest. But when Zanub's armor dimmed to an ashy gray, almost dull silver, Milla snapped back to life. Shaking, reaching, unable to touch him, she pleaded desperately, "Don't die, Zanub, don't die, don't die. Promise me."

He kept a weak gaze on her, lids struggling to stay open, but he didn't promise. He didn't promise!

"Poor Zanub." Lucrecia snaked around to face him. "I rather thought of you as a son."

"Lucrecia, please," Milla said in a hoarse whisper. "Please. Don't do this. I beg you. Help him. Save him."

Lucrecia stroked his metal cheek. "Another child breaking my heart."

"Lucrecia, I'm begging, don't punish him for my deeds. I'm to blame, not him. *Please.*"

Lucrecia smiled softly at Milla. "I'm encouraged you understand this is your doing, Milla." She slit him in two with her wicked claw, up then down, and Zanub's body fanned open, collapsing in a puddle of blood.

Milla screamed and screamed and screamed with all her might, every ounce of angst and rage and heartbreak pouring out of her as she fell to her knees, reaching for her friend. Her king.

Lucrecia clutched her throat, gagging her screams. "Perhaps you remember now, infantile witch, I'm not to be trifled with." Lucrecia released her grip, collected the key, and slithered off.

Milla coughed for breath and sank facedown on the cold, sticky floor of her cell, taking Zanub's lifeless hand in hers. Yes, she resigned along with the Squeeds, fortitude would be wasted here.

CHAPTER TWENTY

THE EXPANSIVE, LUMINOUS REEF jutted jaggedly above the water, not far beyond the inlet. Plum-colored waves swelled as high as skyscrapers, shadowing the reef's incandescence and dulling the cove before crashing down and dissipating in a foamy bath, allowing the brightness to glow again.

Parker estimated a ten-minute swim would get him there, provided he didn't get caught in the undertow of a wave and thrown out to sea. He lowered his eyeshield and scanned the area, hoping some X-ray vision-type magic might uncover a hidden boat or scuba gear, but the beach only offered the beauty of its rich green sands and iridescent boulders. Not even driftwood.

He peeled off his armor and gave himself a moment to acclimate to the freedom, then tucked the metal behind a cluster of crystalline rocks. It shifted and molded into a tidy mound. Fingers crossed it didn't scamper off while he was gone. He tested the water with his hand—warm and thick, like gelatin before it set. Or snot.

Not about to leave the map behind, especially with his rascally metal, he dipped a corner into the gummy brine to see if it would hold up. It did more than hold up, it parted the water, just enough to keep it dry. Astounded, but no time to dwell, Parker pocketed the parchment and entered the purple lagoon. The pebbly bottom disappeared two steps in, as did the warmth, and Parker treaded in frigid jelly. Apparently, water was thicker than blood in Asper.

He dove under, finding the syrupy sea translucent, illuminated by the effervescence of the reef. As he swam, he wondered if the spiked fish twice his size followed him for a reason or if the see-through globules were poisonous or if sharks really were friendly like Milla said. But the fauna kept a respectable distance and that was good enough for him. What he had thought would take ten minutes, took more like two, and he waited for the wave to break overhead, bobbing up and down with the swell, before he rose for one last breath.

Parker descended toward the ocean floor, humbled by the enormity of the glimmering reef. He spotted a sizeable fissure and swam in, finding an underwater tunnel. The emanating glow from the exterior faded the farther he went. With no end in sight, he contemplated backtracking but wrestled with indecision until it was moot. His lungs spasmed and he fought the urge to inhale. Pushing on, he came across a light reflecting from above—an opening—and kicked his feet in a race to the top, gasping as he surfaced.

He was in a pool inside a humid cavern cocooned by the reef. Its radiant exterior didn't provide much light, but sunshine poked through erosions here and there, delivering pockets of illumination. The cavern would be pitch black once the sun set, but Parker hoped to be back at the castle before then. Back with Milla.

He didn't see a *Book of Knowing*. Or a dragon. Or dragon. Or whatever the difference was. He pulled himself out of the pool and onto the mossy ground, thankful to be out of the goop. The cavern was warm and comforting, an obvious ploy to disarm intruders. Nice try. Guarded, he approached a wall with several passageways branching off in different directions. They loved their tunnels in Asper. The reef's interior wasn't charted on his coveted map, so he relied on his own ingenuity.

"My mother hit your mother in the nose," he said, pointing from one tunnel to the other. "What color was the blood? Magenta. M-A-G-E-N-T-A."

He entered the chosen tunnel.

The passageway was narrow and he kept a hand on each of the damp walls, but the farther he advanced, the farther apart the walls became, until eventually he couldn't reach them with his arms fully outstretched. "Yeah, that's not a red flag."

Unable to see well in the dimness, he kept his right hand on the wall to guide him. He lost track of time but traveled long enough for his palm to numb against the roughness, and when the monotony had him convinced he was walking in place, he was proven wrong; another tunnel branched off from the one he was in. He considered taking it for the change of scenery but stayed the course. He encountered another passageway. And another, and another. Unnerved, he backed away from the wall but never found the other side because he wasn't in a tunnel anymore. It was an immense chamber, a trap. M-A-G-E-N-T-A, G-R-E-E-N, B-L-U-E, all paths fed into this chamber.

The dim light vanished, like a snuffed candle, and Parker spun full circle, terrified the dragon had emerged, but there was no movement or sound, maybe just the faint memory of the sea if not the sea itself. Calmed by lasting stillness, he decided the clouds must've crossed the sun, and after everything he'd been through, a little darkness was the least of his worries. He forged on, and promptly tripped over something—a rock?—and fell into the rugged wall and down to the ground. Amused, he brushed himself off and got to his feet. *Thank you. I'll be here all week.*

Daylight sprinkled through the cracks and he saw what had tripped him. It was the *Book*. The *Book of Knowing*. Tossed aside, as if for the taking.

So he took it.

And braced himself. But no boulder barreled toward him, no spikes plunged from the ceiling, not even a fiery dragon snout charring him like a Fourth of July burger. He snickered, a kid with his hand in the cookie jar and no one to catch him.

He brushed the smooth hide of the cover and carefully opened it. Inside, the parchment pages were crisp and pristine. The archaic script looked handwritten by someone with flawless penmanship, and had as many symbols as letters. Parker couldn't decipher a word of it, but a smile plastered his face. He did it. He did what Lucrecia and her army of evils couldn't. He held in his hands the savior of Asper as well as his world. *Suck it, queen.*

A snort, muffled yet close by, snapped the neck of his celebration, and Parker fumbled the prize, catching it as it bounced off the ground. The chamber lit fleetingly from above. He looked up, way up, to the fiery nostrils that illuminated the room in spurts, and saw a dragon, his first, in plain view. The jagged wall he had fallen against was, in actuality, the dragon's massive thorny tail. The gargantuan creature swung its heavy head to survey the situation and Parker froze, *Book* held tightly to his chest. He was daunted and awed in equal parts. He didn't know what he thought a dragon would look like, but this wasn't it. The underside shimmered with a silvery velvetiness while its topside skin shone a brilliant emerald green. Its muscular body was long and lean and slimmed even more at the waist, like a greyhound, and the dragon's forelegs spanned into wings at the elbow, which were fully extended. It stood on its hind haunches, thirty feet tall, easy, and flaunted its tail—willowy and twice the length of its body—overhead. Amazing, except for the angry brow and bared fangs. Oh yes, and the flame-spitting snout.

The dragon settled its gaze on Parker, its opalescent pupils glistening like its belly, and Parker hoped it was blind. And deaf, since he was making wishes. The dragon stopped its fiery breaths and tucked its supple wings close to its side, relaxing into a seated position, and Parker's good luck was beginning to scare him.

He carefully lifted his foot to tiptoe away, thinking he had gone undetected, when the dragon lowered its humongous skull and sniffed, pulling him into the tornado of its robust inhalations. Parker thought he'd get sucked into the giant nostril, but the storm ceased and he hit the ground. Clueless. Did the dragon know he was here or not? He inched away and, in a burst of agitation, the dragon roared, its growl sending shockwaves through the air. Parker was swept in, tumbling and cartwheeling, until he rolled to a bumpy stop. Panting as quietly as he could, he didn't move, not even to assess the burning scrapes and cuts on his arms.

The dragon rested its head on the moss-grown surface next to Parker, the bristly whiskers on its jaws tickling him, and closed its eyes. First, second, and third eyelid, masking its mesmerizing pupils in descending stages. Its breath pounded even temperedly and its nose twitched. Then its back leg. Then its briery ear, as if shooing a fly. It was sleeping.

Not one to look a gift-dragon in the mouth, Parker silently scuttled back, but the dragon slid its giant head to follow, eyes still closed, and

Parker stopped. The dragon did, too, resting close to him. Parker tried again, and again the creature stayed with him the whole time. Baffled, Parker waited to see what its next move would be, and when it didn't budge, he couldn't resist; he stroked its scaly head. The scurfy-looking skin was soft and warm, cushioned, unlike its solid, roughened tail. The dragon sighed pleasurably and Parker spit out a burst of laugher.

"Oh my god, you're just a sweetie pie." With affectionate chuffs and grunts, the dragon rolled on its side for more and Parker was in love. "I might have to take you home."

A bellow—brain-splittingly loud—jolted him sober. The walls, ground, and ceiling shook, raining down sediment, but that was nothing compared to the tremors inside him, a conduit to the reverberations. Low, irate, on the attack, the roar danced around the cavern, impossible to identify where it was coming from. And then: the unmistakable *whoosh whoosh whoosh* of a behemoth in flight. A dragon, colossal, unreal except it was real, emerged from one of the tunnels and landed with distressing grace in the middle of the cave. Its gigantic form masked everything beyond it and its disposition wasn't nearly as sweetie pie as the dragon upon which Parker's trembling hand still rested. This one flicked bursts of blistering fire, strategically singeing him—forehead, cheek, eyelid—as it snorted and growled, its glossy ebony skin undulating with its hostile breaths. Its wings, triple the length of its muscular frame, flapped in warning. The distinction between dragon and Dragon crystal clear.

"You didn't say you were married, you flirt." The fickle dragon padded over to its mate, leaving Parker crouched, his hand hovering over nothing.

Parker took off like a sprinter at the starting line, *Book* forgotten until it flew off his lap. He skidded, turning back for it, and encountered a raging torrent of flames coming straight at him. Parker dove under the fiery limbs and rolled for the *Book*, snatching it up, but Dragon whipped its agile tail, batting him through the air with the barbed tip. The wall broke Parker's flight. Bloodied and speckled with gravel, he slid to the ground, but didn't let go of the *Book*. Dragon was upon him in a single wingflap and Parker steeled himself, but Dragon growled dry, no flames. He was toying with him. Why?

Parker rose slowly and Dragon snarled, low and constant, motivating him to stay put. It opened its mouth, tongue forked and lashing, but it didn't strike. Instead, it lunged, snapping its massive jaw down on Parker, and Parker shrieked, involuntarily, cringing his eyes shut. *Mauled to death by a mythical creature*, was his first thought. Or maybe they all came at once: *Will Milla ever know? Will she think I just abandoned her? What does it feel like to be eaten to death? Will it take more than one bite? I should've told her how I feel about her. I shouldn't have said I came here for an adventure!*

His neck crunched, his lungs compressed, airless, and he shot open his eyes, pain assuring him he was still alive. Dragon's lip, heavy, fleshy, weighed on top of his head, and its fang, which might as well have been a Mack truck, it was as big and reeked of road kill, pressed into him, unrelenting. Dragon was trying but couldn't devour him. The wall was in the way of its giant snout, thank God or the Omniscient or whoever ran this place.

Dragon stepped back and Parker sucked in shallow breaths, his ribs aching, maybe broken. The creature stooped into a predatory squat and lowered its head to size up its opponent face to face.

"I just need to borrow it," Parker said. "I'm not a bad guy. Honest."

Dragon cocked its head, a flicker of comprehension in its titanium eyes.

"You understand? Do you talk?"

The beast rammed him with its nose, corner spikes stabbing his abdomen, and Parker shot out bile as his ribs cracked, for sure this time. But he didn't drop the *Book*. Dragon screeched, brandishing its formidable tongue, and still, no fire from its nostrils. *Why?* Then Parker realized, the *Book*. Dragon had to protect it, and as long as he held onto it, he was safe.

He was right about the first part.

Dragon's talon plunged toward Parker's head. Parker caught on fast and ran even faster. That problem-solver was trying to puncture his skull while keeping the *Book* unscathed. Dragon shot out its dexterous wing to snag him, but Parker dove into a tight cranny between the wall and floor. Swiftly, effortlessly, Dragon swooped down, its head on the ground, sideways, staring at him with one eye. Parker's puny reflection in the dark pupil hid no secrets—his face was painted with terror—but at least nothing on that creature could fit into the cranny. Not its claw, tail, fangs, tongue, not even its bony wing digits.

Dragon dug like a rat terrier after its prey, fervid, possessed, shredding the rocky shelter and splattering silt into Parker's eyes, nose, and mouth, suffocating him. Taking advantage of its fixated burrowing, Parker rolled out of the dirt storm and fled into the nearest tunnel, *Book* in hand, Dragon unaware.

He ran faster than humanly possible and welcomed the closing walls as a sign he was headed in the right direction. He didn't want to jinx his fate, but he almost cried with relief. Then the sickening *whoosh whoosh whoosh* swelled behind him. Dragon had caught on. The current from its wings pushed down the tunnel after Parker, throwing him into a stumble. He caught himself and ran faster, as if that was possible. *Don't look back, don't look back.* He looked back. Dragon tucked its wings and rolled through the air like an eel in water to navigate the narrowing space.

Parker broke into the den by the sea, heading for the pool of water, when a violent jolt shook the entire cave and threw him off his feet. He landed on his coccyx, and a stabbing pain shot down his legs, immobilizing him. The hot breath of Dragon pressed down on him and he was as good as dead. His heart wept, not for himself, for Milla. Failing her tore at his guts, a beast clawing to get out, begging for another chance.

And the unimaginable came true. Somehow, Parker had picked the right tunnel because the opening was too small for Dragon's massive frame to fit through—that was the cause of the jolt—and only its glistening head stuck out, inches from him.

Gingerly, Parker struggled to stand, sciatic nerves searing. The magnificent creature writhed in its earthen confines, thrashing its tail inside the tunnel, trying to free itself. The wall rippled and bowed but didn't give, and Dragon caterwauled in suffering, a cry so mournful—the kind Parker's grandmother hid behind closed doors—that Parker's righteousness succumbed to doubt. Maybe the *Book* was meant to be guarded forever. Who was he to torment the life of a dragon, so pure and honorable? Who the hell was he to interfere with fate?

In an explosion of foam and waves and fury, Vylkrost sprung from the sea like a great white, tackling Parker in a fluid move. Parker let out a shocked groan on impact with him—even without his armor, the captain was solid like metal—and again when he hit the ground. He grappled and slipped on the muddied dirt until he kicked Vylkrost off and scrambled backward into the steam of Dragon's breath. *Book* in hand, he stood inert, caught between honor and evil, and wondered what that made him.

"The *Book of Knowing* belongs to this land," Vylkrost said, approaching.

"Maybe. But not to you."

Vylkrost slammed him up against the wall in wicked speed, propelling the *Book* from his grasp, and smashed his head into a rocky protrusion. Parker crumpled to his knees, then belly. Dazed, he labored to roll over when the contents of his pocket jammed into his thigh. *Ho-ly crap.* He had forgotten about them.

Vylkrost snatched up the Book and held it to his chest with a victorious growl, and Parker let him because he was busy trying to calm his fumbling hands to fill the syringe. As Vylkrost turned to leave, Parker pounced, jamming the needle into his exposed neck. Vylkrost screamed and spun, eyes burning with hate, but hit the ground hard. Parker grabbed the *Book of Knowing*, tucked it inside his shirt, and dove into the purple sea.

The water was heavier with a broken rib and Parker was nauseated and dizzy from the exertion of holding his breath. When he emerged out of the reef, he kicked to the surface, taking the bob of a swell as far as he could, and doggy-paddled the rest of the way, unable to extend his arms without stabbing his lungs. He pulled himself ashore and crawled to the rock where he had hidden his armor. Gone. Every single piece.

Okay, don't panic. He still had the map. He could go back to the Squeed hovel and sneak into the castle that way. He opened the indispensable parchment to locate the Shift, and the coordinates stretched and twisted surreally before him, and somehow, he ended up flat on his back. Maybe he'd rest a minute. He closed his eyes, fading into that semiconscious state, when the sand rippled around him and the black metal emerged from beneath, spreading over him like oil before he realized what was happening. He bolted upright, alarmed, and fully armored. He let it sink in.

His eyeshield was down, fogging his vision with its murky tint, so he raised it even though it occurred to him his armor might be sentient and trying to protect him. But there was nothing else around. Protocol, he supposed. He also supposed the captain's armor was under the sand somewhere and he jumped to his feet, a little spooked. Oddly, his lungs didn't hurt anymore, nor his side. He poked at his ribs, astounded. A byproduct of the metal? The magic? The world?

Desperate to see Milla, he flicked open the map and charted the fastest route back to the castle. Four planes later, Parker had the whole Shift-hopping thing mastered and deemed it more fun than getting abducted by aliens. He emerged in Aelderoy Forest in a full-on sprint—*thank you, junior varsity track*—and was struck by the flank of an armored horse galloping past, knocking him twenty feet in the air. He landed arched backward over a rigid branch as the horse and rider continued, none-the-wiser, before he fell to the ground, shocked silent. It was Lucrecia, heading straight for Queldar's habitat.

Parker stayed low and chased after, fighting through uncooperative foliage the closer he got. Vines circled his legs, pulling him down, but he yanked their roots out of the soil. Breathless, he ducked around back and peered through a gap in the grassy wall. The queen stayed atop her horse as the wizard visibly cowered.

"Why, you traitorous fool," she said, as if complimenting him. "You still have a trick or two up your cloak."

"Traitorous? No, Majestic Ruler."

Majestic Ruler?

She slithered down to him, like a snake, and put her nail under his chin. "I know about the earther."

Parker froze. Hopefully she meant in general.

"As you should," Queldar said. "I instructed Zanub to relay the message. I was merely waiting to see if the earther succeeded before I shared the news. He has the *Book*."

What? Why would he tell her?

"Where is he now?"

Queldar shrugged and shook his head, glancing directly at him through the hole in the wall, and Parker fell back. "I've no idea, my queen. He was aided by Mother Nature. Perhaps she cloaks him."

Lucrecia plucked Queldar up with her finger and dragged him out as she retreated through the forest.

"How does he bring such tribulation to his life?" Aloysius said, causing Parker to jump.

"What the hell? How long've you been here?"

"All my life."

"No. Not… never mind." Parker got to his feet.

"I suggest you bring that *Book* to Milla right away."

"Thanks. I was thinking of mailing it." He scanned the surroundings and turned to Aloysius. "It'd be faster if I had a horse."

"Do not look at me."

"Does your evil master have one?"

"He is neither evil nor my master."

"He conspired with the queen."

"He bought you time. Spend it how you see fit."

Damn know-it-all bird. Parker took off running.

CHAPTER TWENTY-ONE

CURLED INTO HERSELF, fighting the urge to vomit, Milla inhaled quick and shallow breaths. She hadn't heard from Tobly in hours, not since they put the cells in one area to expedite the maulings. The back of her head ached, like she was being bashed against stone, over and over, but it had nothing on her right temple. Throbbing in a way she never knew possible—survivable—it jarred her, rhythmically; ease, throb, ease, throb, but every throb shocked her immobile, breathless. Burning up, damp with sweat, she shivered, chilled. Her eye pulsated with her temple, each beat feeling like a metal spike ramming her eyeball, and she wanted to rip it out. It was of no use anyway; her vision narrowed to a pinhole as bright and blinding as the sun.

She kept her hands over her ears to muffle the yowling 'mongers pacing and ramming their confines. Braulgar had fallen asleep on the bench and the beasts wanted food or freedom. In the cell behind her was all that remained of Zanub—pieces of rigor mortised metal. The cold-blooded sentry had swept up his compatriot like trash and thrown him in with a 'monger. The boy who gave her a reason to smile when she had been brought to the castle; the boy who vowed eternal love; the boy who never thought of himself before her, who lived to make her life better, who never should've been in the castle to begin with—but for her. Gone.

She thought she couldn't possibly have more heartache inside after her father had been killed, but pain was endless. Like love. There was always room for more. She fell in and out of consciousness, her only refuge from the sorrow. The throb. When she awoke, dizzy and weak, she heard footsteps and peered up. Another soldier entered, walking past Braulgar with a nod that went unacknowledged, and approached. She couldn't bear more taunting and buried her head in her arms.

"Milla," he said quietly.

"Parker." She spun to him, overcome. His presence was like a dream. Like hope. Even cloaked in the ugly armor, his humanity emanated. "I thought..." She faltered, not wanting to cry.

"Apparently, I'm incredibly brave. Like a superhero."

She laughed and wiped tears that fell. "The metal has gone to your head."

His lips curved, contorting the helmet into a crooked smile that remained on one side. "Probably. But I'm pretty sure I broke my ribs and they're healed. Is that the armor?"

She nodded. "It's magicked with many forms of protection. Good scraps."

"I could get used to being invincible."

"Such thoughts will get you killed. Besides, the armor might become a detriment now. Lucrecia's sure to awaken every resource."

"Ah, that's okay, it's kinda suffocating. Like pleather. Don't ask." He glanced over at Braulgar, who snored openmouthed, then back to Milla. "So, brace yourself. I have the *Book of Knowing*."

She was stunned. Speechless. Did he say he had the *Book of Knowing*?

"Milla?"

A million scenarios ran past her, but they all came back to, "That's impossible. You must be mistaken."

He retrieved the *Book* from inside his armored chestplate and slid it through the bars, and she laughed. Nervous laughter. Happy laughter. She opened the cover and a rush of runes washed over her, trickling off like a summer shower and disappearing on the floor. "Did you see that?"

"See what?"

She shook her head, it wasn't important, and turned to the first page, allowing the runes to dance off her at will.

Parker tugged on the bars of her cell. "How do you open this thing?"

"The easiest way is a sword through the sentry's eyeshield."

"Really? That's the easiest way?"

"He has a key, if you prefer."

"Yeah, let's try that first."

"If he awakens, trust me, through the eyeshield."

Parker nodded. "Where's the key?"

"It's embedded in his glove."

"Embedded, as in, I have to dig it out?"

"Or go for the eye."

"You're keen on that eye thing, aren't you?"

"He's a monster. He'll lop your head off for the joy of it."

"Good motivator. Anything else?"

"Don't touch a 'monger cage once you get the key."

Parker made his way over to Braulgar who, snoring and wheezing, gripped the handle of his sheathed blade with one hand while the other, the one with the key, rested on his thigh. He reached for the armored glove and stopped short. Milla motioned for him to hurry, but he didn't glance her way. He was occupied taking Braulgar's head and tilting it back, trying to lodge it between two of the modular cells, but the gap wasn't big enough. He laid Braulgar's head against the bars and went around to the side of the cell and pulled. The screech of metal on the stone floor sent chills up Milla's spine, and got the attention of the 'mongers but not Braulgar, who still snored. When the cages parted sufficiently, the sentry's head fell into the gap with a bounce. Milla cringed, but Braulgar didn't awaken. Parker pushed the cell, wedging the helmeted head in place, and flashed a smile.

Maybe he *was* a superhero.

He pried the woven piece of bronze free, palmed it, and sprinted back to her, holding up his hand. "Taking candy." He pinched his brow. "Wait. There's no lock."

"The key works with your thoughts, like the armor. Put it anywhere on the cell."

He did, on the top bar, and the row of bars beneath it evaporated. Milla dove into his arms, metal skin be damned, and he held her tightly, pulling her closer as if she could melt into the armor with him. If only she could.

Get a room!

She leaped back, trembling with relief, and scanned the prison. "Tobly."

Derg.

"Where are you?"

Fourteen rows deep, on the north side.

Milla raced through the maze of cells, skirting the acidic spit of caged 'mongers lunging for her, and found a section of Squeeds, alive. Parker released their cells and they scattered into crevices, except Tobly who dashed over and hugged her.

"Tobly, I've no words to express how glad I am to see you."

Me too.

"No comment," Parker said with a shrug, and Tobly kicked him in the shin. Parker grimaced.

"Already? We just reunited," Milla said, and finished silently to Tobly. *You know that was a tease.*

Yes, but how many opportunities will I get to kick him?

Braulgar grunted and Milla flung Tobly behind her to hide him. He pulled free and she held her finger to her lips to quiet him, but he rolled his eyes.

You think I'm the problem here? He tilted his head to Parker.

Honestly, she communicated telepathically.

Braulgar shifted and realized his head was stuck. He jumped to his feet, releasing himself from his helmet as if emerging from water, effortlessly, sword drawn. He scanned the prison—his face marred with bumps and dents and matted hair—and zeroed in on Parker.

"Traitor!" He leaped over cages in his charge.

"Back inside," Parker said, motioning to an opened cell. Milla and Tobly scrambled in and Parker shot the bars up from the bottom.

Braulgar was on him, sword overhead, but Parker dove behind an empty cell and the blade scraped the back of his armor. Parker stumbled down the aisle and bolted into another, landing himself in a dead end. Braulgar put on a show of swordsmanship, slicing the air expertly as he approached.

Parker smiled. "Nice face." He slammed his keyed palm on the cage next to him, releasing a crazed scentmonger. Braulgar spun in a sprint for his helmet, but the beast pounced, crunching his unsightly head. Milla held her stomach, but Tobly applauded.

"Parker," she called out. "You can't let a 'monger loose; it can't be killed, not even by Lucrecia. You need to cage it."

"That would've been good to know ahead of time."

The beast clawed into the armored shell, which succumbed like fruit rind without Braulgar's will.

Parker grabbed the boot, dragging the suit toward a cage, and Milla yelled, "No!"

The scentmonger whipped its bloody snout into Parker's armored face, snarling. No one moved until, after several surly chuffs, the beast turned back to the gore-lined shell of the sentry.

"You can't take its food. It'll attack any threat, scented or not," Milla said.

"Yep. Got that." Parker slowly unpeeled his fingers from the boot and inched away. "How about magically lifting a cage over it?"

"If I could use my magic in here, I would've escaped."

"Derg," Parker said.

Tobly threw his hands up. *Oh, great. Now the earther is stealing my word.*

"I got it." Parker pointed to the stack of cells against the wall. "I'll lure it in." He bolted to the first cell in the bottom row and pressed his palm on it, dropping the bars. He ran inside and made his way through the entire bottom row of at least twenty cages, leaving them open behind him to create a lengthy passageway.

When he reached the end of the row, he released the bars overhead and hoisted himself into the cell above. He counterpoised and opened the one above that, and the next, until he reached the top row, ten levels up. Leaving each one opened behind him, he made his way to the front, completing a U-shaped channel.

He's clever, Milla said to Tobly.

Meh.

The scentmonger pounced on their cell, startling them, but unable to reach inside, it leaped off and loped toward the exit.

"Parker, hurry."

Parker sprinted back along the top row and jumped to the bottom, ripping off his helmet. The 'monger whirled and leaped into the metal channel in a single bound. Milla shrieked, stumbling back. Parker dropped his helmet and heaved himself up. He was only four cells high by the time the 'monger clambered below him, clawing, trying to climb up. But it couldn't. Parker pulled himself onto the top row and ran, and the 'monger stopped trying to climb and ran in pace with him, but on the bottom.

"*Really?*" Parker about-faced and ran back. The beast followed from below, but it couldn't scale the cages and jumped and swiped the air, trying to snag him.

"Show it how to balance the way you did," Milla said. "But be careful. They learn fast. Very fast."

Parker stretched his legs against the bars opposite him and, counterpoised, slid midway down the next cell. Beads of sweat dropped onto the 'monger's snout and it lapped them up, licking the air for more.

Anyone else hungry? Tobly said, and Milla pushed him without as much as a glance.

The scentmonger mimicked Parker, counterbalancing its massive frame, and clambered up in near wizard speed.

"Run!" Milla yelled, but Parker beat her to it, already on the move.

The 'monger pulled itself onto the top row and galloped after. Parker dove into the last cell as the 'monger lunged for his leg. Milla shrieked. Parker slammed his palm against the open cell and the bars shot up between him and the beast.

Ha! Tobly punched his fist victoriously. *Not for the earther. For the beast being trapped.*

But the scentmonger about-faced, returning back through the maze.

Never mind.

Parker released the bars behind him and dropped to the prison floor, hitting with a sharp moan, as the scentmonger, already on the bottom row, raced toward him. He slammed his key on the cell, but the 'monger sprung the distance of three, shoving its snout out before the bars closed fully. Milla screamed. Parker punched down on its nose and the beast lurched back, startled. The bars shut completely and Parker fell back, scentmonger ensnared.

Milla erupted in a cry of relief and shoved Tobly again, this time in excitement.

Parker turned to her, smiling. "Superhero, right?"

"Indeed."

He got to his feet, removing pieces of armor. "Fun while it lasted, but it's kinda ripe in here, if you know what I mean."

She did and she didn't care. Her heart pounded as the metal dropped off him, the removal of each piece a gift. Shoulders, broad but not boastfully so, and tawny muscular arms, followed by the perfect taper of his torso to a slender V. Strong and beautiful, he emerged fully, his armor dissolving from his hips and legs, pooling on the floor around him. She ached, now more than ever, to feel his embrace. His skin against hers. His lips on her mouth.

Revolting.

She covered her red face, having completely forgotten Tobly existed, let alone stood beside her. *Tobly, no eavesdropping.*

Then think quieter. Please.

Parker winced his way over with the keyed glove, dissolving the bars, and she couldn't wait to leap into his arms, in spite of Tobly's disapproving eyes, but the clamor of soldiers ruined everything. Tobly yanked her with him, and she pulled Parker with her.

CHAPTER TWENTY-TWO

TOBLY BOUNDED UP THE STAIRS, taking two and three at a time, and Milla stayed on his heels for eighteen or nineteen flights—she lost count—but tempered her competitiveness for the sake of Parker. He lagged. Perhaps she shouldn't have made him shed the armor so soon; clearly, he had hurt himself jumping from the top cell in the prison.

Or maybe he's just an earther, Tobly interjected. *And not the super hero he fancies himself.*

Superhero, Milla corrected. *You couldn't possibly understand unless you read their books.*

Snob.

Takes one to know one.

Come up with your own insults for once.

The nerve.

Tobly darted onto the next landing, never slowing, and disappeared around the bend of the narrow corridor. Parker stumbled onto the floor, collapsing to his knees, and Milla turned back. He waved her on, but she hurried to his side and Tobly emerged from around the bend, glaring at them.

"Sorry," Parker said, gasping for breath. "I'm usually awesome at this sort of thing. Ask any dragon."

"No apologies," Milla said. "We'll rest until you regain your strength."

Parker nodded and sat against the wall, but the Squeed threw her a miffed glance. She threw one right back and more. He spun away, arms folded.

"Stop pouting, Tobly. I need time to study anyway. Apparently, I have to learn the history before I can use any spell in this book."

The Squeed threw his hands up. *We're doomed.*

She sat next to Parker, and asked Tobly, "Where are we? I don't recognize it."

Several levels below the Tower, on the north side.

"No chambers on this floor?"

Tobly shrugged. *I suspect the corridor winds in a labyrinth of confusion until starvation ends the journey. But I know a secret exit.*

She patted the floor for him to sit next to her and he did. "You look terrible. Sleep."

You look like a jungle squirrel. But he fell asleep instantly. Amused, she turned to Parker to comment, but he was also sleeping. She got to studying.

The language of the *Book* was older than the ancient spells in her *Quodex*, and the runes, it turned out, deciphered words and symbols she didn't know. She learned that sorcery had burgeoned out of philosophy back when the worlds were one. She read about the Milesian School of Thought, Hylozoists, and Stoics, and realized she had no idea what her father believed. They had never discussed such ideals. Did he believe in destiny or chance? Seemed he had no say in being fated to guard the scroll, yet he encouraged her to face destiny head on and challenge the outcome. Was that possible?

She realized she had no idea what she believed.

She fidgeted as she read about the worlds dividing, anxious to get on with it since she knew this already. Who didn't? Finally, she reached the part that interested her. The scroll. That inviolable parchment that had cost her father his life. If her sketchy understanding of the runes was to be trusted, the Omniscient conceded that the worlds might need to reunite one day. Assuming the *Book* remained safeguarded by Dragon, the Omniscient inscribed the Spell of Unification on a scroll.

No flaws in that plan.

The scroll, unlike the *Book of Knowing*, could be hexed, thus the Omniscient hexed it with a Spell of Protection permitting only the noble to decipher it. But like all spells, even a Spell of Protection would diminish eventually, so the Omniscient gave the scroll sentience to find its protector when that time came; one who would guard it with his own life.

Her father had and yet the worlds were no safer.

The *Book* confirmed what Jovia had told her. The scroll could be released to seek another protector, but it must be done with the proper spell by an honorable sorcerer (she had left out that part) or there'd be cosmic upheaval.

Milla was honorable. Was she honorable? She could use the frankness of her *Quodex* right now. She missed it terribly.

The next chapter recounted history from her lifetime and she thought she had misunderstood the runes at first. But, no, there it was. It chronicled Lucrecia's rise and her ambition to unify the lands, but more importantly, it detailed how Filimore the Protector hexed the scroll. Her father was in the *Book*. She reread every passage about him, grateful to see his efforts rewarded, and she cried softly as the *Book* told of his tragic death.

Her tears were stifled when she read on and saw that history was being written as it unfolded, at least as it pertained to the fate of the worlds. She read about her journey to Clear Rock, the capture of Jovia, the theft of the *Book* from Dragon (though she wished it was referred to as retrieval), her escape from the prison, and then history ended right where she sat. The next chapter depended on her.

She turned the page and found the start of Incantations. Finally. Fanning through the pages, searching for the spell to stop the Unification, she was sidetracked by the hex her father had put on the scroll. The verse was short and to the point, much like her father. *Adeorcian galdorword aet aeghwilc.* Obscure the magic from all. She had inherited it from him, just as she had inherited the spell to unhex the scroll. But no time to linger.

She skimmed the pages again and another verse caught her eye. She really did have the attention span of a bush possum. The spell was naggingly familiar, yet she couldn't place it, only that it wasn't from her *Quodex*. *Mid ors, ond leodscipe, ond peawfaest hyge; alynne seo ymele ond asparest ureu friou.* For some reason, the runes wouldn't assist her. Moving on. Page after page, she searched for the elusive spell and found it as Tobly awakened with a stretch. He urged her to resume the journey before the army sniffed them out.

"Soon, Tobly, I promise." She read through the verse, struggling to memorize it while he shifted and huffed impatiently.

"Shh." She put her hands to the sides of her head like blinders and focused. By the time she knew it from memory, Parker awakened with the most enchanting moans and groans.

He turned to her, groggy eyed but smiling, his hair askew atop his head. "How long was I out? Did I snore?"

"No louder than the hinterland ursine."

"That's a relief." He got to his feet to stretch and Tobly bolted into the darkness. "Subtle."

Milla tucked the *Book* safely into the back of her waistband, under her shirt, and they hurried after, never catching sight of Tobly until they rounded a bend where he waited by a window, tapping his toe. They ran over and Milla leaned out. The air was cool and thin. The vista overlooked the entire mountain below, maybe all of Asper. Above, dark clouds loomed. Parker leaned over her shoulder.

"Wow," he said.

Tobly hopped out, onto a ledge that circled the stone castle, and waved them on.

"Tobly, I'm not leaving this castle without Jovia."

The queen won't kill her, Mill. She needs her to unhex the scroll.

"But if I stop the Unification, she'll think Jovia's to blame."

Valid logic. Unexpected. Tobly hopped back inside. *Perhaps we should visit the Keeper of Evil. Risky, but worthwhile.*

Milla shoved him back in shock. "You know how to reach the Keeper of Evil?"

He shoved her back. *Yes.*

"Keeper of Evil? Sounds like a swell guy," Parker said.

"The Keeper's not a 'he' or 'she' or any kind of person for that matter."

"Like Mirth?" Parker said, and before Milla could warn him, Tobly punched him in the gut, bringing him to his knee. "What'd you do that for?"

"Parker, one does not insult someone's mother."

"Geez. Guess some things transcend dimensions. I was saying she's more than a person. Special, that's all."

That better be what you meant.

"It is."

It better be.

"It is, okay? Can we move on?"

Tobly glared at him. *Better be.* He retreated toward the stairwell having had the last word.

Milla smiled. "He shared his conversation with you. That means his trust is growing."

Parker rubbed his bruised stomach. "Yeah. That's what I took from that, too."

Parker lagged behind Milla and Tobly. Again. And though he was the only one here who had recently outsmarted a dragon and a scentmonger, his ego stung a little bit. Especially since Tobly waited at the top of the next landing, waving him on like a wild ape-kid.

Do I look like a child to you?

Milla laughed. "He's sensitive about his size."

"That's what bothered him?" Parker said.

"What else did you say?" Milla asked.

"I didn't say anything. I was in the privacy of my own head. Which, by the way," he directed to Tobly, "is none of your business."

Tobly mocked him with exaggerated lip movements. *None of your business.* He turned on his heels and disappeared into the corridor.

"I think we're starting to connect."

By the time Parker followed Milla into the corridor, Tobly was at the far end, waiting. Parker did his best to think about rainbows and unicorns, anything to stay on good terms with that little twerp. *Damn it.*

Tobly guffawed sarcastically, then rounded the corner. At least he was out of view. Earshot, too?

You wish.

Parker sighed. Steep learning curve.

In the next corridor, midway down by a window, arms folded sternly, Tobly tapped his foot and his fingers. "He's a pint-sized dude with a gallon of attitude," Parker said to Milla, but shot a look to Tobly. "And yeah, I know you can hear me."

When they reached Tobly, he climbed out onto the ledge and shuffled over to make room. Milla went next and Parker followed. With the ledge barely big enough for his feet to fit sideways, he kept his back pressed into the stony wall. They were almost at the top of the castle. Or mountain. Both, actually, since the castle was part of the mountain, carved from the inside out.

"Tobly, is that the exterior of the tower?" Milla asked. A colossal spire emerged out of the alp above them.

Told you it was risky.

Water churned over a rocky outcrop at the base of the tower, splashing icy droplets and blocking their path. Tobly headed toward it, stopped, and looked over his shoulder to Milla.

Perchance you mastered flight?

"You can fly?" Parker asked.

"No," she said, then glared at Tobly.

Tobly threw his hands up in defeat. *How am I making you look bad?*

"You little vole." She reached out for him, teetering on the ledge, and Parker flung his arm in front of her, slamming her into the wall.

"In case you weren't listening, you can't fly."

Tobly sighed. *Shame. I thought you studied.*

"I did study. I'm excellent at object levitation, I'll have you both know."

"I'm an object," Parker said and Tobly howled with laughter.

Your matter is different than an inanimate object, even if your intellect is not.

"I'm gonna go hang out with the dragons. They were friendlier."

And could fly.

Milla huffed. "Is everyone done? It's established I can't fly. Happy? Now let's proceed on foot."

Tobly shrugged. *I was merely asking. He's the one who made a deal of it.* He advanced into the cascade.

"Did not. You did," Parker yelled after Tobly. He turned to Milla. "He's infuriating."

"Adorably, so." She took Parker's hand with a gentle squeeze. "Don't fall."

"I won't if you won't."

He didn't want to let go, but their fingers parted as she disappeared into the foam. He gave her a few seconds, then stretched his arms along the wall for balance and entered the falls. Much as he wanted to get out of the deluge, he moved slowly on the slick ledge, and when he emerged on the other side, Tobly grumbled. Out loud.

"Nice," Parker said.

Tobly gripped the ledge with his toes and shook himself dry like an animal and hurried into the dense mist ahead.

"That was to impress you with his feral traits," Milla whispered.

She followed Tobly into the mist and Parker followed her. When they caught up to him, he rocked before a wooden bridge barely visible in the fog, a hop, skip, and a jump away from the ledge. It was suspended in midair without tethers.

Parker crinkled his brow. "You're not gonna—" Tobly pounced onto the bridge, causing it to dip slightly. "Never mind."

Holding the rope handrail lining both sides of the bridge, the Squeed advanced into the opaque fog.

"No one knows the castle better than he." Milla readied herself in a crouch and jumped onto the bridge. It dipped more than when Tobly landed on it, which meant Parker might take the whole thing down. He positioned himself and jumped. The bridge sank and rebounded, like a floatie in the pool.

Glistening pearl-sized globules—the mist—parted as Parker walked through but never enough to see past his next step, to see Milla. He reached for a handful of the wafting bubbles and they skirted his grasp. Probably alive like everything else in this weird world. He emerged into a circle of clarity within the whiteness, finding Milla and Tobly waiting for him.

Keeper of Evil, Tobly presented with a righteous grin and a swoop of his arm.

An infinite number of bright points traversed the ebony mountainside, lighting up and dissipating, as if the wall shifted and rippled in constant motion.

"It doesn't look evil," Parker said.

"Of course not. It's the keeper, not the doer, of evil. Within its walls lives the essence of the evil put unto others."

"Why?"

"We believe to right the wrongs when the time comes."

"Oh, karma god."

"Some say it's more powerful than the *Book*, maybe even the creator of the *Book*. It knows not only evil, but good and everything in between. The movement you see is life, is everything, is the universe."

"Crazy."

"Brilliant. Because no evil force, conjurer or not, can mine the knowledge of the Keeper. That's why Lucrecia built her castle out of this mountain. She wants to guard its virtue from those who are noble."

Blah, blah, blah. Do we want to locate the essence of Jovia or not?

"And my *Quodex*."

"How does it work—" Parker began, but an explosion of fury, invisible yet resonating, knocked him back. Milla and Tobly had fallen too but were already scrambling to their feet. Parker pulled himself up as the globules, now swirling angrily, burst apart, making way for the enormous spiky beaks, five or six of them, diving down from the heavens, as if such things could come from any heaven. Corpulent double-humped birds with a small arm next to a large long-clawed talon beneath each featherless wing.

"Wroders," Milla said.

Run!

The bridge flung upward before they could flee and they grabbed onto the rope, saving themselves from the abyss, hanging on as they were pitched every which way, their feet never touching the wooden planks. When the bridge gave up and settled, Parker scrabbled for Milla, locking wrists, but a wroder screaked in his face, flapping its powerful wings with the force to propel him back as Milla was ripped from his grasp by another bird.

"Milla!" Parker lunged for the bird and was snatched up by a monstrous ogre, a salmon in the clutches of a grizzly, helpless. Another clambered out from beneath the bridge and seized Tobly.

The wroder dragged Milla away, half-flying, half-running, until it was airborne with her in tow and it nose-dived into the mist.

"Milla!" Parker screamed, tearing his throat raw as he fought to free himself, but she was gone. Just like that. Parker screamed again, writhing and struggling, but Tobly advised him to conserve his energy. As if there was still a fight to be had.

The wet globules swirled in a sudden tornado and Lucrecia materialized from the mist. Parker panted with anger but controlled himself from reaching out to strangle her, she was that close. He had to stay alive long enough to see Milla.

"At last," she said. "I meet the one who acquired the *Book of Knowing*."

"At last I meet the evil witch."

She smiled. "I had hoped we could be friends."

"That sounds like you."

She lost the pretense, smile gone. "Where's the *Book*?"

"How should I know?"

She vaporized into a spectral mist and a caustic wind hit every cell in Parker's body as her ethereal spirit navigated his entire being. She emerged in her corporeal form before him, irritated, and thrust her nail under his chin, lifting him off the bridge. "Where is it?"

"Bite me."

She growled with a subliminal flash of razor-sharp teeth. "You'd be wise to mind your tongue, earther. Your death can be quick or insufferable." She dropped him to the bridge and dissipated explosively, leaving him and Tobly in the clutches of ogres.

The buoyant globules splattered in Milla's face, not parting fast enough for the speedy wroder. She dug her fingers into the bird's talons, but they were like stalks of woody vines; impenetrable. She screamed as forcefully as she could for as long as she could because she couldn't take it anymore. Her abdominal muscles cramped from the effort and cut her off with a painful jab. Every step forward was a kick in the gut.

She couldn't see beyond the mist and didn't know where the beast carried her; she only knew the Unification was minor in comparison to the cataclysm Lucrecia would breed if she acquired the power of the *Book*.

She retrieved the treasure that she—and every sorcerer in Asper—had ever wanted and held it to her heart, hoping, chanting, praying, that she remembered the verse to stop the Unification. Like jumping off a cliff, she wavered a hundred times, and took that fateful step, the one that could never be undone. She released the *Book of Knowing* into the foggy murk. The pages fluttered grievously as the book plummeted, forever lost.

Milla wept, no longer concerned with the constricting talons around her lungs.

CHAPTER TWENTY-THREE

THREE GLIMMERING MOONS hung in the night sky as if the universe was born of the lineage. Milla pulled herself away from the window. She was banished to her childhood room. Nothing had changed since the day she left, from the lavish bedding down to the child's tea set in the corner. On the vanity, the soft bristle brush lay on its side, its silver handle polished, and crystal bottles brimmed with fragrant perfume. Even her reflection in the mirror looked as lost today as it had that first night here.

"I spent many a twilight in this room waiting for you," Lucrecia said softly.

Milla spun around. "Concealing your reflection only illustrates your deceit."

"Habit. Apologies." Lucrecia's reflection shimmered into view in the mirror. "Why did you never return, Milla? I know you loved me. Could a cheap spell bury all that we had?"

"You speak so much of love and yet you hurt me every chance you get. Love is selfless, Lucrecia."

"I have been selfless. It pains me you don't recognize that."

"You stole me from my father."

"What would you do if your child was kept from you?"

"I'm not your child."

"We must get past this point, Milla, if we're to make any strides. Yes, Jovia carried you, but she carried you for me."

"Your desire for a child has corrupted your memory. She made no such deal with you."

"Is that what she told you?"

"Yes."

"Perhaps her memory is corrupted by the joy a newborn, a fortune she thought she would never have."

"You can't force me to love you."

"I never did."

Blasted witch.

"I gave you all I had as a mother. I worked tirelessly to raise an educated, well-rounded sorceress who could face the world. I suffered the heartache, greater than a sword to my belly, when I had to resort to punishment. I do not lie when I say it pained me more than you. You were my princess. And every morn, I awoke with thoughts of how I could better your life. Yes, I was strict when I schooled you to be heir to my throne, but great power doesn't come effortlessly. It's earned. Achieved. Fought for. I strove to impart such values on you."

"The wrong values, Lucrecia."

"Don't start with this again. We can quibble all our lives over the definition of evil."

"You killed Zanub. There's no quibble."

"What kind of ruler would I be if I allowed a traitor in my army?"

"Please, Lucrecia, as your blood, I beg you, forego the Unification."

Lucrecia shook her head. "Groveling like a common witch. I raised a better daughter than that."

"I'm not your daughter."

Lucrecia twisted Milla's wrist, forcing her to her knee. "Do not siphon what sentiment I have left for you. It's all that keeps you alive." She released her.

Milla got to her feet and held her stinging wrist.

"After traveling the portal and learning a new lesson or two, you still see the world in one color, Milla. Before I ruled, the king was overthrown by his army. Soldiers ran wild, slaughtering for sport. It was I who restrained them. But sorcerers everywhere had already developed a hatred. You're too young to remember the despair. There was no going on in peace. I only stole their magic to prevent more deaths. I couldn't have known they'd perish without it. I didn't know it was part of their souls."

"Our souls."

"Yes, our souls. But we cannot go back, can we? Now, I must protect our future. There are battles in Asper and beyond that threaten us all. I must fight for my leadership, for my leadership is the protector of the masses."

"You're not noble, Lucrecia. You're power hungry. You fight for your leadership? I fight for your downfall. I fight to see your reign taken from you because you've spoiled a world of beauty with your ugliness. You've destroyed a loving family with your misery. And you've stolen hope from this world. I fight to see hope restored."

"Quite moving. You should orate. Now give me the *Book*."

"Is that what you came for? Under the guise of motherhood and love?"

Lucrecia materialized in her face. "I'm tired of your games."

"I don't have it."

Lucrecia whipped through Milla with ethereal fervor, causing her to sway from the force. She emerged empty-handed and angry.

"Do not play me, child. You've already run my nerves further than most."

"Now who's naïve?" Milla said. "Did you expect me to keep the *Book* knowing you'd take it from me?"

Lucrecia snarled. "Then we're back where we started." She marched out, effortlessly passing through the heavy chamber door.

Milla stared after, making sure she left, when the door burst open and two soldiers grabbed hold of her.

"Release me! Let me go!" Her feet never touched the ground as she kicked and fought until the soldiers threw her onto the diminished pile of armor in the incinerator. She scrambled, but the groan of the trapdoor stabbed her ears, and she was sucked into Inferno. She screamed as the conflagration engulfed her.

Milla clambered in every direction, but was swept into the tide of Inferno's grasp. She was thrown from one flame to another, the blaze dancing as gleefully as it had when it incinerated the soldier. Flickers lashed her face and retreated with cackling amusement. Fiery sparks teased and taunted, singeing but not marring her arm, her neck, her cheek. She fought back, punching and kicking, and was smothered momentarily—black smoke—for her efforts. To think, they were once playmates. With a harrowing jolt of speed, Inferno wound through the castle in record-time and hurled Milla out. She slammed onto the cold floor and slid twenty paces, jumping to her feet for another attack, but the bully was gone. *Brainless sycophant.*

Milla was in the Hall of Magic. So much for intimidating the evil witch; Lucrecia was inviting her to test her powers with anything she could need at her disposal. Everything but a 'monger tail. She surveyed the cauldrons and sniffed their contents, some bubbling, some ballooning and popping with a splatter, and some stagnant. She ran her finger across the books on one of the shelves, longing for her *Quodex*. She turned to the translucent rock in the center of the chamber and it beckoned to her with a wistful shimmer. She looked over her shoulder, then back to the rock. As if there was anyone else. But what would the crystal want with her? She had never graduated to Beholding and her father had never insisted she learn, unlike her other studies. Once a soul left its bodily form, there was a risk it might get lost, forever trapped inside, and no crystal wanted that. Could she take that risk? The truer question was: how could she not? The castle was impervious to wandering souls from the outside, cloaked in protection, but in here, this Beholder, the queen's rock, could penetrate all walls.

A soft glow misted off the surface, and Milla approached with the resistance of a river crossing, neck deep in water. The wispy air enveloped her instantly, pulling her aura into the ethereal world with the sensation of falling. She flitted about, unable to control her astral exploration. She spread her arms to slow her journey, but the places blurred past in a sure descent into oblivion. She was at Lost Creek one moment, her shack an instant later, then in Clear Rock, Lost Creek, Rose Garden, her shack, Walter's Antiques, Lost Creek. Her essence shuddered and stopped abruptly, in the prison at the castle. Parker was in one of the cells. *Parker.*

His furrowed brow brought warmth to her. He'd find a way out;

he conquered a dragon, after all. She was emboldened by his courage. He was honorable and fearless. And he believed. Believed in himself. Believed in her.

She reached out to touch him but couldn't feel anything. She wafted over him, enveloped him in her soul. He looked up, sensing her presence, she knew it, but a barking 'monger broke their bond. The beast's cage slammed up against his and Milla screamed but had no voice. The sentry unsealed the scentmonger's bars and Milla, frantic, wrapped her essence around Parker. The bars to his cell disappeared and the 'monger bolted in.

Milla fought, her essence flailed and shattered and converged in the mayhem of the charge. She screamed and screamed, voicelessly. Anything, anything but this! Parker grabbed onto the scruff of the writhing animal and straddled its back, but the 'monger rammed the bars, smashing Parker's head against the metal. *No!* He hit the ground but kicked and punched the snarling snout. Milla's essence was caught in the melee, the horror, grasping helplessly, giving him nothing, as the scentmonger ripped into his arm, his legs, and punctured his flesh. She screamed in agony. His blood showered her essence. *No, no, no!* She begged with her entire being, she offered herself, but the 'monger clenched its massive jaws around Parker's ribcage and Parker went limp. She wailed in anguish, her soul shattered, and her essence fell to the ground as she lost consciousness.

Milla lay motionless on the floor before the Crystal Beholder, helpless, paralyzed. Her aura seeped out of the stone and back into her body and she jolted up and ran for the door.

"Jovia is next."

Milla spun and slipped to the floor in her effort to stop and face the witch. Lucrecia stroked the Crystal Beholder, cleansing it.

"You monster!" Milla charged and Lucrecia halted her with a single finger, sending her slamming into a cauldron. She fell to her knees—depleted of energy, insides aching—and cried, slumped in defeat. She had no words anymore. No will, even.

"Do you see now, you cannot defeat me?" Lucrecia said.

Milla nodded. Her failure was abundantly clear.

"My goal is not to hurt you."

"How can you say that? You take everyone I love."

"It's all you respond to."

"You have no heart."

"I must, for that sentiment cuts me deeply. Some things are bigger than us, Milla. Bigger than family, than love. Accept that. I have. And I'm willing to suffer the heartache for the greater good. But I'm not evil as you believe."

Lucrecia wrapped her cold fingers around Milla's wrist and, in a wicked flash, her aura shot into the Crystal Beholder, taking Milla's with her.

Parker, alive—*alive*—rocked inside one of the prison cells. Milla reached for him but was back in the Hall of Magic on trembling legs.

She cried again, cried with hope. "He's alive?"

"For now."

"I don't understand. I saw him attacked."

"You journeyed to the future. Cooperate and the future will change."

"Change? How can you change the future? Destiny has spoken."

Lucrecia smiled. "Sweet girl, destiny and I are old friends, but nothing written cannot be unwritten when one has the power. Change your course, Milla, change destiny."

A rush of heat washed over Milla and she felt faint. Maybe it was the past, maybe the future, one of them made her sick. All she knew was that Parker was already dead. Unless…

"Unhex the scroll so I can perform the Unification," Lucrecia said, "and the boy and Jovia will be released unharmed. My oath."

"I'll remove the hex."

Lucrecia touched her cheek warmly, eyes shining with love. "Was that so difficult?"

Milla dropped her head, ashamed. *Yes. Yes, it was.*

CHAPTER TWENTY-FOUR

THE PRISON TEEMED with newly captured Squeeds, Tobly among them, and unlike Parker, who rocked in his cell, they remained motionless.

We need a plan, Parker shouted in his head but got no response from the Squeeds. *I see, all talk and no action.*

Not a single one took the bait. He twirled the syringe inside his pocket. It was half-filled with sedative, the last of it, but should be plenty to take out the sentry. Unfortunately, hoping for a bullseye into the open eyeshield from across the prison floor fell into the same category as winning the lottery.

"Hello? Excuse me, Mr. Guard?"

Mr. Guard? Tobly snorted.

At least, he assumed it was Tobly. *Well, what would you call him?*

'Monger spore. Desert trash.

Helpful. "Hey, Guard. Can you hear me?"

The sentry turned to him with an irritated sneer. "Quiet."

"Okay, good, you can. I have something important to tell you."

The sentry ignored him.

Clever. Bore him to death, Tobly said.

Parker gritted his teeth. "It's about the Unification."

The sentry turned to him. "What of it?"

"It's kind of a secret. You have to come closer."

The sentry sat on the bench and kicked his feet up on a nearby cell, ignoring him.

You understand the 'mongers will be here soon, Tobly said.

I'm trying to gain his trust.

No one trusts an earther. Get him over to you.

Parker clenched his jaw to stop from growling at the little runt. "So I guess you don't want the page I stole from the *Book of Knowing*," he said. "The one with the verse for the Unification."

The sentry's armor faded briefly. "You have the verse? Where is it?"

"Right here. I'd bring it to you, but you know…"

The sentry scanned the surroundings, drew his sword and marched over. He wasn't in arm's reach when an infestation of Squeeds shot out of the crevices and rushed him into Parker's cell, pinning him there. It happened so fast, Parker was still fumbling to get the syringe out of his pocket.

Hurry, Tobly shouted.

The sentry thrashed to free himself, sending several Squeeds careening across the prison floor, but the rest of the pack smashed his face against the bars.

Must I define 'hurry' for you?

"Shut up." Parker uncapped the needle with adrenaline-rushed hands and jammed it through the eyeshield with such force, it broke off and lodged in the sentry's eyeball. "Gross."

The sentry screamed and his knees buckled, taking him down along with several Squeeds. Parker grabbed his palm and unsealed his cell as a Squeed lopped off the sentry's hand. "Okay, that's extreme."

The Squeed ran down the rows, releasing his clan, and they funneled into the crevices. Even Tobly.

Footsteps boomed from the stairwell and Parker dove to the ground for cover. Vylkrost marched in, spotting the unconscious sentry immediately, and followed the trail of blood to the abandoned gloved hand at the end of the row. He snarled and scanned the prison ward, his gaze passing over Parker's head, and returned his attention to the sentry, rolling him onto his back. He must've seen the broken needle in his eye because he roared with anger and kicked him hard enough to propel him down the aisle before storming out.

Idiot, Tobly said.

Parker jumped to his feet with a gasp. The damn Squeed was huddled right next to him. "Don't do that."

Parker and Tobly ascended the stairs in a run. "We should split up. Cover more ground that way."

The worlds will be unified by the time we search this castle. We must wait below the Tower and intercept Milla as they transport her.

"To the all-hell-will-break-loose ceremony? Isn't that cutting it a bit close?"

We're past 'close.' We're desperate.

Tobly darted into a corridor and Parker had to backtrack to follow. *A little warning, please.*

He rounded the corner and slammed into Tobly, who stood motionless in front of an openmouthed Queldar. Parker rammed the warlock against the wall by his neck. "Where's Milla?"

"I've no idea."

"You're lying. I saw you spill your guts to the queen like a sniveling little lackey, you—"

Vile sack of dung.

"For good cause, to protect Milla. But I can't be obvious about it."

"Then tell me where she is."

"My oath, I don't know. I was presently searching for her myself."

Parker released his grip and Queldar straightened his cloak.

If only there was such thing as a Beholder to aid you.

"I haven't my tools, boy, not even my *Quodex*."

Boy? Tobly kicked him in the shin.

"Watch yourself. I can still enchant a spell or two without my instruments."

Tobly gnarred.

Queldar turned to Parker. "Perchance you can direct me to the Hall of Magic where I may find some resources?"

"Perchance *I* can? Who would know this castle better than you?"

"Settle down. We fight the same fight." He nodded to Tobly. "Have you ever come across it?"

Never.

Queldar sighed and thrust his cloak outward, disappearing inside, before the cloak itself vanished.

"Are you kidding me? He can do that, but he can't find Milla?"

Sorcery is complex. Tobly took off again, sticking to the interior stairwells until they were near the top. *Run faster than an earther,* he said, bolting into the atrium.

Parker entered the atrium, faster than an earther, he was pretty sure, and sprinted into the corridor after Tobly. He heard a plaintive whine calling out to him and slowed, listening.

Tobly, he called silently. The Squeed returned from around the corner, nostrils flared.

Desperate. Remember?

I heard something. Maybe it's Milla. The soft cry wafted into the corridor. *Did you hear it?*

Smells like a trap.

Parker followed the moans to a vast black marbled room with a black marbled throne. A shiny void in space and time; a black hole. Tobly stopped him by the hand before he could enter.

She's not here.

Parker entered, slowly at first but built into a run, following the cries to a podium where Milla's *Quodex* fluttered. Excited, he turned to call Tobly, but the Squeed was by his side.

Well, take it. Derg.

Parker grabbed the *Quodex* and the book rippled with a soft breath that was cut short by the onslaught of galloping horses in the corridor. Parker dove behind the throne to hide, Tobly beating him there.

Quiet, the Squeed said.

Derg.

Stop saying that. It sounds ugly from you.

Several soldiers guided their horses inside the room and spread out but none of them as far as the throne before disseminating back into the stairwell.

So much for the element of surprise, Parker thought.

Worse. The queen is on the hunt. I'll distract, you get Milla.

Before Parker could protest, Tobly charged into the corridor and flames shot past with a screech, giving chase. Parker made a beeline for the stairwell but pulled up when hundreds, maybe thousands of soldiers on horseback ascended and descended in strict formation, filing in and out of the various levels. The fortress groused and groaned as if it would topple from their aggressive charge. Parker ducked into the shadows of a recess and remained stock-still in the darkness, cold armor brushing against him from soldiers filtering past. He was about to flee when he caught the dim-witted torches taking turns looking left then right, alternating watch. Getting away undetected was out of the question, so he ran for it.

With a shrill, earsplitting scream, the flames flared out toward him, joining together in a singular blaze. The heat baked his back, sizzling his hair, but he escaped into the stairwell, jumping down five, ten steps at a time. The torches squealed in tattle and the stairs melted into a grungy slide, throwing Parker on his face and tossing him into the atrium. He reached out for something to grasp onto but caught nothing and plummeted several stories to the dungeon. He landed on his stomach, the wind knocked out of him, eye to eye with the enormous cockroach. The surly vermin hissed, but Parker hardly cared about their feud anymore and jumped to his feet, his body stabbing with pain.

He scanned the myriad of stairwells leading out of the dungeon, looking for the darkest one with the least amount of torches, when the racket of falling armor jarred him. He hit the ground for cover. Metal showered down from the incinerator, loose pieces bouncing from the flames. He waited for Inferno to scarf them up, but the blaze stood erect, like a fiery channel reaching for the highest point in the castle. Parker scrambled for the pieces, slipping into them as if he'd been wearing armor his whole life. A simple plan, but the torches were simpleminded.

Milla huddled in the darkest cove of the Hall of Magic, far away from that deceitful rock. In a room full of spells, potions, and powders, there was nothing to help her. She thought she was hallucinating when Queldar approached from the shadows, floating in his shapeless cloak. His face brightened.

"Milla." He materialized before her, kneeling to take her hand, but she pulled it away.

"What do you want?"

"We must leave."

"I'm not going anywhere."

"Milla, Lucrecia mustn't unify the worlds."

"The fight is over, Queldar."

"Your father wouldn't want you to give up."

"How dare you presume to know anything my father would want, you traitorous imposter."

"I don't ask that you forgive my deeds, but I beg you, do not unhex the scroll. Lucrecia will be the ruin of all that is good."

"If you're so keen to stop her, why do you serve her? You're the one who told her of the Unification."

"I did it for love, my dear. For family. I thought I could—"

"You know nothing of either," Milla said.

Queldar smiled with dismay. "If I had a 'monger tail for every plan miscarried, I'd be flush with brew, your father used to tease. Some things never change. I'm victim to my own failed plans, Milla, but my intentions were honorable."

"You knew Jovia was alive but kept silent to hide your own deception. Where's the honor in that?"

"She was determined to keep her pact with Lucrecia for your safety. How could I betray that? Of course ideas flooded my mind—reunite child with mother, husband with wife—alas, such thoughts were best kept quiet or everyone would suffer in even the most optimistic outcome. I feared for her life."

"So you chose her suffering for her?"

Queldar dropped his head.

"Hasn't she suffered enough?" Milla said.

"Yes."

"So you see, I can't refuse the queen."

"Your father believed good would prevail."

"He was wrong." Milla held tears in her eyes. "The world is already evil. Look about. There's no wonderment, no joy. Every sorcerer has been killed. Why stop her now? The world has already succumbed to her terror."

"I still have hope, Milla."

"The world would've been better if you left things as they were."

"I disagree. Yes, had I known your father guarded the scroll, I might not have bartered for your freedom, but I'm glad I didn't know, for if you stayed, you'd be like her, would you not? A child needs a moral parent."

Milla buried her face in her hands and Queldar rubbed her shoulder in comfort.

"Lucrecia is not the only evil this land has seen," he said. "We've endured worse in our history, yet we survived. My heart aches knowing you may lose everyone you love if you do as I ask, but you mustn't unhex that scroll. If you do, the universe of our lineage—the Rising—will merge with Lucrecia. That is how the worlds unite; through her. She's nothing compared to what she will be if that happens. You have the strength, Milla, and I gladly offer my life to give you the chance to prove it. Your mother would do the same. Trust good to prevail over evil, as your father did."

A rat sprung onto Queldar's back, its wicked claw primed to slice his throat. Milla grabbed it by the scruff, but missed the opportunity to break its neck as the beady-eyed vermin metamorphosed into Lucrecia. Her sharp talon graced Milla's throat now.

"So, you've reconciled," Lucrecia said with a snarl.

"Release Queldar of his charge or I won't unhex the scroll."

Lucrecia stroked Milla's neck with her claw. "You cannot amend our deal, child."

"I just did."

Lucrecia turned to Queldar. "Shameful you would sacrifice her young life so readily, Queldar. Have you no loyalty to anyone but yourself?" She flicked him away like a gnat and Queldar disappeared within his cloak, the wrap following thereafter. "His debt will be cleared when the scroll is free of the hex," she said to Milla, and dispersed in a shower of radiant dust.

Milla wiped the trickle on her arms, thinking it was the magical remnants of the queen's show, but it was the awful glint of her memories escaping. *No.*

She scraped her nails into the floor, grappling to stay present.

CHAPTER TWENTY-FIVE

THE CAGE SLAMMED INTO A ROCK and tipped over. Milla landed upside down on the back of her neck. The metal box fell open, like a blossoming flower, and the bars disappeared. She crawled out, onto the mossy ground, barely recognizing her flimsy shack. It had been more than four years since she saw that ratty nest of twigs and vines. It was smaller than she remembered. The stink of root vegetables and cabbage brewing on the fire pit curdled her stomach.

The white crow must have thought it was clever, spying on her from a thick pine, but she flailed her arms at it and it soared out of the shadows and into the clouds. She entered the shack and her lungs tightened from the claustrophobic confines. Her once-favorite blanket was stretched over her cot, its corners tucked with precision, and at the foot of the bed was a folded pair of pants and top. Both burlap. Itchy, reddening burlap.

Her father's cot was stored up flat against the wall, predictably, allowing room to study. The candle on their lopsided table flickered and Milla ran to it. "Inferno?"

The flame glided from her breath but didn't respond. She blew it out with a sharp puff and spun away from it, arms folded, and fought her quivering lips. The dusty floor had soiled her sandals and was making its way up her royal gown, which had already unraveled to her knees like a cheap dress of strings. Why was she being punished?

She fled deep into the forest before her father might return. She'd rather live among the beetles and bears than in the squalor of that dump.

Her orientations were coming back with every leap over fallen trees and shallow streams, and she made sure to bypass Lost Creek. That would be the first place he'd search if he was expecting her. She scrambled over a reedy bush and was knocked into the air from an invisible force, nose-diving into a muddy patch. She twirled to her feet, but out of nowhere, dirty, craggy arms thrust her to the ground and held her there. "Release me at once!"

The creatures obliged and she jumped up, swinging and kicking, keeping them at bay. They were horrid—a pack of wood-foliage-dirt boys, smaller than her, clad in nothing but a cloth hiding their indecency. They had animal teeth and obviously hadn't showered in ever.

Have so, she heard from somewhere in the crowd. *And you're welcome.*

"Who said that? Welcome for what?"

A boy stepped forth and, without moving his lips whatsoever, said, *I did*, while the others bobbed on their toes, licking their lips like they were getting ready to pounce.

"How do you speak without moving your mouth?"

This forest is not for children.

"I'm not a child, I'm a princess."

The animals sprung on her and she was on the ground, being dragged away before she knew it, but just as quickly, they retreated as the one boy shook his finger madly at them. Riled, they kicked the leaves and punched the air, and some even turned on each other, shoving and snarling.

The boy leaned toward her. *You don't smell like a princess.*

Milla sniffed herself. "My perfumes are at the castle."

I mean to say, evil.

"Because I'm not."

Not yet, perhaps. Take yourself home then. And quickly. I reserve my anthropoidal appetite to soldiers, but my brothers will eat any being.

"You're disgusting."

Takes one to know one.

The wood-foliage-dirt boys disappeared, as if scattering into a hundred Shifts, but there were none in the area. Scared, Milla ran nonstop, back to her shack, and by the time she arrived, her father was at the fire pit, stirring the soup. He dropped the ladle and materialized before her, scooping her in his arms.

"Milla. My sweet, sweet Milla." His tears splashed her shoulders and he didn't let go until she pushed herself free.

"Please," she said.

He held onto her hands but trembled so much, she wished he would let go. "Did you escape the castle? How did you get here?"

"Vylkrost. How else?"

"Vylkrost?" His eyes widened in fright and he looked over his shoulder, both ways, and said, "Hurry. We must make our home elsewhere."

He scrambled into the shack, taking her with him by the hand, and circled the small room like a feverish raccoon. He collected potions, powders, a journal, and other essentials as he said, "Gather your belongings. Never mind. We'll make do." He rushed to the door, but Milla didn't follow.

"I wish to go back to the castle."

He dropped everything in his arms at once. "What do you mean?"

"I wish to be with my mother, the queen."

He grabbed her by the wrist and pointed his finger in her face. "Milla Saofia Joviana Langstromer, I never want to hear those words from your mouth again. Do you hear me?"

She erupted in tears but said, "Then close your ears because it's true and I'll say it until you take me there."

His face went redder than the crimson berry. She thought he'd explode, but he took it out on the rickety table, shattering it with a swipe of his hand. Milla shrieked and covered her head from flying shards of wood but found herself beneath a cloak as fragments bounced off. When the debris settled, her father summoned his cloak and it retreated from her, slipping back over his head. His cheek trickled blood from the scratches.

He heaved heavily but spoke softly. "Forgive me. You've endured more than any child should have to."

"I can go home?"

"Your home is with me."

A branch crunched outside and Milla darted her eyes fast enough to see Queldar's fat head duck from the window. She ran out after him. "You!" she called as he scurried away. "Stop, you weasel." He slumped.

"Don't make a deal, Milla," the wizard said.

"This is your fault."

"What is?" her father asked.

"He promised a scroll in exchange for my return," Milla said.

Queldar shook his head, but his brow twitched.

"What scroll?" her father asked Queldar.

"Mere rumors, brother. Nothing of true concern. I spun a convincing tale from forest chatter."

Her father approached Queldar, nose-to-nose. After uneasy silence, he asked, "So now you serve the queen?"

"I had to offer her something, Filimore."

"Your soul?"

"A sacrifice worth making, brother, for you were sure to die of a broken heart. Every day, every failed attempt brought you closer to death."

"We're no longer brothers."

"But—"

"Go now, Queldar," her father said.

"Filimore, please—"

"I'll use force if I must."

Queldar left, sagging more than his baggy cloak, and Milla had a twinge of regret for ratting him out. Her father destroyed the shack with magic and fire, to be sure no remnants remained, and moved them to a forest she'd never been to before. He built their new home by hand, saying magic could be traced and it was imperative they never be found, and then they didn't live in the shack; they lived in a secret chamber accessed through a tunnel from a hidden door carved into the wall behind their cots. Total darkness save for a candle or two, and no reference to count the days. She missed her lavish chamber at the castle and Zanub more than that. She missed her fancy clothes and tasty food but Zanub even more. Worse, she was sad all the time, and lonely. Her father tried to cheer her with an amulet, but it didn't compare to her jewels at the castle.

"Your mother wore the other half. It was going to be a gift for your thirteenth birthday, but now seems more fitting, does it not?"

Milla curled her lip and took the amber gem. It wasn't surrounded by rubies or diamonds and dangled unglamorously on a rope softened by time. He tied it around her neck. At least it itched less than the burlap.

"You do so look like your mother."

Indeed. She and the queen were strikingly similar.

Her father eventually deemed it safe to move into the main quarters, but he wouldn't let her play outdoors. Obsessed with studies, he insisted she bond with her *Quodex*. The book seemed nice, but magic only reminded her of the castle, so she pretended more than she studied.

When he slept one night, she paced the shack, thankful it was bigger than the hidden room, and snooped through his wooden trunk. Among textiles, powders, and dried herbs, she found a stack of exotic books.

"Those belonged to your mother," he said, startling her to her feet.

"I thought you were asleep."

"Only with one eye."

Milla laughed.

"She enjoyed Earth books," he said. "I never indulged."

"Too busy studying, I suppose."

"So you've not forgotten everything about me."

"I didn't forget you, Father. I studied as well as you. I was due to graduate to Beholding the day of my release." The pride in his eyes made her feel worse. "I can't sleep. May I read?"

"As long as you want."

Milla struggled through an entire book, left to imagine what some of the earthly objects were that she'd never heard of before. She fell asleep at some point because she awoke with the morning light, the book heavy on her chest, and stretched with a moan. She jumped up, ready for studies, and wobbled from the current of disappointment when she realized where she was.

Her father placed a bowl on the table for her. "Come eat your porridge."

Milla sat in the sagging straw chair and nearly retched at the sight of the slop. Not even a seed or berry to brighten it. And no juice? She pushed the bowl away. "Are we to live like this forever?"

"If we're lucky."

"I should rather die."

"Milla."

"I don't see the point. Imprisoned in a stinky shack. No one but each other to pass the time. It's not fair, Father. Why won't you allow me to return to the castle, if only to be with my friend?"

"Your friend is evil."

"You take that back!"

"Everyone in the castle is evil, my daughter."

"I was in the castle."

"Against your will. You were stolen and tricked."

"You think very little of my will."

"I think greatly of you. Like it or not, you're still a child and the queen has swayed you with false charms."

"I miss my friend. He's kind and honorable. I must see him again. He's my prince."

"Be patient. The days will ease your pain."

But they didn't. She ached deeper and lost interest in everything but sitting on the grass and gazing into the woods.

One morning, the mosquitoes were extra feisty and Milla sought refuge inside the shack. Her father must've gotten used to her spending the days outside because he didn't notice. Seated in one of the fraying straw chairs, his back not quite to the door, he was bathed in the sun and squinted from the peripheral glare. He retrieved a plain wooden box—silvered, unnaturally smooth as if polished—from inside his cloak and placed it on the table before him. He hesitated twice before unhinging the clasp and opening the box. He removed an iridescent scroll bundled with lace woven from strands of gold, much like the queen's gowns.

Gently, he untied the lace and unrolled the scroll onto the table. The parchment settled with a ripple, lying flat, and the symbols on it shimmered. Her father gathered his journal from another pouch in his cloak, mumbled a prayer to the Omniscient, and opened the book. He went back and forth between pages before gathering two sprigs of a woody herb he had apparently hidden in the underside of the table. He crushed the dry sprigs between his fingers into grains and sprinkled them onto the scroll. The shimmering symbols dimmed, then returned to their full glow.

"*Aheordest se ymele,*" he said, and Milla braced herself, for what she didn't know. But nothing happened. Nothing at all. Her father dropped his head and his cloak sagged with him.

"You have the scroll," she said, causing him to spin in midair, his cloak creating such a fuss, she was blown onto her backside.

He hastily rolled the parchment, tucked it back inside the box, and stuffed that deep inside his cloak.

"Why?" she asked as she got to her feet.

"Forget you saw this. It doesn't exist."

"But it does. Did Queldar know? Tell me."

After much stalling, he reluctantly told her the story of the doves, and the years he had spent trying to release it to find another protector, to no avail. With Queldar unwittingly setting the queen on the hunt—he didn't know her father was the protector—he urged her to never speak a word of this no matter how dire the circumstance. Be it life or death. He admitted it was too much to put on a young sorceress, but the worlds depended on it, everyone's lives depended on it, and he must depend on her. She gave her oath, because his heart seemed heavier than a winter's rain, but she couldn't help think this scroll could also return her to the castle.

At dinnertime, she forced a bite or two of the bland stew and readied herself for bed, claiming exhaustion. Soon after, her father climbed into his cot with a grunt, and she couldn't deny he had aged much more than the years she was gone. She pushed the guilt aside and waited, hoping to hear snores not weeps, and when she was rewarded, she tiptoed out of bed and into the garden to read by the moonlight. She had found one of Jovia's journals while sifting through the Earth books. Having heard many stories while at the castle and of course stories from her father, she longed to read the truth from the woman herself, the woman she barely remembered, in her own words.

Five pages in, and Milla's head bounced, ready to nod off. Jovia wrote about the dullest things—afternoon strolls in the woods, collecting berries, crafting sandals. *Boring.*

Tell me about it.

Milla fell off the rock she was sitting on and tumbled in a backward roll to her feet, heart pounding. The dirty rough-skinned little imp pointed at her and laughed. *Graceful.*

"Stay away from me, you disgusting flesh-eater."

Don't flatter yourself. You've no flesh to chew on. He salivated. *Though I do enjoy gnawing on a femur. Good for the teeth.* He took a step toward her and she held out her hands threateningly.

"I know magic."

I should hope so. You're a sorceress, after all.

"What do you want?"

He shrugged. *'Sides food? Not much. Someone to climb trees with.*

"A princess doesn't climb trees."

Luckily you're not a princess.

Milla huffed. "Say it once more and I'll bloody your nose."

Many sorries, your highness. I was misled by your castle. He leaned against the rock she had been sitting on and his skin changed color and texture, making him practically invisible.

"You," she said, astonished. "You're the boys in the prison, who look like the walls."

Derg.

"You match your surroundings."

Double derg.

"How do you do that?"

He shrugged. *Just do.*

"Go over there." She pointed to the sooty fire pit and he obliged, camouflaging perfectly with it.

"Who are you talking to?" her father asked from the doorway, stealing her attention, and when she turned back to the fire pit, the boy was gone. Or maybe elsewhere, where she couldn't detect him.

"No one."

Her father approached. "You found her journal."

Blasted. She forgot she was holding it. "I wanted to know her better."

"And do you?"

"I didn't get far."

He patted her shoulder. "Take your time." He went back inside. Milla waited for the craggy brat to show up again, but he didn't, so she cracked open the journal. Halfway through, the delightful stories of being with child, giving birth, and raising a baby were replaced with the horrors of being hunted. Jovia had lived fearful that her misguided sister would find them, would take her baby. They had moved from forest to forest, living in makeshift hovels that were quickly assembled and disassembled to hide their trail. Pages and pages and no smiles in her words anymore, just tears. The last entry was addressed to Milla.

My precious daughter, the depth of my love goes beyond words, beyond life itself. If we do not find one another again, know that you filled me with more joy than most have in a lifetime. You'll be with me always. I love you.

By the time Milla finished reading, the salt of her tears reached her tongue and the morning sun blinded her with a rainbow of iridescent dots—familiar and soothing—dappling the forest. And she remembered. She remembered her mother used to dangle the amulet, no matter where they had fled to or from, no matter what terror they had escaped, no matter, she dangled the amulet for Milla, catching the sun and enticing her to nap with the colorful dance of light.

Milla clutched the gem with one hand, and hugged the book to her chest with the other. She crawled into her cot and stayed there for days. Perhaps it was starvation, perhaps guilt, but she began to recall other moments with her mother, moments she didn't know she had saved until now. Tickles and cuddles; baths with more bubbles than water; being swathed in cloth scented like the forest.

Milla had betrayed her—forgotten her—for perfumes and jewels, silver gowns and plush covers. She cared only about greedy comforts while her mother had suffered and died for her. She dozed scant minutes at a time and allowed her father to trickle water on her lips, but by the fourth day, when she was too weak to roll over, he insisted she rise. He pulled her up to a seated position, stacked his pillow and blanket behind her to support her, and gathered a tray of herbs, powders, and potions.

"Life is cruel," she said, her throat drier than the desert sands.

"Where there is life, there is hope, Milla."

"How can you say that?"

"Because it's true." He whisked ingredients into a bowl and held a spoonful to her mouth.

"Smells putrid."

"Then it smells better than I expected."

"I'm not hungry."

"One bite. You'll feel better. My oath."

Milla blocked her nose and swallowed the rancid paste. The room imploded at the pace of a wasteland turtle on its last leg, sucked slowly into a pinhole until everything was nothing, light or sound, and an explosion of kaleidoscopic clouds, vibrant and bold, swirled into a whirlwind of streaming color and noise.

CHAPTER TWENTY-SIX

MILLA WAS ON THE EBONY TOWER, no recollection how she got there, and the Rising had begun. Bursts of brightness thundered and rang amid the blackened sky over the castle. The three moons—their lineage—traveled faster than time. The crescent became the half, the half the full, the full the crescent, and thusly they continued in the chaotic sky. Encircling Inferno's flume, three crystals mirrored the moons in motion and shimmered with energy. Inferno, erect from the depths of the dungeon, frolicked in the clouds.

Vylkrost dragged Milla to the prancing fire and Inferno retreated from the skies, teasing her with flickers and embers. She stared down the fire, having been through too much to be intimidated. But Lucrecia stepped out of the flames, startling her—villainous witch, always had a trick—and held out her arms like she owned the universe. Her golden gown shone beneath the active sky, enveloping her in a radiant glow, as if she were honorable. She breathed a soft sigh of exhilaration.

"Glorious, is it not? The elements beg us to mend the broken worlds and we shall."

Milla had nothing to say. Or perhaps too much.

Lucrecia stroked her cheek softly, then held her face firmly in hand. "Now is not the time to deceive me," she said in a whisper. "Do you understand?"

"I understand."

Lucrecia released her and five droplets of blood trickled onto Milla's lips. Milla wiped them off as the witch entered the flames and took her perch on a white marble throne levitating in the center.

Inferno parted further, revealing Jovia on the farthest side of the tower. Emotion swept over Milla as if the years hadn't passed. As if she'd never been kidnapped and raised as a princess, as if her father had never confiscated her pain. It all disappeared at the sight of Jovia, the woman who sacrificed everything, surrendered her own life, so Milla could be safe. Now flanked by rows of soldiers, wrists bound behind her back with metal cuffs chained to the wall, and ankles manacled with a single restraint; her suffering never ended. Vylkrost stepped next to Jovia, drawing his sword, and Milla grabbed her stomach to stop the sick from coming up. The thought of unhexing the scroll was unbearable, but watching Jovia die was unfathomable.

The sea of sinuous armor parted and Queldar emerged, his frail frame tremoring as violently as the wind, but he managed to make his way to a dais equidistant between her and Lucrecia, stumbling twice. He unrolled the scroll and held it high, white-knuckled against the determined gusts, for her to see.

Golden, dappled with flecks of light, magnificent. In the years her father had guarded it, she never once appreciated its beauty, its meaning. Now, its presence enchanted her. Its splendor brought forth the noblest devotion to protect it, as if her choice hadn't been difficult enough.

"Unhex the scroll," Lucrecia said.

Afeorsian cneowrim afol. The verse coursed Milla's veins, but she was unable to release it into the ether. Her conscience refused. Punishment, for choosing evil, for turning her back on all her father had fought to protect.

Lucrecia slithered her torso off the throne, face to face with Milla, and said, "You're nervous. Perhaps this will help." She slid her eyes to Vylkrost and he backhanded Jovia's face, ripping it bloody. Milla shrieked, awakening her vocal cords.

"Marvelous. Now proceed." Lucrecia slithered back to her throne.

Milla turned to Jovia, desperate to beg forgiveness. She yearned to explain that she didn't have the courage to endure another heartache; that her soul would bleed out. She wanted to promise she'd study every minute of every day to somehow undo the horror she was about to commit. She had so much she needed to say before she betrayed everything her father stood for, but she saw only love in Jovia's eyes. A mother's love. Unconditional. The same her father had shown even when she relinquished the scroll that terrible day.

Milla's insides stung with the heartrending revelation; she must stop Lucrecia, no matter the price.

"I won't do it, Lucrecia."

Inferno screeched, but Lucrecia quieted her pet with a stroke. "So you're prepared to see the witch die?"

"I have no fear—" Jovia began, but Lucrecia flung her into the wall with a twist of her wrist while never taking her gaze off Milla.

"Death will be on your head, Milla."

"It already is. You killed my father. Zanub. Our lineage. And now you want to unite the worlds so you can kill them, too? I won't let you—"

Lucrecia clutched Milla by the throat in sorcerer speed, crushing her windpipe and cutting off her air.

"No. Lucrecia, no!" Jovia struggled to free herself of the chains. "Please. Have mercy, dear sister."

"I see not everyone possesses the newfound strength you have, Milla." Lucrecia plunged her wicked nail into Milla's jugular, so swiftly, so superbly, Milla thought it was a bluff, feeling nothing, but Lucrecia ripped it free—jagged like the serrated edge of her knife—and blood spurted out. Milla froze—shocked—then gagged, unable to breathe. Jovia buckled in grief, her confines keeping her from crumpling to the ground. Queldar reached out, but Lucrecia immobilized him in midmotion. Milla wheezed, unable to fill her lungs.

"I'll unhex the scroll," Jovia called out. "Please. Save her and I'll unhex the scroll. You have my word."

Lucrecia slammed her palm onto Milla's neck, clotting the blood instantly, sealing the wound, and Milla sucked in a breath that very well brought her back to life.

"Like mother, like daughter," Lucrecia spat out.

Milla swung her eyes to the queen. "Finally," she whispered, her throat burning from the wound.

Lucrecia glared at her. "Ingrate. You wouldn't exist but for me. I gave you everything a mother could. And you cling to that weakling who hid all these years because she wouldn't fight for you? You cling to the memory of your father who not only failed you, he failed his fate as protector of the scroll? You're a disgrace, undeserving of the lineage."

Yes. Yes, she had been. "I'll remove the hex."

Lucrecia's nostrils flared. She looked to the tumultuous sky where the moons were in place and would soon move on in their journey. Inferno wafted edgily.

"I'm your better choice and you know it," Milla said. "The verse is ingrained in my blood. She must rely on memory."

Lucrecia snarled with a flash of ugliness. "One more betrayal and I will kill you and let her suffer the pain. You've proven yourself unworthy of my love."

Milla nodded. "And you of mine."

Lucrecia faltered but composed herself. "You always knew how to hurt me, Milla." She flicked a finger and Queldar unfroze, falling to his knees. He shook terribly but lifted the scroll for Milla to see.

"*Afeorsian cneowrim afol*," Milla said. Short and to the point. She thought of her father, of course, and her heart warmed.

Glistening runes—the hex—rose from the scroll and scattered in the bluster of the Rising, leaving the parchment clean. As with the *Book of Knowing*, they were invisible to everyone else. The naked parchment, now unhexed, shimmered and the Unification Spell bled into view. The elegant script flowed like a dance on the parchment, beautiful and poignant, as the silver cast of the moons undulated in wait. This was it. Everything Milla had fought for ending in failure.

But more words drifted off the scroll, hovering, unaffected by the gusts. *Mid ors, ond leodscipe, ond peawfaest hyge; alynne seo ymele ond asparest ureu friou.* The verse from the *Book of Knowing*, the one the runes wouldn't decipher, floated before Milla, beckoning, unseen by everyone else. The realization hit like a shockwave. This verse comprised the words her father had entered, piecemeal, in his journal. He had dedicated his entire book to that one verse—his entire life. She nearly cried. She knew what it meant.

She looked to Queldar, but he mistook her concern and reached out in condolement only to be startled back by Lucrecia plucking the scroll from his hands. The witch returned to her throne in the center of the flume and, encircled by the radiant crystals, wasted no time.

"*Seo ymele paerbig abracede geagne sum galdorcraeft fwifeald,*" she read off the scroll.

Electrical impulses fired through the sky, depositing the energy of the universe into the queen. Her face flushed with delirium, from beauty to horror and back, as winds wailed and swirled, threatening to whip everyone off of the tower.

"*Alor craeft geamearced be pe hwa peon heald.*"

Iridescence, invisibly visible, flowed from one crystal to the next until the three stones were joined by a lucid aura, and the energy shot up from the crystals, uniting with the moons. The sky exploded in verve, cracking and shattering and converging.

And then Parker. *Parker!* He sprinted onto the Ebony Tower, throwing metal off his frame, scanning the crowds. The army didn't notice him, their focus on the roiling environment and their mighty queen becoming mightier with each stanza. Milla swayed with the urge to run into his arms—to feel his touch, smell his scent, lose herself in him. Instead, she marshaled every ounce of strength to wait for his gaze to catch hers. And like a bolt of energy, their eyes met across the pandemonium. No words, only a slight motion of her head, and he slowed to a halt, as if they were of one mind.

"*Warne alor deorcnes, alor almaegen, alor hatheort,*" Lucrecia recited.

Flames erupted overhead, shooting its passion into Lucrecia, sparking the three moons on the curve of her back to shimmer synchronously with the moons above. She was the conduit to the elements: the energy, the fire, the moons, the crystals. Everything was Lucrecia and, ablaze, Lucrecia was everything.

"*Hede seo craeft rihtlice laest ryneu beo sip demere.*"

Lucrecia held out her arms with rapture, fire eddying around her, and Milla pounced. The world blurred in colorful streaks and thunderous groans as Milla was on her in sorcerer speed—her first time. Grabbing Lucrecia's wrist, shocking her out of her reverie, Milla snatched the scroll while reciting the verse her father had worked on his whole life: "*Mid ors, ond leodscipe, ond peawfaest hyge; alynne seo ymele ond asparest ureu friou.*"

She leaped out of the funnel of fire as Lucrecia yowled in agony, the blaze no longer friendly. The golden threads of her gown melted onto her frame, embedding itself in her flesh. Her three moons scarred. She broke free and rushed Milla, but Milla raised the scroll overhead, ready to rip it in two, and Lucrecia stopped, aghast. Inferno, too. The sky churned in confusion. Three moons clung to the formation of the crystals on the Ebony Tower.

Lucrecia softened. Her hand quavered. "Don't be a fool, child. Consider the horror you'll bring by destroying the scroll. All will be lost. Our future will vanish."

"You've always underestimated me, Lucrecia. I don't need to end our world to stop you. I've studied the *Book of Knowing*. I am my father's daughter." Milla ripped the scroll in two.

Lucrecia screamed in anguish as the two halves of the sacred parchment floated sublimely despite the fracas above Castle Hill. Each piece blossomed into a dove, somehow, somewhere along the way, and together they soared into the burning sky. Inferno's ferocious blaze withered and Lucrecia shuddered on feeble legs, her hope of unifying the worlds gone.

Milla smiled despite the turmoil. *Take that.*

The sky cracked and shattered and broke into pieces, leaving black fissures to suck away the vibrancy. The castle shook, toppling turrets; their huge stones breaking apart the tower deck. Soldiers fled in panic, except Vylkrost, who rammed through the throng for Lucrecia. She shunted him aside and, in a blinding flash, seized Milla by the throat. Parker charged, but the witch sent him airborne with a guttural roar. Queldar, too, was thrown into the stone wall.

The queen panted with ire, the vein in her neck snaking up to her forehead. "I may have failed as a mother, but I will not fail as queen."

Milla locked eyes with her. *Beon gan o bodig and gemynd.*

Lucrecia's hand hardened to stone and lost its grip, but she vaporized in an ethereal mist, catching Milla by surprise. Coalescing behind her, she grabbed Milla by the hair and spun her to the ground. Milla used a levitation spell to propel a chunk of stone into the attacking witch, launching her across the deck.

Milla scrambled to her feet, but Lucrecia was faster, and Milla encountered a vengeful maelstrom of flames rushing toward her. She fought back with the Zaephyr Spell, sweeping the firestorm into the cyclone's tempest and spinning it up into the chaotic sky, spitting out a show of arcs and flashes.

Lucrecia screamed louder than the spectacle, her bony face pulsing with veins. Hands clenched until she dripped blood from her own palms, she transmogrified into a corpulent bird form, baring deadly talons and razor fangs, and dove for Milla. Milla corralled the powerful twister, sucking the evil bird into its vortex and pitching it across the tower. The bird screaked in rage, crashing into the throne with a bone-crunching thud, and transfigured back into Lucrecia, pathetically, as if her magic had run out.

Milla fizzled the twister into sparks and approached the impotent queen. "There's no Unification to be had, Lucrecia. It's over."

Lucrecia quivered, her lips unable to hide her sadness. "I wanted this for us, Milla. I thought you, of all, understood me. Have you forgotten our plans?"

"You said yourself, I've grown."

"Away from me." Lucrecia's shoulders slumped. Milla reached out in peace and Lucrecia shot a venomous bolt of lightning toward her. On instinct alone, Milla raised her hands to deflect the bolt, and it struck Lucrecia in the chest. The witch had a look of disbelief, perhaps motherly disappointment, as her sinewy frame convulsed with electricity. She tried to claw her way out of the current but fell backward into the fireless pit.

Milla lunged for her but was too late—the queen's roar dissipated into the dungeon. Milla dropped her head; she didn't want it to end this way, but it was over. The Rising had passed. The three moons were withdrawing, fading, taking their silvery glow, and the crisp cerulean sky was emerging from the blackness. The scroll was free, free to find its next protector. Even the evil castle was crumbling. Soon, perhaps the Keeper would be unfettered for the noble and ignoble to try their luck.

Queldar scurried into the ash of the collapsing tower, having unbound Jovia from her shackles, and Milla called after him. His peculiar bird, fluttering alongside him, glanced back, a sparkle in its snowy eyes, but Queldar disappeared without a word. Milla took Parker in one hand and Jovia—her mother, she reminded herself—in the other, and fled.

Milla, her mother, and Parker tumbled down the earthen shaft, kicking up silt and sediment until they landed before the embers of a smoldering fire. Milla helped her mother to her feet, and Parker shielded them protectively, but the Squeeds weren't interested in skewering anyone. Hundreds of tunnels had caved-in and most of their habitats had collapsed. The tiny hunters labored to bring order back to their home, cleaning debris, containing fires that had spread, and rescuing those who were trapped.

Milla scanned the packs for Tobly and found him somersaulting boastfully out of one of the tunnels and landing on her toe.

"Ow." She shoved him back. "Show-off."

Says the princess who took down the queen and her castle.

Milla blushed. *Oh, you noticed?*

Tobly laughed and pulled her in for a hug.

The wall shifted into Mirth, consoling many of her younger offspring with gentle rubs. "I trust from the plight of my home that you've succeeded in your journey."

Milla nodded. "Lucrecia's reign is over, but I don't know what will come of the future."

"One never knows what will come of the future, Milla." She retrieved the journal from a crevice and gave it to Milla.

"My father's… but I don't understand."

"We did a little swap," Parker said. He took the coveted map from his back pocket and gave it to Mirth. "Seems like an understatement, but thanks."

"Thank you, mortal, for returning hope to our world." She sank into the wall, disappearing.

Milla's mother leaned into her. "That was odd, yes?"

"You get used to it."

Parker yelped and grabbed his back. "Geez, a nudge would've sufficed." He removed Milla's *Quodex* from his waistband. "Someone's anxious."

"Beast." Milla squeezed the book to her chest and it chuffed and snorted and wiggled unlike its usual grumpy self. Milla turned to Parker. "What else do you have back there?"

"Wouldn't you like to know?"

Yes. Very much.

"So, what now?" Parker asked.

Easy as that, Milla's joy, gone, shredded. Extracted from her soul and dispersed into the universe for someone else. It was inevitable, but still, her heart fell to her stomach, heavier than stone. How she held her tears was a miracle. "Now you go home."

He laughed, as if she was joking, but then caught on. "Wait. Are you serious?" He led her away from the others before she could answer, sparking everything inside her with his touch. "I thought… I mean… I don't understand. You want to go our separate ways?"

"I'll never forget you, Parker—"

"Don't give me that crap."

"Did you liken my emotion to beetle dung?"

"Yeah, that's pretty much what it's worth."

Tobly clapped his hands. *Fight. Fight. Fight.*

Milla and Parker swung around, glaring, and both said, "Stop eavesdropping."

Make me.

Parker grumbled and led her farther away.

"They're telepathic, Parker. You can't get far enough away."

"I can think of one place."

If only. "This is my home. And I can't leave my mother. I just found her."

"Then I'll stay."

"What of your grandparents?"

"Stop ruining all my good ideas."

She laughed softly, but said, "Perhaps this was our time, Parker. Fate brought us together when we needed each other, and now we must move on, the better for it. At least, I am."

He shook his head, folded his arms, paced in a circle, brushed his hair back with both hands, making him even more irresistible, and shook his head again. He was killing her with his beauty. He leaned in close, so close his soft breath warmed her face, and when she thought she'd melt from the intimacy, he said, "I followed you here because the second you disappeared in that mirror, I couldn't breathe."

You couldn't?

"Not to escape. Not for excitement. But because I couldn't imagine not seeing you again. *You* make me feel alive. I don't want to go back without you, Milla. I don't want to do anything without you. Please, come with me."

He kissed her. Finally. It was more intoxicating than she'd imagined. His lips were soft and tender yet burned with passion. The strength of his body against hers, the pulse of his heart, quickened like hers, transported her to a place within that she never knew existed. Dizzy, flushed, wanting. Euphoric. She tingled, body, mind, and soul. Oh yes, she was going back with him.

Tobly rolled his eyes. *Derg.*

ABOUT THE AUTHOR

Rhonda Smiley lives in Glendale, California with her oft-writing partner, James Hereth, and their bossy dog, Jojo. She graduated from Concordia University in her native Montreal, Canada with a major in Film Production, and has written for many shows, including *Ninja Turtles*, *Tarzan*, and *Totally Spies*! When not writing for television, she's tackling her own projects, like the animated feature *Race*, which she wrote and produced.

Currently, she and James are working on their graphic novel, *Blowback*, due out in 2018.

Asper is her first novel.

Visit her @ rhondasmiley.com

Lightning Source UK Ltd.
Milton Keynes UK
UKHW010721121021
392079UK00001B/341